PEPYS IN LOVE:
Elizabeth's Story

PEPYS IN LOVE:
Elizabeth's Story

PATRICK DELAFORCE

BISHOPSGATE PRESS

FOR JILL

British Library Cataloguing in Publication Data

Delaforce, Patrick
Pepys in love - Elizabeth's story.
1. Pepys, Elizabeth 2. Authors, English
& Wives—England—Biography
I. Title
942.06′6′0924 DA447.P4

ISBN 1-85219-000-0

All enquiries and requests relevant to this title should be sent to the publisher, Bishopsgate Press Ltd., 37 Union Street, London SE1 1SE

Printed by Whitstable Litho Ltd., Milstrood Road, Whitstable, Kent

CONTENTS

LIST OF ILLUSTRATIONS

INTRODUCTION

The great historians have written the definitive story of Samuel Pepys. His famous diaries have been read and will be re-read with the utmost pleasure by millions of people round the world.

Every book that has been written about Pepys has, of necessity, been based on his ten year diary, which also spans the last ten years of his marriage to Elizabeth le Marchant de St. Michel. This beautiful talented Huguenot girl has been completely overshadowed by the man who *subsequently* became great and respected, for during the time of his relatively short marriage, he was certainly not that!

This book attempts to redress the balance.

Pepys described her family as follows: 'Anjou gave her a father out of the illustrious family of St. Michel: Cumberland gave her a mother out of the noble race of the Cliffords' (by whom she was related to the Mountagus, Pepys' patrons). On her tombstone her epitaph, composed by him, said 'Wife of Samuel Pepys (Secretary of the Royal Fleet) who educated first at a convent, then at the French Court, shone in the virtues of both at once. For beauty, accomplishments, languages most highly esteemed without having borne issue, because she would not produce her equal. When at length she had peacefully said farewell to this world (having hardly completed her journeying in the more pleasant places of Europe) departed, returning to wander in a better world'.

Pepys' own philosophy of the time, in his words was 'The truth is, I do indulge myself a little the more in pleasure knowing that this the proper age (he was then 26 and she was 19) to do it, and out of my observation that most men that do thrive in the world do forget to take pleasure during the time that they are getting their estate, but reserve that till they have got one, and then it is too late for them to enjoy it'.

Perhaps John Dryden put the concept of the Pepys marriage more succintly

> 'A very merry, dancing, drinking
> Laughing, quaffing and unthinking time'.

But Elizabeth, who died tragically of a fever in their Seething Lane home, aged 29, would have said 'Eat, drink (and be merry) for tomorrow we shall die'.

Samuel Pepys never married again.

CHAPTER ONE

EARLY DAYS

"And they in France of the Best Rank and Station
are most Select and Generous"
William Shakespeare

My name is Elizabeth Pepys.
My brother Balthazar (Balty) and I were born in Bideford in Devon – he in 1639 and I a year later.

My father's family came from Baugé in France, just north of Saumur. His name was Alexandre le Marchant, Sieur de St. Michel, and he was the only son of the High Sheriff of Baugé, a town of about 5000 people. He was always a wild, restless and extravagant man. But he *was* handsome. Balty called him 'Extreame Hansome' and 'allsoe of mightey winning Courtely Partes'. He was a gentleman 'extremely well-bread being of a very good house in ffrance'.

From what I have learnt and what Balty tells, my father was more than a gallant and reckless soldier of fortune 'being bread to Nothing but the Sworde'. He soldiered in England, Ireland, Germany, the Low Countries and in France.

My father's family had always been strong and fervent Catholics and it came as a terrible shock to them when my father, aged 21, then serving in one of the German state armies, turned Protestant. This must have been about 1623. Thereafter he was often dubbed 'that Damned trublesome Hugenot', by his friends and enemies at Court.

When his army service finished in Germany he returned to Baugé, only to find that his father, my grandfather, was dead and that he had been disinherited from the family fortunes – such as they were. His sister, my aunt, was the sole legatee. News of my father's abjuration had reached Baugé and this was the result. It came to him as a great shock which stayed with him for many years, but he never moved an inch from his Huguenot principles.

Nevertheless the family still cared for this black sheep. My great-uncle was a distinguished and wealthy cleric – a canon in

Elizabeth Pepys by J. Hayls by permission of National Portrait Gallery.

Paris – and he was so fond of Alexandre that he promised to make him 'his Aire' and a reversion to his estate of 200,000 Tournois pounds (about £20,000 value in 1620) if my father would abjure his Protestant religion and 'but goe to mass againe'. I often wonder why he refused this fortune. After all our dear Roi Henri Quart thought that Paris and the French throne was worth a mass. Was my father wrong to stay with his new religion?

My father's life was an everlasting game of snakes and ladders. Now that he was desperate, his luck changed and his friends came to his rescue and gained for him an appointment at Court.

Henri Quart's daughter, Henrietta Maria, was betrothed to the English King Charles I – a marriage arranged by the perfidious Duke of Buckingham. In 1625 my father was appointed to her retinue in England as a Gentleman-Carver, a rôle which I am told required great presence and his famous charm, but little responsibility. I do not know for sure whether he actually carved the French Queen's gigot, but if he did, be sure it was done with great panache.

All went well for some time and my father was happy at the Whitehall Court, until it was time for a snake to replace the ladder.

The Queen's Catholic 'friers' reported to the Queen that 'he came not to Mass, was by it imediattly known to be what he was, viz a very stronge and firme Protestant, soe that the Queen dismissed him his imployment, hee having in discourse and Controversy of religion struck a frier'. His soldier's fiery temper had got the better of him and there was no possible way to avoid disgrace. As Balty once said 'the cloudes of his Misfortunes frowned on him againe'.

Alexandre then found a military command under Cromwell in Ireland. There he met and married my mother, a widow of the Clifford family and daughter of Sir Francis Kingsmill, an Anglo-Irish gentleman.

They returned to England after their marriage, to Bideford in Devon where Balty and I were born.

Despite objections from my mother's family and friends, including Lord Moore, my parents raised a sum of money (probably all borrowed) of £1500 and set off for Anjou to reclaim all or part of the family fortune. As Balty put it 'to indeavour by law with his sister and to recover if possible some parte of his fathers Estate'.

But alas another snake – related by Balty 'at sea hee and all their goods were all tooke by the Dunkirckers and hee also prisoner some months, so that hee and my mother were againe to begeen the World'.

After his release from prison in Dunkirk Alexandre 'took many very Honourable Comissions both in France, Holland and Germany as well as England. He caried a Company of foote under his Comande by order of Englande, to Assiste the frenche against the Spaniards in the taking of Dunkirck (at which he was much pleased) and in 1648/9 of Arras'.

I was a child of eight at the time, and then we lived a few years in Paris. In 1652 my father's fortunes were at their usual low ebb, and it was there that he first conceived some ideas which might restore his fortunes. Balty said that 'he grew full of wheemsies and Propositions of Perpetuall Motions etc to Kings, Princes and Others which soaked his pockett and brought all our famely soe low by his not minding any thing elce spending all hee had or had gott and getting no other imployment to bring in more'.

In Paris my mother met a 'Rich Counselors wife' called Madame Trouson and a Monsieur Duplesis, a 'Rich Advocat of the Parlement and many other pretended Devouts'. Almost certainly they were friends of the rich Parisian canon, my father's great-uncle.

Between them all a conspiracy was hatched. My mother, poor woman, must have been sadly distraught. She agreed to leave her husband in return for which the 'Devouts' would bribe her, 'fitting a Gentle-woman of her Quality, Give a Rounde some of moneys'. !

But worse was to come! As part of the agreement to leave the 'Damned trublesome Hugenott', I was to be made a nun and Balty made a Page to the Pope's Nuncio. As he said later he might have become by now a Cardinal!

All went well for the conspirators. Madame Trouson in one coach carried off my mother and I, and Monsieur Duplessis carried off Balty on 'the appointed day and Hower, as sweete as litening ffor ffeare of my fathers interest and furies'.

First we were taken to the 'Nouvelle Catholique of Weemen' and Balty to the equivalent for 'Garsons'. And later I was removed to the 'Nuneries of the Urselines' where I was received with much gladness! It was the 'stricktest Nunery in all Parris'. Dear Balty described me, then aged 12 or 13, as being 'extreme Hansome'.

But the intrepid soldier of fortune quickly discovered the plot. After about twelve days at the Urselines convent in Paris my father 'by some stratageme or other' rescued all three of us, 'hee having bine allmost distracted about it Poor Deare man and gott us all for England againe'. My mother, probably reluctantly, concurred with this sudden change of plan.

We then went to live in St. Martins in the Fields. Meanwhile

Alexandre took out patents for curing smoking chimneys, for purifying water, for moulding bricks, and for keeping pond water clear and fit for horses to drink.

Sir John Colladon, the Huguenot physician-in-ordinary to the King, who also lived in St. Martins in the Fields, and Sir Edward Ford of Harting in Sussex were partners with my father in the patent for curing of smoking chimneys.

In 1655 when I was 15 I met and married a handsome, sparkling young man of 22 called Samuel Pepys, son of a modest tailor of Salisbury Court, who had just left Cambridge. He told me that he was Secretary to his cousin Lord Edward Mountagu, who was I believe, related to my mother, since he frequently called me cousin. But in truth I am sure that Samuel was not only running errands for my Lord Mountagu, but also worked with his father – delivering suits and clothes made by his father for various customers, of which, alas, later he was much ashamed! Nevertheless young Samuel knew almost as much about tailoring as his father did and took a very lively interest not only in his clothes but in mine too!

My father, according to Balty, had said how glad he was that I was marrying a Protestant like Samuel 'that she had by matching with you not only wedded wisdom, but also one who by it, he hoped in Christ, would quite blow out those foolish, Popish thoughts she might in her more tender years have had of Popery'. But I told my father 'Dear father' (and kissed his handsome eyes) 'though in my tender years I was by my low fortune in this world deluded to Popery, by the fond dictates thereof I have now joined with my riper years which gave me some understanding, a man to my husband, too wise and one too religious to the Protestant religion to suffer my thoughts to bend that way anymore'.

Samuel later told me of his early loves for Betty Archer and Elizabeth Whittle. But they counted for nothing now. He must have known that my family was poor and likely to remain that way. He certainly cares for Balty and is kind to my parents.

He is a small man, we are much the same height – both about five foot tall. He has large eyes, a long, rather Roman nose and wide, rather pouting, sensual lips, and lots of brown hair – not I suppose as handsome as my father or Balty, but such a lively, sparkling, enquiring intelligence! One can sense his ambitions. He has so many friends and such a large family – cousins everywhere. And there is no doubt about this, he really *likes* our sex as well as loving them.

So we were married at St. Margarets Church, Westminster. The banns were read on 10th. October and we went before a magistrate on 1st. December for the civic ceremony which Cromwell's new laws insist upon. Samuel bought me a ring at the goldsmiths near the New Exchange and we ate our wedding dinner afterwards on Fish Street Hill.

The Register of the church shows our marriage as 'Samuel Peps of this parish, Gent and Elizabeth De Snt Michell of Martins in the ffields, Spinster. Published October 19th., 22nd., 29th. (1655) and were married by Richard Sherwyn Esq. one of the Justices of the Peace of the Cittie and Lyberties of Westminster. December 1st (signed) Ri. Sherwyn'.

CHAPTER TWO

THE OLD SOLDIER'S TALE

"The warrier who cultivates his mind polishes his arms" Boufflers

When the four of us – my parents, Balty and I – were living in Paris in the period at the end of the Civil War in England, the year before King Charles was beheaded, my father used to recount to me, aged nine, tales of his youth. As a loving daughter I believed them of course, although they seemed far-fetched, even unlikely. But my mother confirmed that they were all completely true!

Once upon a time – which is the best way to start – our French family in Anjou produced a very early Protestant, converted to the new faith in about 1540. He went to Ireland and founded a line of St. Michels in County Kildare. My father told me that Christopher in 1560 was Baron of Rabane and Norraghe, and Edmund St. Michel was in Queen Elizabeth's service in 1570. Amongst other activities he imported large cargoes of red wine from Gascony for sale to the troops. He knew Sir William Cecil in the London Parliament. His son Walter St. Michel, who was a lieutenant in the Queen's Army in 1587, knew Sir Robert Cecil in the English Parliament. He described himself as 'a poor distressed gentleman, but her Majesty's subject born in Ireland employed myself in her Majesty's wars there'. By 1602 their lands and estates had been much diminished by litigation. The family lived at Castle Reeban, and were called the Barons of Reeban. I think my father met the surviving family in about 1635 when he was courting my mother shortly after she was widowed.

My father was born at the time when King Henri IV – le roi galant – acceded to the French throne. As he grew up his dearest wish was to serve his famous King. In 1610, aged just 17, he was appointed 'Gentilhomme Ordinaire' to the King, to his absolute delight.

That month of May produced warm spring days. He was a young dashing cavalier, and was entrusted with the supervision of the King's escort in an open carriage through Paris from the

Tuileries towards the Arsenal. He had not a care in the world and failed to notice that the King's guard had lagged behind the carriage. They had reached the Rue de la Ferronerie when suddenly a young man leaped from the admiring crowd onto the step of the carriage and plunged his drawn sword into the King's side, mortally wounding him. The speed of the sudden vicious attack took my father and the guards by surprise. Within seconds however he had disarmed the young man, taken his sword and struck him to the ground. My father took the dying King to the Duke of Sully's home near the Arsenal. Poor dearly beloved Henri Quart died almost immediately. The wretched assassin, François Ravaillac from Angouleme, was put to death with horrible tortures a few days later. My father was desolate and blamed himself bitterly for the King's death. In fact the King's guards were casual and lazy and totally to blame.

My father was still a Catholic then, but a few years later he went to soldier in the Protestant Princes' armies of the Palentinate and Bohemia, where he was converted. At the age of 21 he had failed to regain his inheritance from his father and uncle, but was accepted back into Court and became Gentilhomme Ordinaire to the young King Louis Treize. The King was obsessed with hunting and much preferred to chase game rather than attend to the stuffy affairs of state. One day in May 1624 he and my father were riding in the countryside outside Fontainebleu. A large hare was put up and was chased helter-skelter across the countryside until they came across a small river. The King's horse stumbled and threw him heavily into the deep water. Quick as a flash my father jumped from his horse and scooped the King up into his arms from the deep flowing river. An hour later, having carried him back to the palace on his horse, he was delivered into the safe hands of Jean Heroard, the King's doctor, who pronounced him unharmed. Alexandre might have failed to protect the father, but he certainly saved the son!

My father is very proud of the fact that he has served three sovereigns.

Henrietta Maria, who was born in 1609 to Henri Quart and Mary de Medici, had her own Court, to which my father transferred on her marriage to King Charles the First in 1625.

My father has tried to explain his relationship to the Queen of England to me. Having served her father and her brother so faithfully for fifteen years, he was an obvious choice for a courtier at the time of her marriage.

He was then twice her age and very attractive to women (so he says, and I do not disbelieve him). By her marriage treaty she was entitled to have a French retinue of 70 in London, including 29 'resolute papist' priests and a dozen musicians. But in April after her marriage her Court had increased, mainly at Somerset House, to no less than 440 – including my father. He told me that the many court scandals and the terrible plague of that year were probably related! Several members of the French retinue died from the plague. The scandals were so great that King Charles forced the Count de Tilliers, the Queen's Lord Chamberlain, to send several hundred of the French courtiers and their families back to France. The Queen's brother Louis XIII complained of their treatment and sent M. de Bassompierre to London as Ambassador to mediate. Although my father was included amongst those sent back, he remained a Gentleman Carver to the Queen and Courier for a number of years. The tragic siege of the Huguenots at La Rochelle took place in 1625. I think Alexandre wished that he had been with Buckingham's fleet that tried to save them.

The Queen was a devout Roman Catholic and her court was dominated by her chaplain, the Bishop de Mende, and her eight remaining Capucin priests, including Father Sancy and Father Berulle. Father Fogarty, an Irish priest, joined her entourage later on and became friendly with my mother and myself, much to my father's indignation. The Queen knew that Alexandre was brought up as a Catholic. She guessed that he had been converted, but he was sufficiently tactful not to embarrass her. – at least not until his patience had been exhausted by the bullying Fathers Sancy and Berulle.

Three years after her marriage, the Queen entrusted Alexandre with a very delicate mission. Two of her sisters – one the Princess of Piedmont and the other Christine, married to Emmanuel, the Duke of Savoy – sent her valuable and costly gifts. My father was entrusted with the task of collecting these gifts in Paris and transporting them to London. They were valued at 200,000 crowns and included a large Italian chest made of 'cristallo di rocca' inlaid with gold and silver and containing many crystal vases and glasses. There were gold and silver cloths for her boudoir and containers of 'acqua di Gelsomino' or Jessamy scented water for her toilette. Undeterred by bandits on land and pirates in the Channel, he brought his precious cargo safely to his royal mistress. On the 9th April the Queen wrote to the Duke of Savoy, her brother in law, and thanked him for the 'temoignages d'amitié qu'il lui a envoyé par le Sieur de Saint-Michel'. He carried out many such missions for the Queen both in England and France. That was the year of the Duke of Buckingham's assassination by John Felton. After the discreditable affair of my father's affray with the Queen's Capucin monks, his title of Gentleman-Carver was taken away from him and he was succeeded by Raphael Tarterau in 1639. Court life bored him and promotion to Captain of the Queen's Horse was much more to his liking, especially as the clouds of war were fast gathering.

My father told me about his romantic courtship of my mother Dorothea, who was the youngest child of Sir Francis Kingsmill. My grandfather was born in 1570 and knighted in Dublin in 1603. They are an old Hampshire family, also owning estates at Ballybeg Abbey in County Cork and at Hermitage Park, Lucan in County Dublin. My maternal grandmother was Dorothea, daughter of Sir Conyers Clifford, and thus we are related to the powerful Cliffords of Cumberland. My mother was born about 1605 and initially married Thomas Fleetwood in 1620. He died young in 1632 leaving my mother a widow with two children. She was swept off her feet by my father who was serving in the Army in Ireland, and married him when she was 30 and he was 42. The Kingsmills and the Cliffords and Lord Andrew Pooley (one of Queen Henrietta Maria's couriers) all strongly disapproved of the match. As a result she was cut off from all their wills and had to rely all her life on her husband's intermittent earnings and other people's generosity (including that of my husband Samuel and the French Huguenot Church in London!) They obviously thought that Alexandre was an adventurer (which he was), who was after my mother's fortune (which he was not).

Shortly afterwards they went off on their abortive mission to claim *his* inheritance via Dunkirk! Every month the Dunkirk privateers captured English travellers and made them prisoners, and this happened to the St. Michels. After a few months of unpleasant captivity they were exchanged and allowed to continue their journey to see the "Archpriest" St. Michels in Paris to negotiate terms. But since Alexandre was adamant that he would not abjure his new religion, his quest was hopeless.

In the period 1638–41 we were living near Bideford on the borders of Devon and Somerset, where Balty and I were born. Louis XIII died in 1642 and was succeeded by Louis XIV the next year, so my father's influence at the French court diminished for a time. The Queen was in Paris in '43 and eventually went into permanent exile six years later. Her gallant naval attack on Yorkshire in '43 was abortive, and she was back at St. Germain the next year, living on a small pension from Queen Anne of Austria, her sister-in-law.

At the beginning of the Civil War Queen Henrietta formed her own regiment in England of mainly French soldiers. Colonel Sir George Goring was the Master of the Queen's Horse and my father was his second in Command . Colonel Goring had commanded an English regiment in the Low Countries under the States of the United Provinces in early 1639 and my father had been with him on that campaign. In 1643 they fought some battles in the West Country and besieged Bristol. On the 29th March of that year the Queen's forces defeated the Parliamentarians under Sir Thomas Fairfax at Seacroft Moor. At the end of '43 Colonel Goring went to France as Ambassador in Paris to be with his Queen in exile.

My father recounted two adventures in the English Civil War. In late September of 1645 Cromwell's troops defeated the King's troops near Winchester. My father, who was the Captain of the Queens Troop of Horse, was captured. He was wearing a beautiful silk scarf which the Queen took from her own neck and gave him to wear as his Colours. I think this story indicates the love and trust that existed between the two of them – the Queen fighting for her Kingdom and my handsome middle aged father fighting for his life. Under a military term called 'composition' the fight was not severe and the prisoners later exchanged, in a very gentlemanly fashion.

The next episode does not, I am afraid, credit my father with much honour, although he still thinks differently. It was reported in the 'Weekly Intelligencer'.

January of '47, two years before the King was beheaded, before Cromwell overthrew Ireland and before his patron had fled the country, saw Alexandre in France again. Near the Pont de Neuilly, two leagues into the forest of Boulogne, a bloody duel was fought on horseback between four Royalist officers – on a matter of honour! My father was Captain of Horse for his Majesty and Mr Wittfield was a Scottish gentleman of Prince Rupert's Horse – and they were firm friends. One evening on their travels my father won at cards the sum of 60 pistoles from Colonel Sir Thomas Sandys and Colonel Ambrose Jennings – both of them officers senior to my father. Their quarrel was simply because Sandys refused to pay his debt or to give my father a bill in writing 'alleging in derision that he could not write'. It was an out and out insult and a duel (on horseback with pistols) was inevitable. My father therefore challenged Sandys 'being come to the Rendezvous with their seconds, having charged their pistols, one before the other: at the first discharge Col. Sandys received five bullets into his arm'. My father was hurt 'and fallen down by the fear of his horse, in raising himself struck with his sword the same Colonel in the arm and both the seconds did so well pistol one another that a few hours after they died both. A priest who went by boasted that the said Mr Wittfield whom he exhorted, who professed to be a Protestant had been converted by him and was Roman Catholic'. But he still died. My father was in disgrace after this discreditable affair – which was one compelling reason why the St. Michel family were back in Paris at the end of that year.

Cardinal Mazarin and then Cardinal Richelieu were in control of the country. Henri IV's two young grandsons – the Prince of Wales, shortly to become King Charles II in exile, and his 13 year old brother James, Duke of York, had joined their mother in Paris. Henrietta Maria baptised the 'little Monsieur', as Phillip, Louis XIV's brother was called. When Charles left Paris for the Hague, his mother went into the Carmelite convent of St Mary de Chaillot, although her small court, including my father, was at the Palais Royal. Ironically enough my father's Anjou family were notable Carmelite Brothers. Antoine was Louis XIV's Almoner and wrote religious books about the Protestant Churches.

It was in the year of the horrible bloody Royalist duel that my father as usual did the unexpected! I may have given the impression that he was a gallant, a courtier, a roistering soldier – but there was more to him than that: he was and is an author! On the few occasions that he was at home, wherever that might be, according to my mother he was working on something quite different. He had translated 'The Life of St. Eustace, martyr' from the Italian into French. Giovanni Baptista Manzini would have been proud of it. So at the end of 1647 the Parisian printer called Charles Lambin produced my father's opus, which ran to nearly 250 pages. Italian is a cousin language to our own French 'bien sûr', but nevertheless when I was 13 and living in Paris I read it with enthusiasm and love. But I doubt that he made much money from the publication. His Catholic cousins, Maurile and Jerome St. Michel, both prelates, wrote and published several books.

One of the Queen's intimate friends in Paris was Walter Mountagu, originally a Protestant, and then a Catholic priest, who later became an Abbot of St Martins, Pontoise. He was a strong Royalist, brother of the Earl of Manchester, and was the second son of Sir Henry Mountagu. He was also attaché at the British Embassy in Paris, and later became Ambassador. He was contemporary in age with my father, and although not friends, they met frequently over the years. He was a distant cousin to Sir Sydney Mountagu, "My Lord's" father. Sir Sydney was also a fervent Royalist; was expelled as such in 1642, and died two years later. Through Walt Mountagu my parents met other Royalists in exile: Sir Samuel Tuke, another great favourite of the Queen's, and also Edward Somerset. He was the 6th Earl of Worcester and Earl of Glamorgan. He arrived in Paris with a man called George Leybourn, at the same time as our small family did in 1648. The Somerset estates in England were sequestered but as he had an introduction to Cardinal Mazarin he was able to live comfortably for several years in Paris. Rather rashly he returned to London in October 1654 and was promptly sent to the Tower of London.

Edward Somerset was a famous inventor. In the year of Balty's birth he had invented, and had shown to King Charles I, a great wheel fourteen feet in diameter, which he claimed was of perpetual motion. He invented a form of engine driven by hot water steam which he called a water commanding engine. And he wrote a famous book called 'Century of the Names and Scantlings of such Inventions, etc'.He became firm friends with my father, who was converted to the mysteries of 'INVENTIONS' I doubt whether either of them earned anything from their strange inventions but they certainly enjoyed making their discoveries. Edward's only son, Henry Somerset, was with him in Paris in exile. I more or less grew up with him in the years 1648–53, by which time I was thirteen, quite mature enough to like Henry very much, although he was ten years older than me. He always told me that he was going to be a Duke when he grew up, and I suspect he will be!

CHAPTER THREE

MY BROTHER BALTY

"Am I my brother's keeper?" Genesis

Balthazer St. Michel is my only brother, a year or so older than I am, born like me in Bideford, Devon. He has many characteristics of his father – handsome, vain, dashing, full of charm, particularly with my sex, always in some trouble, usually through his impetuosity, and, again like my father, finding somebody (usually my Samuel) to help him on his way. During his career Balty, as he is always known, soldiered in Ireland; and in the Low Countries during 1664, when he was 25, with the Duke of Albermarle's Guards. Subsequently Samuel secured for him the appointment of Muster Master in the Navy at Deal.

In the early years of our marriage, Balty was often on our doorstep asking me for money, and Samuel for help in finding him a place. As Samuel said, 'I perceive he stands upon a place for a gentleman that may not stain his family when, God help him, he wants bread'. The false pride of our family! He had many mistresses, and I remember in 1661 he and his French servant came to see me and wanted me to visit his latest mistress, whom he described as young, rich and handsome. As Samuel said rather cynically 'but not likely for him to get'!

The following year he introduced the two attractive Gosnell sisters to us. He was in love with one or even both of them. They were half-French and fond of singing and dancing. I think their father was a well-known actor and they both wanted to go on the stage. One of them indeed came to us for a few weeks and Samuel was much impressed with her songs and country dances. We called her 'our little Marmotte'. But Balty had promised her a more exciting life with us than she actually found, and she soon left us for the stage.

Rather to our surprise in the winter of '62 Balty did marry a girl called Hester Watts, whom he had been courting all that summer. She was reputed by Balty to be worth £500. Samuel described her as 'most little and yet, I believe, pretty old girl, not handsome, nor has anything in the world pleasing but they say she plays mighty well on the Base Violl'. I told him that he was damning her with faint praise.

Poor Hester, she patiently bore Balty five children and their eldest boy was christened Samuel, of course, for my husband became his godfather.

In February of '64 Balty went to Holland, like his father, to be a soldier and make his fortune. Samuel kindly gave him ten shillings and a closebodied light coloured cloth coat with a gold edging in each seam, lined with lace from my best petticoat, that I had when I was first married. But Balty returned from Holland and came to see us early in the New Year telling us sad stories of what he and his wife had endured. In July Samuel spoke to Sir William Clerke on Balty's behalf for another Army appointment, but to no avail. However in October Samuel actually visited the Duke of Albermarle to ask for a place for Balty in his Guard.

In December of that year, Balty came to see us and to our delighted amazement he told us that not only had be been admitted to Albermarle's Guards on present full pay 'and other marks of special respect', but that the Duke and Sir Philip Howard had so directed that Balty should be 'put as a right-hand man', whatever that means. It certainly sounds as though – thanks to Samuel – Balty has at long last fallen on his feet – for a change! In the new year he even attracted the attention of the King's brother, the Duke of York, through Samuel's recommendation that Balty should be made a Muster-Master in the Navy. The Duke enquired who he was and whether he was a stranger (foreigner I suppose) by his two names, both strange. Of course Balty would use *all* the family name of le Marchant de St. Michel. As a result he was awarded not only the entitled pay as Muster-Master, but part of the other officer's salary as well. His luck continued. In the spring of '66 Samuel's request to Sir Philip Howard was agreed, that Balty could go to sea *and* save his pay in the Duke's Guards at the same time.

Nothing succeeds like success. Balty had become of age, and now Samuel for the first time treated him like a man; almost, but not quite, as an equal! When Balty dined with us in April Samuel reflected that he was now 'become a good serious man. I hope to do him good being sending him a Muster-Master in one of the squadrons of the Fleete (which will be worth £100 this yeare to him besides keeping him the benefit of his pay in the Guards)'. I was so proud of my two men then – my young brother (I always think of him as young) and my kind helpful husband. And so it fell out,

Balty received his commission from the Duke of York as Muster-Master under Rear-Admiral Harman. Samuel was so pleased that he took Balty off to John Hayls to see my painting which was almost finished.

Balty's life, like his father's, had its 'événements'. In May '66 Hester lost a newborn child by some fall or fit. And in June Sir John Harman's ship the 'Henry' was involved in a battle with the Dutch fleet. Samuel told me that the 'Henry' sailed into the main body of the Dutch fleet. Harman then made his way through them, was set on by three fireships, one after another, fended two of them off and disabled the third: his ship was set on fire upon which many of his men leapt into the sea and perished: the English lost above 100 men and a good many women too. I did not realise that the Navy took women to sea; presumably not for their cooking ability. We thought at first Balty must be lost. On the 8th June however he returned unhurt after the utmost imaginable danger he had gone through in the 'Henry', being on the quarterdeck with Harman all the time and for which service Harman commended him most seriously and most eminently to the Duke of York. Samuel took Balty to his Office and there talked a great deal of this great sea battle. Samuel was mightily pleased with the bravery of Balty, who rejoined the fleet almost immediately.

In the summer Sir Philip Howard, who now was almost Balty's patron, told him that before he could re-muster he must bring a certificate of his swearing the oath of Allegiance and Supremacy, and having taken the Sacrament according to the Rites of the Church of England. The French Huguenots are often asked for these certificates before they can be granted high office, so that our loyalties to our new country and countrymen can not be suspected.

Balty next decided to go into a venture with Samuel's colleague, Anthony Deane, a leading shipwright, and others. They formed a partnership to borrow from the Navy the sloop 'Hunter'. With permission from the King, the sloop would become a privateer to prey upon the Dutch shipping during the third war with the Dutch. Samuel himself was involved in these little ventures, so there was nothing unusual. But the 'Hunter's' captain, Thomas Swaine, took it upon himself to license the ship in a French port to prey upon the English ships as well as the French. Even worse, one of the other captains called Mohun, either out of revenge or need of profit accused Deane and his partners, including Balty, of treason. It luckily came to nothing but Balty was lucky to escape from that fiasco. The adverse publicity even affected Samuel's good name and reputation.

During the terrible fire which swept London at the end of '66,

Balty at long last was able to return some of Samuel's kindness to him. It fell out like this. On the 11th of September when the fire was at its height, Balty arrived at our house from sea and Samuel was glad to see him. Samuel put him in charge of guarding the Office all night against the fire, whilst he came down to see me at Woolwich, where he had sent me for safety. Balty stayed and helped, and two days later he and Samuel, with labourers recruited from Deptford went to Tower Wharf to get Samuel's goods and chattels safely away. I came back to Samuel and we put Balty and his wife in the best chamber on the ground floor, whilst Samuel and I slept in the old closet upon the ground! Balty that autumn often seemed ill at his home in Leigh (near Sheerness). Samuel thought he was consumptive and I pray he is not.

The following February after the fire was over, Balty told us how worried he was about our parents, who depend on his generosity and the French church subsistence, and that they live on only £20 a year. Samuel promised to help Balty by getting him made Deputy Treasurer of the Fleet, so that he could better support our parents. In April '67 this was resolved with the Duke of Albermarle and Sir William Coventry. Balty and Samuel actually counted out the gold pieces of eight together on the 11th. and the following day Balty went back to sea. Samuel told me that he gave Balty much good council and had "great hopes for him that he will make good use of it and be a good man for he finds him willing to take pains and very sober!"

We saw a lot of Balty and Hester during the next few years. She is much better dressed these days as Balty gets more prosperous. Samuel described her as 'mighty fine in a new gold lace 'just a cour'. Samuel's French is very good but what he meant is 'juste au corps' i.e. fitting well and cut close to the body.

In May '68 Samuel took Balty off to see the Duke of York and told me that the Navy Board had written the Duke a letter about Balty and that the Duke is 'mightily pleased' with him, about which we are both delighted. In November '68 Samuel was so depressed with the prospects of the Parliament not renewing his Admiralty office, that he suggested to me that we go to live with Balty and his family in Deptford until he could clear his accounts, live cheaply and 'out of sight'.

At the beginning of '69 Samuel cleverly arranged a deputy for Balty as Muster-Master and a new appointment as well for him, to do with the Store Keeper's Account, which the Duke of York has allowed.

In the summer of that year Balty joined Samuel and I on our visit to Holland and Flanders and Paris.

CHAPTER FOUR

OUR EARLY MARRIED LIFE

"A very merry, dancing, drinking/laughing quaffing unthinking time" J. Dryden

After our wedding we went to live in a garret at the Wardrobe, in "My Lord's" lodgings in Whitehall. We were much in love and one room, some food and wine seemed, initially, to be enough – more than enough.

Samuel in many ways behaved like a student. Having just left Cambridge, he wanted that gay irresponsible life to continue. His part-time work on Mountagu's business and social affairs brought him into contact with many new interesting people: The Pickering family, who are relatives of the Mountagus; "My Lord's" ménage of courtiers and servants; crafty John Creed, his secretary; the ebullient Will Howe, his boy; the Crewes, Mountagu's in-laws; his musical companions, friendly Mr Spong, Hill, Purcell and Lock; his cousins the Turners, and many others.

His gregarious nature took him most evenings away from me to his own pursuits. This was an appropriate description, because be ogled and kissed every pretty girl within his reach. Certainly Mountagu's maids were easy prey, little Sarah in particular, and probably Betty as well. But one girl seemed to me to be a problem. She was called Catan Stirpin and she sold children's clothes and coats in Cheapside. She was pretty and she seemed to be willing. One evening I was so lonely and jealous that I followed Catan and Samuel to see what they were up to, but discovered nothing untoward. Curiously enough, a few years later, she married a Frenchman, Monsieur Petit, and in '60–61 they came several times to dine with us as friends.

Back in our little room I cleaned and scrubbed everything in sight. I washed and mended Samuel's clothes, and trudged to market. I cooked the rare meals we had together. We played backgammon and read books in the evening, and Samuel fiddled on his bass viol. I recited French poems to him and he sang and sang. One cold winter night we had no coal and no money for coal, so hand in hand we walked to his parents in Salisbury Court and spent the night there. Sometimes I was happy but most of the time I was discontented and sad at Samuel's neglect. Aged 16 or 17 I expected marriage to a debonair, handsome young man to offer me much, much more than I seemed to be receiving.

Samuel's family in London were not what I had expected of a Cambridge graduate. Tailors, turners, blacksmiths, weavers, fishmongers, butchers and joiners are not the people that my father and mother had brought me up to meet and understand. Samuel is a snob in many ways, and I am no better. What it meant to me was that I had no real friends, and my best friend of all spent most of his time about town. He knew that I had no money or allowances from my parents and was entirely dependent on him, unless I went to work, which his pride would not allow. The Mountagus and other friends ask me from time to time to act as interpreter in French and English, which I do willingly. I could possibly have earned my keep by interpreting and translating from English to French (that is easy) and from French into English (which is difficult). We both have expensive tastes for clothes and good living, but had not sufficient money from Samuel's two jobs with which to indulge them. Once Samuel had to pawn his lute for 40 shillings to pay for our food (or his gadding about). 'La bonne table', and the 'milieu' of the Court were the basis of my dreams. My father's tales of his Court life as a Gentleman-Carver to the Queen had produced so far unfulfilled desires, which a young tailor's assistant and household manager looked unlikely to achieve for me.

Our sexual love for each other is always strong and warm. However my monthly periods have usually been heavy and difficult, and our hopes for a child are rapidly fading although occasionally some false expectations are aroused. I am quite surprised that Samuel took this fact almost nonchalantly. He is a survivor of eleven children born to John Pepys and Margaret Kite. The majority of their children died in childhood: Samuel has grown accustomed to young deaths in his family and constant mourning and grieving. In his heart of hearts I do not believe he really wants a child. It is possible that his disease of the stone (which his brother John also suffered from) may affect his fertility. Who knows? The result is that it looks as though we shall continue to be childless. Initially I was more worried for Samuel than for myself. My discontents grew as a result of all these problems – Samuel's evening out with his various friends and his musical club, and occasionally the girls that he met and flirted with. Our lonely little room became more clean and more scrubbed. I was therefore easy prey for predatory Captain Robin Holmes when he came into my life again. He was a dashing young soldier, I think a marine. Certainly he had a magnificent uniform and the panache to go with it. I made the proverb clear to Samuel about what is sauce for the goose . . . I flirted outrageously with the gallant young captain, and Samuel was horrified, vexed and angry. I pointed out my reasons for discontent and sorrow, and swept out of our sad little room! My parents were overseas so that I had nowhere to stay, but friends of mine called Mr and Mrs Palmer had lodgings in Charing Cross and I went to stay with them for several weeks. By this time Samuel was desperate. His family and friends had disturbed him with their laughter and criticism. He was 'en effet' guardian and ward to the young Mountagu children – Jemimah and Edward – in "My Lord's" absence at sea. What was Samuel's patron going to say to him about my disappearance? 'My Lord's cousin has vanished, My Lord'. So I was in a very strong position. I had called Samuel's bluff! He wanted me back, and back on almost any terms. His pride was torn into shreds and tatters that I should actually nerve myself to leave him. 'Our Differences' he called them then and ever afterwards.

I was not in any way happy without Samuel. He was my first lover and I wanted to go back to him – on my terms. The fair young Captain meant nothing to me. He was a friend of Mountagu and afterwards was knighted. He served his purpose in our life, which was to warn Samuel to pay more heed to me, his wife. So we made it up, were friends and lovers again, but still at the Wardrobe. At the end of '56 Samuel was given more responsibility by "My Lord". To look after his lodgings and family, to monitor all his monetary affairs, that is, to keep his creditors at bay. Both John Creed and Lady Pickering gave Samuel helpful and considerate advice. The Mountagu family, much aware of our poverty, were now very kind to me after our reconciliation. Geese, turkeys, and other produce and delicacies were sent to us from their great estate at Hinchingbroke.

Samuel's declining health had been a worry to us and the Mountagus. Eventually in the spring of '58 he was operated on by Thomas Hollier of St Thomas hospital for the cutting out of a stone. The operation could not be done in our little garret, nor in his father's house, for lack of space. The Turners of Salisbury Court very kindly made room at their house for the crucial operation. Mrs Jane Turner is the daughter of John Pepys of Ashtead.

Ever after, the Turners – all of them, including Theophila the eldest daughter, about my age – are welcome in any house Samuel and I may live in. I thought he was going to die. A huge stone was removed, which he keeps as a grisly souvenir. Luckily Mr Hollier knew what he was doing and Samuel recovered quickly. I helped in every way to nurse him better.

Our fortunes turned in that year of 1658. After the successful operation, Mountagu pulled his puppet strings and Samuel that summer became 'a mean clerk' as he described it, at £50 per annum to crusty Mr George Downing in the Tellers Office at the Exchequer in Old Palace Yard. Samuel did not like Mr Downing and was frightened of him, but it was the first step on the ladder of the Civil Service or so we hoped.

The immediate result of this promotion, and Samuel still served "My Lord" as well, was that on 26th August we moved from our one little room in Mountagu's lodgings. Mr Valentine Wanley was the Huguenot church pastor, well known to my parents, and from him we took the lease of a small house in Axe Yard. It was on the west side of King Street, Westminster, in walking distance from the Office.

Can you imagine our pride and delight in our 'new' little house? Samuel was 25 and I was 18, and we moved from squalor to grandeur in a day. If you counted our cellar (for coal and wine) we had three floors and *five* rooms! Our new bedroom was as big as the room we had lived in the last three years. There was a dining room, a spare room for Samuel's books and papers, a dressing chamber and a garret with space for several maids'. And a garden yard at the back with some grass on it. I felt as though I had been let out of prison and entered heaven. But there was more to come. Samuel had carefully added up his two incomes and decided we could afford a MAID. Little Jane Birch was now part of our household, someone to talk to, someone to help me in our newly acquired grandness. All for £3 per annum. Our 'Differences' were forgotten and Samuel and I were beside ourselves with love and laughter and pride.

My parents were living again in London and I saw them each month, and also Samuel's parents each week on Sunday. Of our various neighbours, the Hunts were kindest to me, particularly if Samuel was out on the town for whatever reason; we played cards together.

That year we were living and eating in the garret whilst Samuel had the main house refurbished. Once we dined at home in the garret where I dressed the remains of a turkey and in the doing of it burned my hand! Our meals were now more ambitious although my cooking skills were still very limited! And still are for that matter.

When Oliver Cromwell died shortly after we moved into our new house and was succeeded by Richard Cromwell, Samuel was very anxious and worried, as perhaps was most of England, not knowing what was going to happen next. Matters seemed to get worse and worse, but we were isolated in our little nest. Then came Richard Cromwell's downfall, and all was in the melting pot again. Mr Downing asked Samuel if he would go to Holland with him. Samuel gave him an ambivalent answer, and shortly afterwards Mr Downing offered Samuel a post as one of the Clerks of the Council! Samuel thought it not safe to change his current employment with all the Parliamentary difficulties, and the offer came to nothing. Just as well – General Monk and his army occupied all London, and Samuel sang his new song 'Great, Good, and Just' to me and anyone else who would listen to it! My Nero fiddles whilst Rome burns . . . When "My Lord" Mountagu, recently disgraced, was restored to power as Admiral in '59 he asked Samuel to go to sea with him as secretary. Samuel wanted me to go and stay with his cousins the Bowyers, at Huntsmore in Buckinghamshire and leave our sweet little house. I fought him tooth and nail, but he held the pursestrings and he did not want me left alone in London during his absence. It was no consolation to me that he made his will before he left-everything to me, except his books in the English language. I took coach to the country in mid-March, very sad and much alone. The Bowyers were kind to me. Their son William was older than Samuel, and their four daughters were so fond of Samuel and, to a lesser extent, of me, that he called their parents 'father and mother'. Even brother Balty visited them in the country and left his horse to graze there.

I wrote many times to Samuel at sea. He was meeting the King and Duke of York, and helping his grand cousin "My Lord", now Admiral of the fleet under King Charles II.

On the 19th June little Jayne Birch, Balty's black dog, which he had given me, and I, returned to London and were re-united with my loving Samuel after three months apart. He had brought me back his love and a Dutch basket! Better still he received from the King a sum of 60 ducats and seventy guilders, and from "My Lord" an even better appointment as Clerk of the Acts which was worth £350 a year (although he charitably agreed to give £100 away to old Mr Barlow, who had a prior claim on the warrant). So now our rented house in Axe Yard was too small for us and we moved to a larger house in Seething Lane.

My admirers continued to woo me! Both "My Lord" and Edward Mountagu his eldest son have tried to court me, faithful Will Hewer of course, William Batelier, 'my William', even Samuel's young clerks. John Burr sent me a pair of turtle doves, and Captain Curle, of the ship "Maria", gave me a silver can but he was really thanking Samuel for a new commission. Captain Robin Holmes was still trying to gain my attention. I let some of them kiss me from time to time, but that was all. In August '61 I encountered a young man at the Theatre – Lord John Somerset's son, 'a pretty gentleman' as Samuel described him. I had flirted with him in France a long time ago when I was 14 or 15. He tried to woo me again with sweet words and a bracelet of rings. For several weeks he sent me secret messages by his footman before he realised that I was no longer interested in him. A pretty woman in 17th century London on the fringe of the Court was considered 'bien entendu' fair game.

Samuel and I were in and out of the Wardrobe most days. One day Lady Mountagu was endeavouring to hire a French maid and they could not understand each other, so I was asked to interpret (My French is still better than my English, even after five years of marriage to Samuel). I dined there alone with "My Lord" who called me 'Cousin' and took a great deal of notice of me. Samuel later referred to it as 'a just esteem', and much satisfied with "My Lords" discourse and respect to my wife. It was *much* more than esteem, but I kept quiet!.

Apart from my health problems each month and my wretched teeth, although the Huguenot dentist La Roche had done his very best for me, I was very happy then – with life, with my friends and admirers, and above all, with Samuel.

At the end of '63 – November I think it was – Samuel promised for both of us a trip to Calais or some other part of France next summer. I was longing to go back to see 'la belle France' again, perhaps in Samuel's small yacht, the "Bezan", or in one belonging to one of his friends.

That was about the time when Samuel, rather foolishly in my opinion, wrote to Lord Mountagu about his mistress and his absences at Court. I feared for Samuel and his career. Despite our close relationship to the Mountagus and our warm friendship with both "My Lord" and "My Lady" and their fine children, although they do not behave like children, particularly young Lord H., I was much disturbed. What my Lord Sandwich did not realise was that John Creed, his trusted secretary, was gossiping to Samuel. The two Mountagu daughters were sent by their father to Chelsea to

Mrs Betty Becke as an excuse for their erring father to go thither, as a pretence to see *them*, pack them out of doors to the Park, and stay behind with his mistress. Oh the perfidy of men! And "My Lord" went on seeing her again – a married woman with loving husband and children. On the last day of the year Samuel told me 'My Lord Sandwich did ask me how *his* cozen, my wife did, the first time he hath done so since his being offended and in my conscience he would be so glad to be free with me again'. So Fate continued to be with us! In the New Year Samuel was planning to ask the Sandwich's to dinner in *our* house!

On Easter Day in '64 Samuel was not at all well, and though I was eager (in my Easter finery) to go out, we stayed at home. Samuel read Dr Fuller's book to see what he says about my mother's family, the Cliffords and the Kingsmills to see what our heritage might be. He found but little. Samuel made a new will and Testament that year, and for some strange reason tore up many old papers including a romance called 'Love is a Cheate' which he wrote, a student, still at Cambridge. I often wonder whether his journal that he writes so secretly at night – or so he says – is but another Romance!

In September '64 I was not well and I thought I was with child and Samuel 'en effet' said that he neither believed me nor desired a child. I was pleased at the possibility of pregnancy, but alas as usual, my 'monthes' arrived a few days later. We had been married nine years by then. He was gadding about town then, more than ever before.

Sometimes I keep copies of my letters to Samuel. One from the Wardrobe was about my discontent at the time of our separation. I re-read it to him some years later. He found it 'so picquant and written in English, and most of it is true of the retiredness of her life'. He was so angry at this reminder of our early life that he forced the letter from me and tore it up.

In the spring of '65 we all had dinner with the Mountagus, I in my new lace whiske (a women's tippet) which "My Lady" thought mighty fine. "My Lord" looked as though he also agreed. He showed us his new silver plates by Burston.

That summer the terrible plague of London started and Samuel sent me across the river to Woolwich, to lodge with Mrs Sheldon. In August, to my surprise, he gave me a diamond ring which had been given to him by a naval purser! Perhaps it was to celebrate his new appointment as secretary of the Tangier Committee. I was worried for my father, as he was ill, but luckily it proved not to be the plague. The fathers of both Will Hewer and Tom Edwardes died. To my shame I must admit that during those terrible Plague months, with dear Samuel so exposed to danger in the City, we – my servants and friends and I – did have a merry time in Woolwich, safe, or fairly safe, from the sickliness on the other side. Samuel also, I believe, amidst that terrible death, enjoyed himself. One night, he told me, he and two (male) friends spent the night on his shrimp of a boat, the "Bezan", playing cards and drinking and talking. In November I ventured to Town to see Samuel, which he said was boldly done, but he came frequently over the water to see me. And we were happy on those occasions. He was much preoccupied with the victualling contract for Tangier at the time. At the end of November I came home, and we were very loving together as always after a separation.

It is hard to believe we have been married for ten years. Happy years despite the lack of children, and Samuel's gadding about. We have enough money (or almost). Samuel's career at the Office has made him well-respected, and despite some misgivings we love each other dearly.

CHAPTER FIVE

MY PARENTS, THE ST. MICHELS

"Oh what a noble mind is here o'erthrown, the courtiers, soldier's, scholars eye, tongue, sword"
William Shakespeare

A few years after we were married, my father and mother lived in Hind Court and then moved in 1662 to lodgings in Covent Garden, and in 1664 they were living in 'an ill-looked place in Long Acres'. My father told me he was going into Germany to fight against the Turks which made me sad but gloomier still that he and my roguish brother were going to Holland as soldiers. They went and they returned safely. In September 1665, at the height of the Plague, my father fell ill. Their house was shut up and I was desperate, but Samuel sent them 20 shillings help, as always, by Mr Russell his boatman. So I visited my parents in Long Acres among all the brothels. Samuel was troubled at it to see me go thither, and in April he wrote 'My wife had messages from her mother today who sent for her old morning-gown which was almost past wearing and I used to call it 'her kingdom' from the ease and content she used to have in the wearing of it. I am glad I do not hear of her begging any thing of more value'. But Samuel again sent 20 shillings that year to my father, Alexandre, at his house in Long Acre. Early in '65 I took my mother some apples, neat's-tongue (ox tongue) and wine – old people never know how to feed themselves properly.

My parents moved yet again and in 1666 were living in Deptford and I went there frequently to see them. Kind Samuel wrote, 'my wife to her father's to carry him some ruling work which I have advised her to let him do it: it will get him some money'. Paper for preparing accounts, I believe.

The next year my parents were receiving 4 shillings a week from the French church in London as a subsistence grant. In that year my father petitioned the King, asserting that he had discovered King Solomon's Mines of gold and silver. He also described himself as a Captain and a Major in the English troops in Italy and Flanders. My mother was equally eccentric. When my brother

Balty was serving in the army in Ireland she pawned all the things he had obtained there while serving under Oliver Cromwell, and then ran of her own accord, without her husband's leave, into Flanders. My parents were, of course, Royalists and were ashamed of any connections the family might have with the Protector.

In April my sweet Samuel took Balty one evening into the Park and out of pity for Balty's father, told him what he planned to do to help him financially – that is, to make him Deputy Treasurer to the fleet, by getting Sir George Carteret's consent and an order from the Duke of York for £1500 to be paid to Balty. Balty promised the whole profit to be paid to me to be disposed of, as I see fit for my father and mother's relief.

And in June I showed Samuel a letter from my father who was going overseas and that afternoon would take his leave of me. Samuel sent him three Jacobuses in gold having real pity for him and my mother. My parents then lodged with a Frenchman called Monsieur Prin in Charing Cross, who played the trump-marine (trumpet). Then Samuel commented in January 1668 'My wife this day hears from her father and mother: they are in France at Paris: he, poor good man! thankful for my small charities to him. I could be willing to do something for them, were I sure not to bring them ever again hither'. This is a rather cynical comment. Samuel was treating my parents as 'remittance people', in effect discouraging them from returning to London. He knew that I was devoted to them. In fact they were back in Deptford the next year and I visited them in April.

At Christmas in '68 I visited my parents as usual. My mother was as worried as I was about Samuel's eyes and told me she often prayed for him and his future sight. When I told Samuel, he replied 'I am glad to have friendship with them, believe they are truly glad to see their daughter come to love so well as she do'.

I know that Samuel and his family regarded my parents as being irresponsible and unreliable. Indeed they probably were. All their life they were on the move, driven by my restless father's need for action and of course, for money. Being married to a serving soldier is not an easy life. I certainly sympathised with my father's ideas for curious inventions. Apart from the ridiculous plan for discovering King Solomon's Mines, all the others had some merit. Chimneys do smoke; our filthy water does need to be cleaned and purified before drinking it; bricks do need to be moulded into sensible shapes for building. All credit to him for his attempts to do something to make our lives easier and healthier.

They are my parents and, knowing all their aggravating ways, I still love them and Samuel knows that.

CHAPTER SIX

EDUCATION AND OTHER TALENTS

"Though her Mien carries much more Invitation than Common, to Behold her is an Immediate check to loose behaviour. To Love her is a Liberal Education". Sir R. Steele

When, in 1655, Samuel married me, an ignorant, naive, but not innocent young woman of 15, he must have realised that my schooling had been limited. Our travels from Bideford to France and back again had not been conducive to my education, certainly by comparison with Samuel's years of work at Cambridge. I have some talents. I am bilingual in French and English. I can write in both languages, although my English grammar has its limitations. Samuel married me because I am an attractive woman. My mirror tells me so. Samuel tells me so. Other men tell me so. But he also admires my sense of dress and dressmaking. His father being a tailor, and Samuel having spent some time in helping at the tailor's shop, has given him a distinct taste and admiration for fine clothes, which often clashes with his instinctive Puritan feelings. I have certain domestic skills. I have made Samuel a woollen cap and knitted him pairs of stockings, mended his clothes, and made shirts and smocks. I can also clean and dress wounds. Samuel once saw me dressing the head of Emanuel Luffe, "My Lord's" German footman and a theorbo player, injured in a brawl with Thames watermen. Samuel called it 'all of a goare of blood'. Doctors rarely were needed in our small household. But he was determined, and I acquiesced in his wish, that I should obtain additional knowledge. This is how it began.

Once he said of me 'My wife, poor wretch is troubled with her lonely life which I know not how without great charge to help as yet, but I will study how to do it'.

Samuel is an insatiable collector of books. Some of the books he purchased at Allestry, Martins or Kirtons the booksellers, were for me and for me alone, such as 'Polixandre', 'Imposture', L'Illustre Basse' in four volumes and 'Great Cyrus' by Magdeleine de Scuderi, French romances by the same author, and the Epistle of

Cassandra, a romance by Sieur de la Calprenede. When I recounted some of the longwinded dramas of the Grand Cyrus to Samuel on our travels, he did get bored and then cross with me! However occasionally Samuel read some little French romances!

Another category of books he bought were for both of us to read – often aloud to each other. One was 'Life of our Queen, Henrietta Maria' which he read to me 'but so sillily writ that we did nothing but laugh at it. Also a 'Masse' book which cost 12 shillings, which Samuel read aloud to me. After it was finished I told him that I was long ago acquainted with it.

Over Christmas '62 Samuel bought for me as part of my 'education' Ovid's 'Metamorpheses'. We took it in turns to read to each other. Rather difficult. He also bought French books for *both* of us to read, 'Delices de Hollande', Cardinal Mazarin's long Will and a French translation of 'Nepotisme'.

As Samuel's eyesight deteriorated, so of an evening I read more and more to him. For instance Mompesson's very curious 'The History of the Drummer of Mr Mompesson' – a strange story of spies and worth reading, Chaucer, 'The Siege of Rhodes', Boyles' 'Book of Formes', 'The State of England', John Wilkin's 'Reall Character', young William Penn's 'The Sandy Foundation Shaken', Sir Henry Vane's 'Trial' etc. Most of these are serious books intended to be interesting and educational, but not so with a ridiculous book 'History of the Taylors Company' by William Winstanley.

Occasionally, and this pleases me immensely, although at the same time I feel sorry for Samuel in his sad state, he asks me to read his Navy Office papers to him at night. One was a copy of what the Surveyor offered to the Duke, which the latter had presented to Samuel. It is a new practice to have the ships' captains accountable for all stores and victuals.

On another occasion I read out the Duke of York's correspondence with Lord Brouncker, Sir William Penn and Sir John Minnes, which papers concerned Samuel's duties. He says that I am mighty useful to him. I can also recite extracts to him of Hamlet's 'To be or not to be' and other Shakespearian speeches of renown, which pleases him. About my letterwriting he is not always complimentary. Writing once to Lady Sandwich and her French companion 'Mademoiselle', Samuel examined my letters before they were sent off, 'they were so false spelt that I was ashamed of them'. However throughout our married life we have written letters on every occasion when we were apart – wher Samuel was at sea for instance.

Subjects dear to Samuel's heart are mathematics and geography. After all as Secretary at the Navy Office he needs to know both subjects well. In July '62 he engaged Mr Cooper, mate of the great ship 'Royal Charles' to teach him arithmetic, starting with the multiplication tables. He read the classics at Cambridge, but was strangely ignorant of other subjects. Even I could do my household accounts quite well, and Samuel knew little more than I in the basics. All through that month Samuel and Cooper were hard at work on their tables! In the spring of '63 Samuel started to teach me astronomy. Then he realised that I should be taught the principles of geography and then of mathematics. So in September '63 he purchased a 'payre of globes' for £3.10s from Moxons. He was delighted to teach me geography, because he was 'en effet' teaching himself as well. He admitted that he bought the globes *principally* for me! He read me a lecture in geography which 'she takes very prettily and with great pleasure to her and to me to teach her'. By December '63 'she is come to do Addition, Subtraction and Multiplication . . . propose not to trouble her with Division'. Samuel's division was not a strong point. Throughout January '64 we had our evening lessons, followed by prayers, followed by bed. When Samuel felt that he had taught me something he was content that our bed was a fitting and happy ending. But looking over my house accounts in September '64 he found things that seemed somewhat doubtful, and grew angry. I confessed that when I do miss a sum for a purchase I add something to the other items to make the total up to the correct amount. He was not angry at my sums, just discontented that I could not remember every household item purchased! Handsome Henry Sheres also tried to teach me the rules of perspective to help with my drawing, but found I was ignorant of the whole principle of lines. He was also a talented poet, and I valued the 'rhymes' he had written to Samuel.

I am athletic and though small, strongly built. Samuel and I walked great distances in the parks and fields around Town, and in the country at Brampton. I remember foot races in the park with Theophila Turner, and over the bowling green at Jamaica House, Rotherhithe with other young girls. I am also a good horse rider and rode side-saddle upon pretty mares that Samuel hired for me, 'she rides very well . . . she got a fall but no harm' he wrote. Balty and I learned to ride early on – my father was anxious that we should.

Samuel and I played backgammon in our early married life, and we played cards with our friends the Bateliers, and with the Mountagus at the Wardrobe. It was an amusing social occasion that Samuel and I both enjoyed.

But dancing was another matter. When I first met Samuel at the age of 15, I could dance in a rudimentary fashion but not of a standard for the 'haut monde'; not that marrying a tailor's son I ever expected great dancing skills! When I was 23 and had been married eight years, we began mixing with Lords and Baronets and their ladies, and it was time, I felt, to take some lessons. Samuel could not, or would not, dance.

Recently, in the spring of '63, young Mary Ashwell came to us as my maid and companion. She was musical, played the harpsichord – a merry jade, Samuel called her. She had a good carriage and inevitably she could dance, and dance well, better than I could. So Mr Pembleton, my new dancing master, came to start to teach me the coranto and country dances on the 25th April. Soon Samuel thought I was too conceited about my modest skills. Mr Pembleton came most days to teach me, on the 4th May I remember now, he persuaded Samuel to try the steps of a coranto. I begged him to try and thus he began and became Mr Pembleton's 'schollar', and therefore had to pay him 10 shillings 'entry money for the course'! Samuel told me 'the truth is I think it (dancing) is a thing very useful for any gentleman'. Four days later Samuel was positively preening himself after we had stayed late dancing with Pembleton. 'They say that I am like to make a dancer' he said smugly. I liked young Pembleton, who was now coming to teach me twice a day. 'Folly' said Samuel, but by mid-May he was dancing 'La Duchesse' 'which I think I should with a little pains do very well'. At the end of May Pembleton's course of lessons finished. I paid him off, but not before we had danced country dances and single dances all evening. So Samuel and I were now launched into society.

Samuel's passion in life is music. I simply do not know where he obtained his skill, his knowledge and his sheer depth of feeling for all things musical. Probably it was from his father, who played the bass viol well, certainly not from my mother-in-law. It was inevitable that Samuel would try to impart some of his musical skills to me. Not that I minded. I can sing, but in a totally untrained way, not in Samuel's opinion, near his own high standard. Perhaps the surprising thing is that Samuel delayed until the autumn of '66, when we were an old married couple of eleven years standing, before it was agreed that I should take singing lessons, since I had already been singing with him on many occasions. Samuel has composed several songs which show his real feeling. One is called 'It is Decreed' and another 'The New Droll', and of course 'Beauty Retire'. He employed a Mr John Berchinshaw, an Irish music-master, who quickly inspired 'Gaze not on Swans'.

Thus, John Goodgroome, composer, music master, and a Gentleman of the Chapel Royal, related to Theodore who had taught Samuel five years ago, arrived in October to teach me how to sing better. Samuel, honest as ever, has always told me that my ear for music is not good (I agree) and that I will come to do 'something after some lessons'. He also said to me that he has not enough patience to teach me, or to hear me sing now and then a note out of tune. He made me fearful to sing in his presence. The singing lessons continued well into '67, when Samuel noted 'find Mr Goodgroome whose teaching of my wife only by singing over and over again to her and letting her sing with him, not by herself to correct her faults . . . content that I do think she will come to sing pretty well and to trill in time which pleases me well'. High praise indeed from my master. The lessons went on, but at the end of August Samuel was dissatisfied that I was learning so few songs of Goodgroome. He therefore struck a new bargain with my patient teacher: he would now pay him 10 shillings for every song I learnt. The lessons did help me, and the result gave Samuel pleasure. He told me how at Audley End in '67 we did sing together to his great content, and in '69 he said how pleased he was with my singing with him.

Samuel also insisted that I should take music lessons. In the autumn of '60 he was giving me my music lessons in which he took as much pleasure as I did. But he became more ambitious on my behalf and a Mr Gregory, later Clerk of the Cheque at Chatham, came to teach me to play on the 'Viall'. Samuel was glad that he was an amiable and sober man, which obviously made him a better teacher! This went well and during '67 Samuel hired Thomas Greeting, a master teacher of the flageolet to come and teach me, and paid him 4 pounds. In May he said that he was pleased 'with my proceeding, though she hath lost time by not practicing, that I am resolved for the encouragement of the man (Greeting) to learn myself for a month or so'. Samuel really wanted an excuse to play music 'ensemble'. He was, to my untutored ear and eye, as good as Greeting. Anyway he paid 20 shillings a month to Greeting to come and play with him and me. That summer Samuel admitted to me that I now play 'very prettily with him' and by the end of August Mr Greeting was paid off, 'having as much as he can teach *us*!'

So with my retinue of Mr Cooper the mathematician, Mr Pepys

the geographer on the globes, Mr Henry Sheres on lines of perspective, handsome dancing Mr Pembleton, Mr John Good-groome the song bird, Mr Gregory the fiddler, and Mr Greeting the woodwind-master, I feel a very well-schooled and educated young woman.

What else? Yes, of course, there is *my* painting.

CHAPTER SEVEN

TO PAINT AND BE PAINTED

"Le nez de Cleopatra: s'il eut eté plus court, toute la face de la terre aurait changé" Pascal

It is the fashion now to have oneself painted, perhaps for posterity, if one has a rich husband, lover, or just a plain admirer. London has many fine painters and teachers of painting. Pictures and prints mean a great deal to both of us. In our early married life we bought pictures at Mr Cade's. Samuel is almost as knowledgeable about painting and prints as he is about his music. That is to say that he has a good eye and listens to what the fine 'paynters' have to say about art and craft. But he cannot paint himself. Although to do my clever little husband justice he probably would paint well *if* he chose so to do.

Samuel has already commissioned for £3. 10s. Mr Emmanuel de Cretz, whose father Thomas was Sergeant-painter to King James I and Charles I, to copy (and that is what de Cretz is famous for) a painting of "My Lord" Sandwich by Peter Lely, who lives in the Piazza. Mr de Cretz showed Samuel his copies of the King's paintings by Raphael and Michael Angelo, and Samuel has now borrowed a painting of Queen Elizabeth by Mr de Cretz for our house.

It all started just before Christmas '61 when Samuel's fortunes seemed so well set that he asked Savill, the painter, to paint my face. It was the first time that I ever sat for a portrait.

On the 23rd November Samuel commissioned Mr Saville to paint both of us. Four days later Samuel started to sit for him, and two weeks before Christmas I too started to sit for him. Samuel commented at the end of the first day that he found the 'dead colour of me is good, above what I expected'. The last day of the year I sat for the final time. Samuel stood beside me and gave poor Mr Saville advice 'on some little things to do, that now her picture I think will please me very well: and after her, her little black dog sat in her lap, and was drawn which made us very merry'. But Lady Sandwich, although liking Saville's portrait of Samuel, was much 'offended' with mine, with which Samuel of course agreed; 'And it do much wrong her . . . but I will have it altered'. So, four days later, back I went to poor Mr Saville 'where we staid very late to have her picture mended which at last is come to be very like her and I think well done, but the paynter though a very honest man I found to be very silly as to matter of skill in shadowes', – thus spake the master.

In February Samuel decided that Mr Saville was a good enough painter to portray him 'in little' (in miniature). Later that month Saville came to our house with his two pictures of us, which we hung up in our dining room. 'It comes now to appear very handsome with all my pictures' quoth Samuel proudly. In June Saville came again to varnish both pictures and get payment of £3 for Samuel's miniature.

Samuel that summer had been to visit Sir Peter Lely's studio, where he saw paintings in progress of the Duchess of York 'her whole body sitting in state in a chair in white sattin', and another, also unfinished, of the King. Samuel gave Lely a small present and promised to visit him again. He also visited the studio of Michael Wright, a Scottish painter, 'but Lord! the difference that is between their two works'. Later he met Captain Brewer, another 'paynter' but talked about the Presters in coffee houses! Samuel has purchased engravings of William Faithorne, of Hollar, Thomas Symons, and the Frenchman Nanteuil (through William Batelier). Visiting a painter and sitting sessions are now regarded as part of the social scene. When we sit for our paintings our friends accompany us, amuse us and distract the painter.

It was not until the spring of '65 that I myself decided to start to paint in all seriousness. Dear Thomas Hill, Samuel's musical friend, and my Huguenot friend, James Houblon, the merchant introduced me to one Alexander Browne. I had been experimenting quietly for some time without telling Samuel, for fear he would decry my efforts, until on 7th May my painting teacher appeared at our house. I was seen 'to learn to limn of one Browne, which Mr Hill helps her to, and by her beginning, upon some eyes. I think she will do very fine things and I shall take great delight in it'. This was Samuel's initial rather dubious and cautious assessment of the new situation! The next day Alexander stayed and dined with us. I was busy in learning to paint as Samuel said 'with great pleasure and successe, especially one fine womans Persian head, mightily finely done: beyond what I could expect of her'.

So far, so good. Samuel, enthused with my painting efforts,

"Elizabeth Pepys being painted" by A. Elmore, by permission of Mary Evans Picture Library

visited James Huysman from Antwerp and saw several good pictures at his studio, and intended he should draw or paint me. But that summer of the Plague year found me over the water at Woolwich, and so my own painting continued. 'Very curious' said Samuel, which from him was a noncommittal phrase. One day after a painting lesson Alexander Browne was having dinner with me in our house – Samuel arrived and was most vexed that my painting master was sitting at table for a meal with me! In August he looked at Pegg Penn's paintings (she is also a pupil of Alexander Browne's) and tactfully commended them, 'but Lord so far short of my wifes as no comparison', which is what a loving husband should say. In September back in London Samuel brought Lady Penn and daughter Pegg to our house to see my paintings 'which did mad Pegg Penn'. Excellent. At the end of the month Samuel admired my picture, now finished, of Our Saviour. He promised me a £60 necklace of pearls in two years or less, if my paintings pleased him. Lots of 'ifs' and 'buts'. Our friend Thomas Hill persuaded Nicholas Lanier to bring 'two or three of the finest prints for my wife to see that ever I did see in all my life'. That was in October and the Plague was still raging.

John Hayls, the portrait painter, was considered to be Lely's rival and was noted for copying Van Dyke. He was commissioned by Samuel on February 15, the day after St. Valentines, to paint me in the style of Saint Catherine, a fashion complimentary to the Queen. Whilst Hayls was actually painting me, Samuel, Mary Mercer my maid-companion, and lovely treacherous Mrs Knipp, were singing away in the studio. Poor John Hayls. The Plague showed no sign of diminishing but the sittings continued and Samuel commented 'my wifes picture pleases me well, and I begin to doubt the picture of my Lady Peters my wife takes her posture from, and which is an excellent picture, is not of his making – it is so master-like'. Samuel was 33 that day, and flirting with that baggage Mrs Knipp, who had come to see me, *her* friend, at Hayl's studio. The next day for another sitting, with not only Mrs Knepp, but also lovely Mrs Pierce, and my Mary Mercer and Samuel singing and being merry (singing Samuel's new song 'Beauty, Retire'). Samuel was vexed that day that the painting was 'not so like me as he had expected, having finished one part only of my face'.

Early in March Samuel now liked the portrait and said 'mightily and very like it will be and a brave piece of work, but Hayls do complain that my wifes nose hath cost him as much work as another face, and he hath done it finely indeed'. I cannot think why

Hayls could not paint my nose right the first time. It is a fairly usual, normal kind of nose! On the 8th March Samuel thought that my face and neck now finished 'do so please me that I am not myself almost in consideration of the fine picture that I shall be master of'. In mid-March the great 'oeuvre' was finished 'a most pretty picture and mighty like my wife'. Samuel particularly liked the way Hayls 'draws the heavens laying a dark ground and then lightening it when and where he will . . . the price not a whit too dear for so good a picture'. Hayls was paid £14 for the picture and £1. 5s. for the frame, and promptly started to paint Samuel in an Indian gown. A few days later Samuel watched Lely (Lilly to Samuel) paint the Duchess of York, and was delighted 'to see that there was nothing near so much resemblance of her face in his work as there was of my wifes (by Hayls)'. On the 16th May both of our pictures and one of Mr Hills were received of Mr Hayls, and we hung them in our home.

Samuel and Balty between them persuaded Samuel's father to be painted by John Hayls, which took place in June. Meanwhile I was still painting, hard at work, and in August showed Samuel the Virgin's Head that I had just finished, with which he was 'mightily pleased'. In November Samuel bought me some prints by Faythorn to copy, or to give me ideas for my winter painting. He paid another visit to Peter Lely and decided that his paintings are much better than John Hayls!

Dear William Hewer had by now secured paintings for himself of Samuel and me copied by Abraham Bosse, the Huguenot copier.

In March Samuel went to see Hayls and Samuel Cooper's studio. He is famous for his miniatures 'which is all in little, but so excellent as, although I must confess I do think the colouring of the flesh to be a little forced, yet the painting is so extraordinary as I do never expect to see the like again'. Samuel saw the miniatures of Mrs Stewart, Duchess of Richmond, as a young maid before her smallpox attack, The Lord General, Lord Arlington, Lord Ashlys, Lord Chamberlain and many others 'being infinitely satisfied with this sight and resolving that my wife shall be drawn by him when she comes out of the country'. Meanwhile Samuel commissioned John Hayls to paint our friend Harris, the actor.

In July 1668 I was painted by Samuel Cooper. On the 6th July, accompanied by Samuel, Will Hewer and Deb Willett I had my first sitting. 'A most admirable workman and good company'. We found he was not only an excellent painter, but to quote my Samuel 'now I understand his great skill in musick, his playing and setting to the French lute most excellently, and he speaks French (that means he is a gentleman!) and indeed is an excellent man'. So excellent that we had a great Artistic Evening. We invited Mr Samuel Cooper, John Hayls, a cousin of Samuel Cooper's and Mr Butler, the author of Hudibras – 'all eminent men in their way'. On the 10th August Samuel and I and Deb visited Samuel Cooper's for him to finish my protrait, although my Samuel was not satisfied 'in the greatness of the resemblance nor in the blue garment, but it is certainly a most rare piece of work as to the painting. He hath £30 for his work – and the chrystal, and case, and gold case comes to £8. 3s. 4d. which I sent him this night that I might be out of his debt'.

At the end of August John Hayls was asked to repaint my hand in his picture of me, which he did in early September, also Harris was painted in his habit of King Henry the Fifth.

In January '69 we both visited Henry Dankers, the great landscape painter, to ask him to paint panels in our dining room. We wanted paintings of the four Royal households at Whitehall, Hampton Court, Greenwich and Windsor. In the event, instead of Hampton Court, we asked him to paint us a landscape of Rome!

That same month, for the first time ever, we gave a dinner party in honour of my Lord Sandwich. With him came Lord Peterborough, Sir Charles Harbord, Lord Hinchingbroke and his brother Sidney Mountagu, and Sir William Godolphin. With two of my persistent admirers there I was a little uneasy. After a dinner of 6 to 8 courses and an excellent variety of wines, Samuel showed them *his* books and pictures and *my* drawings and paintings, which they all praised.

In the spring of that year Balty came to see us. He knows two Dutch painters, both in St James' market. So the three of us set off in our new coach to visit them. First we went to see John Loton, a famous landscape painter, who has I gather been painting in London for some years. He then introduced us to one Simon Verelst, newly come over from Holland, living now in the same house. Samuel recounts what Verelst showed us 'a little flower pot of his drawing, the finest thing that ever I think I saw in my life, the drops of dew hanging on the leaves so as I was forced again and again to put my finger to it, to feel whether my eyes were deceived or no'. Verelst's price for it was £70, and Samuel then had 'the vanity' to bid him £20 'for a better picture I never saw in my whole life; it is worth going twenty miles to see it'. The next day Samuel took Henry Sheres to see the fine flowerpot. The price was then reduced to £50!

Late in May Alexander Browne, my teacher presented Samuel

with a book of his original drawings, which cost Samuel 20s. A Mr Bushnell also painted me that same year.

For nearly nine years now I have been given very great pleasure in being painted and drawn by London's best and finest painters. Even greater has been my own delight in endeavouring to produce paintings, not only for my enjoyment, but for Samuel's pleasure as well.

CHAPTER EIGHT

LES GRANDS SPECTACLES

"Les grands seigneurs ont des plaisirs"
Baron de Montesquieu

I still think of myself as a Frenchwoman, despite being born in Bideford and with an Anglo-Irish mother: but Balty and I are pure French in temperament. We get excited too quickly, too easily amongst all these stolid Londoners. But the English do manage to provide 'les grands spectacles' of one kind or another. Samuel and I will always go to them given half a chance, if we have the time. Most of the spectacles are free.

All of us are born with a capacity for enjoying other people's misfortunes, and Samuel and I are no exception.

I remember well the executions of the Regicides in the autumn of '60. Samuel went to see all of them, and he persuaded me to see one of these grisly sights. We went to Charing Cross to watch poor Major-General Thomas Harrison butchered. He was hanged, drawn and quartered in front of our eyes. As Samuel said at the time he looked 'as cheerful as any man could do in that condition'. After he was hanged his body was cut down and his head and heart shown to the people – including us – at which there were great shouts of joy. On the following days John Carew, Colonel Francis Hacker, Daniell Axtell and others were executed in the same way. Samuel went to see the limbs of our 'new traytors set upon Aldersgate which was a sad sight to see: and a bloody week this, there being ten hanged, drawn and quartered'.

The horrible sequel to the Regicides' execution took place on the 30th January following. At the invitation of Lady Batten, wife of Sir William, the Navy Surveyor, who was much senior to Samuel at the Navy Office, I went with her to see the final degrading end to the late Protector, Oliver Cromwell, his son-in-law Judge Henry Ireton, and John Bradshaw, another great judge. Their bodies were dug up and then hanged and beheaded, and we saw them buried at Tyburne. Their bodies had been drawn on a sledge from Holborn. I should not have gone to see that fearful, horrible sight.

Even Samuel did not go. He thought Cromwell a man of great courage, and this final deed done to him most dishonourable.

Three years later Samuel sent me to Aunt Wight's to secure a place to see Colonel Turner hanged. He had been condemned to death for robbing Mr Tryon, a merchant in Lyme Street, of about £5000. Samuel knew Colonel Turner and described him as 'a mad, swearing confident fellow well known by all, and by me'. Samuel paid a shilling to stand upon the wheel of a cart in great discomfort. The Colonel delayed his fate by an hour by 'long discourses and prayers in hope of a reprieve. A comely-looked man he was and kept his countenance to the end. I was sorry to see him die'. Thus spake Samuel. We were part of a crowd of 12 – 14,000, who saw the poor wretch perish. I felt ashamed of our own blood lust afterwards. We were sensible, peaceful law-abiding citizens of London.

There were more cheerful occasions. The city celebrated General Monk ending the so-called Rump Parliament with bonfires (Samuel counted 31 between St Dunstans, Temple Bar and Strand Bridge and near home in King Street), and with all church bells a-ringing. The butchers made a great to-do 'burning and roasting and drinking for rumps'. That was in February '60. Three months later London celebrated again 'the happiest May-Day that hath been many a year to England' as Samuel put it, on news of the King's decision to return to govern England. Samuel was irked at so many people drinking the King's health in the streets upon their *knees*, 'a little too much', he said.

Late in November of that year Mr Stephen Fox, one of the King's agents whom Samuel met at sea on the famous voyage to the Hague to bring the King back to England, brought Samuel and I to Court. We went into the Queen's presence-chamber. I was placed behind the Queen's throne (more of a chair really) and watched whilst she and the two young princesses had their dinner. Samuel told me he thought little of her 'a very little, plain old woman and nothing more in her presence in any respect nor garbe than any ordinary woman'. We thought the Princess Henrietta was very pretty, but Samuel expected her to be more so. Nor did he like her hair dressed 'frizzed short up to her eares'. I was standing next to the Princess, with one of my fine dresses and my fashionable two or three black patches on. My courtier husband remarked to me that he thought me much more handsome than the young Princess. We then had a princely dinner provided by Mr Fox and his wife. As Samuel said, 'all provided for me and my friends, I bringing nothing but myself and wife'. Afterwards I recounted my day at

Court to my parents. It is difficult to realise that my 'old' father was Gentleman-Carver at Court a long time ago to this little, plain old woman, the Queen. Mr Stephen Fox's wife was formerly Elizabeth Whittle. As a precocious student Samuel used to make up anagrams on her name!

At the King's Coronation on April 23rd '61 Samuel secured for me in Westminster Hall a little stall on the right hand: it was full of fine hangings and scaffolds 'one upon another full of brave ladies'. I was one of the brave ladies who watched the King come into the Hall with his crown on and sceptre in hand. He walked under a canopy borne up by six silver staves, carried by Barons of the Cinque Ports. There was a sumptuous feast and Samuel went from table to table talking to Bishops and many others. We had no food served us, but Lord Mountagu sent us rabbits and a pullet and some bread from the Lords table. The outside ground was covered with blue cloth. The Heralds and the King's Champion were in armour on horseback, with spear and target carried before them. Samuel obtained great pleasure looking at the grand ladies and listening to the 24 violins. I stayed the night with Mrs Hunt – on the way meeting a lot of drunken gallants, who forced us to drink the King's health upon our knees, on a faggot – a strange frolic indeed! Vive le Roi!

Over the years of theatre going Samuel and I have seen the King and his mistress, Mrs Palmer, Countess of Castlemaine, at close quarters many times, also the Duke of York and his mistress. They often looked at me. The next year we saw Lady Castlemaine close to at the theatre. Samuel and I agreed that she was 'not now so handsome, now begins to decay'. Quelle tristesse! I wonder when I shall be seen to decay?

In April 1665 we went to Court on a Sunday to the Whitehall chapel by coach and heard the King's chaplain, Stillingfleet, whom Samuel knew at Cambridge, preach a good sermon. It was the anniversary of the King's coronation, and a grand occasion.

There were many naval events on the Thames, which Samuel took me to see. Some were poignant and sad, others grand and pompous with much ceremony. In December '60 a sudden storm sank two ships at anchor at Woolwich, the 'Assurance' and the 'Kingsale', manned and victualled to sail to the Guinea Coast. Samuel and I went by barge to Woolwich to see the wrecks. Twenty sailors were lost in the accident. Samuel was sad because he knew both the Captains and had been on board the 'Assurance' on several merry occasions.

The first time I ever went on board a Navy ship was on

Valentine's Day in '61. We went by barge with the Battens to Deptford to see Mr Pett's yacht, then to Woolwich to board the 'Rose-Bush'. The ships captain was Captain Arthur Browne, a son-in-law to Sir William Batten. We had a fine dinner on board and 'great mirth and all things successfull' as Samuel put it. It was a very small boat and I was glad that I was not a sailor nor married to one.

Another time the whole Pepys family, including Will Hewer, went by boat to Woolwich to watch the launch of the new great warship called the 'Royal Catherine'. Samuel spent most of the time talking to the King and Duke of York. It was a great success – the new ship floated and did not sink. The Queen and her Maids of Honour also came to see the launch. It was very rough and they were all very sick coming by water in their barge! The spring of the next year I took the young Mountagu girls to see the wrecked ships in the Thames – the 'London' and others. It was another unpleasant journey, rough, and both children scared of the waves.

On the last day of '62 Samuel and I went to Whitehall to see the Queen in her presence-chamber. We saw too her Maids of Honour and the young Duke of Monmouth playing at cards. My cavalier at my side pronounced a few of the court ladies to be very pretty in their velvet gowns. We slept that night at the Wardrobe, in "My Lord's" bed as he was absent from town.

Early in '66 on a cold February day, Samuel and I and Mary Mercer went by coach to Windsor for the day, to the ceremony of the Order of the Garter (such a funny bedroom English title). Samuel's friend there is Dr William Childe, organist of St Georges Chapel. He met us and installed us among the Knights' stalls. Cushions were brought to us and a chorister gave us the anthem sheet to sing. The choir were as good as Samuel expected. A high service with everybody, including the new Knights, bowing frequently towards the altar. After prayers we were shown the chapel plate, the Knights' robes and the Knights' banners hung up over the stalls. We saw the tombs of the late King, that of King Henry VIII, and poor Queen Jane Seymour. Then we visited Windsor Castle. Samuel said it is the most 'romantique castle that is in the world', the prospect and views from the Queen's apartment balcony 'being the best in the world'. I was very happy and well pleased at the ceremony and grandeur of the Castle and the royal Chapel. Samuel was pleased at my obvious pleasure.

A few weeks later Samuel took me to Westminster Hall 'where I purposely took my wife well-dressed into the Hall to see and be seen': this during the great plague.

The next awful disaster was the Great Fire of London. The 2nd of September was the worst day of all. I met Samuel and John Creed in St James Park. We went in Samuel's boat on the river to see the flames and the smoke, as hundreds of houses perished. We were almost burned with showers of fire-drops. We stayed as long as we could on the Thames, and then went to a Bankside alehouse until it was dark, and from there saw the fire grow in corners and upon steeples and between churches and houses as far as we could see up the hill of the City, in a most horrid, malicious, bloody flame. After it was dark the flames and the crackling of the houses and their ruins made a horrid noise. Both of us went home with sad hearts. There was little sleep for either of us for several nights, as we laboured to move all our valuables to Bethnal Green, and on a lighter to Tower Hill. We all worked without stopping. Once at two in the morning I woke Samuel to tell him of yet new cries of 'Fire' at Barking Church which is at the bottom of Seething Lane, near our house.

Later that month I went with Samuel through the City to see the ruins and debris caused by the fire.

In mid-November we went to see the Ball at Court to celebrate the Queen's birthday. We climbed up to the loft and Samuel and I watched for hours. The King was in a rich vest of silk with silver trimming, as were the Duke of York and most of the male dancers. Mrs Steward of course far outdid the Queen. She wore black and white lace, and her head and shoulders were dressed in diamonds – but the real Queen wore no jewels at all. The ladies were dressed in rich petticoats and gowns, with diamonds and pearls. They danced the Bransles, then a Corant, and then a French dance, including one which the King called the 'New Dance'. Samuel commented to me 'the business of the dancing itself was not extraordinary pleasing. But the clothes and sight of the persons were indeed very pleasing and worth my coming, being never likely to see more gallantry while I live, if I should come twenty times'. The ball finished at midnight – so away home.

The following spring I went to Whitehall, it being Maundy Thursday, to the Royal Maundy. But the King, of course, did not wash the poor peoples feet himself. He made the Bishop of London do it for him instead. Le Roi le veut!

One of the greatest events in our lives happened in the spring of '68. Samuel was working hard preparing his great answer to the Parliament for the Navy Office about seamen's tickets . . . with these thoughts he lay troubling himself till 6 o'clock in the morning and at last getting me to talk and comfort him. I knew that this was perhaps the most important event in Samuel's life. It would break his career if his speech and defence went wrong, and make his career if all went right in Parliament. So I comforted him in the best possible way.

One of the most frightening things of our lives – including the dreadful plague year and the time of the Great Fire – was the week when the Dutch fleet were in the Medway. We expected an invasion, another burning of London, perhaps even the occupation of the country by a foreign power. The French I might have accepted, but definitely not the Dutch, although they behave better to their prisoners than either the English or the French do.

Samuel was an administrator – a civil servant – not a fighting sailor, and he had no responsibility for the terrible 'débâcle' of the Medway, although I suppose he shared in the overall poor reputation of the Navy Office for allowing our ships to be captured, burned, and sunk. I think that all England felt that shame. It started on 8th June 1667. We had a excellent dinner that day – a ham of French bacon, boiled with pigeons, an excellent dish à la français. Eighty Dutch sail were reported off Harwich. The King was doing something about it. The militia were buzzing about in the provinces. As they did not seem to know where they were going, Samuel made Lord Barkeley, the militia Colonel, a present of his six maps of England, I suppose to point the troops in roughly the right direction. Samuel thought about fireships. Soon the Dutch were up as high as the Nore at the mouth of the River Thames. 'But, Lord, to see how backwardly things move at this pinch . . . ourselves being used to be idle and in despair . . .' My husband's words, not mine. The Dutch were now at Sheerness, and there were fears for Chatham . . . At home on the 11th Samuel had a great deal of serious talk with me about the sad state we were in. The trained bands of London were called up. I went to see my mother to try and reassure her. I told her that Samuel was sure to find a suitable solution. All depended on the boom across the river to protect our great ships. There was no thought that the great ships might sail out and actually give battle to the Dutch. Samuel told me, and his father, who was staying with us, that the Dutch fleet had broken the boom-chain and burned or captured our great ships, including the "Royal Charles". He said to me 'I do fear so much that the whole Kingdom is undone . . . I give up all the money that I have in the Kings hands for lost. So God help us!' He thought he had done his 'full duty, I am sure'. I am not sure; I think he could have *done* much more. He had powerful friends at court. He had the ear of the Duke of York, even the King. Each night he came home to bed with a heavy heart. He felt some violence would be offered to the Navy Office because of the disgrace of the English Navy. All the King and the Duke of York could do was to command the sinking of more and more of the Royal Navy ships. Even I could see that you do not win battles by sinking your own ships. So Samuel made his will and sent all his gold away - and I his loyal, loving wife joined in the panic and helped get his gold safe to the countryside. Of course the unloved, unpaid, uncommanded seamen were at the root of the problem. Why die for your country whilst unloved, unpaid and uncommanded? Why indeed. The Dutch eventually withdrew in triumph. Our humiliation remained. I asked Samuel 'why were our Navy seamen not paid?' And he answered me 'The King's government granted us no monies. We have no navy'.

Samuel took me afterwards to see our ruined fleet. The once proud ships lay in ruins on the banks of the river Thames.

Tout passe, tout casse, tout laisse . . . les grands spectacles.

CHAPTER NINE

MY HUSBAND'S FAMILY

"A wise son maketh a glad father" Proverbs

I never dreamt when I first met Samuel Pepys late in 1655 that he had such a large family. All I had in the world were my lovable eccentric, wandering parents and my charming irresponsible brother Balty. Samuel was one of eleven children, of whom most died young. He cared little for the surviving brothers and sisters, and most of the time did not even like his own mother. There were uncles and aunts and cousins 'partout' – like little rabbits popping their heads out of their burrows. They were in London, Cambridgeshire, East Anglia, Surrey, Ireland and elsewhere. Rumour has it that there is a Pepys family from France, from Languedoc and the Gironde, and another in Holland.

A few of this huge tribe I liked, but most I felt nothing for, one way or another. Samuel was even more vehement in his likes and dislikes, certainly in private, although in public he always was remarkably polite to them.

Some were passing rich and well connected, such as the Irish family, whom I never met. Samuel's great uncle Talbot Pepys was the patriarch of the family and lived in style in Impington in Cambridgeshire, were he died in March '66. It was his sister Jemimah who had married Sir Sidney Mountagu, "My Lord's" father. The old man Talbot had two sons; Dr John Pepys I saw little of, but the elder son Roger, Samuel and I knew well. He was an uxorious, flamboyant man, who married three times, and often – man to man – consulted Samuel about his next match. He was a successful, worldly lawyer, and helped Samuel in the long silly family legal battles of '61 over Uncle Robert's will: Samuel hoped to be named heir to Uncle Robert's estate. I kept well out of the squabbles, but Roger gave Samuel a great deal of helpful advice. He was a Member of Parliament, and during Samuel's early career told him lots of gossipy news of who was in or out of favour. No doubt they gossiped about the Royal mistresses too – most of whom Samuel and I saw at the theatre. He also warned Samuel of any dangers on the horizon at the Navy Office, for he knew his way round Whitehall. Roger and Samuel were alike in many ways, and he always treated me as one of the Pepys family.

The rest of the large family who came into my life were quite unremarkable. Besides tailors and a washerwoman, there were weavers and turners. The mother of Thomas the turner, Mary Syvret, was a Huguenot like me. Her two other children Charles, a joiner, and Mary, both married Huguenots. The Angiers cousins of Cambridge were also of Huguenot origin. Samuel was surrounded by them!

The Pepys women married tradesmen – Thomas Fenner the blacksmith (and the awful Joyces). Samuel's aunt Elizabeth Kite, his mother's sister, had married a fellmonger, and his uncle Kite was a butcher. William Wight was a fishmonger – more of him anon: Thomas Stradwick was a confectioner, Frank Perkin a miller, and so on.

Once there was a game of cards called 'Families' or 'Happy Families' where all the trades families had to be matched up. It took me a long time to work out who was who, as Samuel patiently explained his myriad relations to me.

Samuel's favourite, and mine too, was his father John, who was worth more to him than all the rest put together.

Little old John Pepys was two different men to me. Before my in-laws and Samuel's sister, Pall retired to Brampton countryside in '61, he was still working as a modest tailor at Salisbury Court. Samuel and I saw his parents once or even twice a week. A Sunday dinner with them was usually a happy, jolly affair for everybody. His father came to London, Samuel told me, as a young tailor's apprentice at the age of fourteen, and had stayed there ever since. He always had a twinkle in his eye for me. He was also a mysterious man. Several times he went overseas to Holland and Samuel signed permits for him to go there. He went there the year after we married. He had no business there and no customers. A Thomas Pepys was educated at Leyden University. My belief is that there was a Pepys family living in Holland. In January '66 Samuel went to enquire after his father whom we had given over for lost coming from Holland. He was an old man of 65. What was he doing in that country? Did he have a 'petite amie'? I hope so, because his wife Margaret Kite was a sour old puss, if ever there was one. I know that Samuel had to act as peacemaker on more than one occasion – their maid being the cause. Like father, like son. Samuel spoke of his father in his latter years so sweetly and tenderly 'a poor melancholy man that used to be as full of life as anybody . . . my heart never being fuller of love to him nor admiration of his prudence and pains heretofore in the world than now'. Each time Samuel visited Brampton his old parents were overjoyed to see him 'my mother ready to weep every time she looked upon me'. When Samuel asked John Hayls to paint his father, then aged 65, he said 'it joys my very heart to think that I should have his picture so well done, who besides that he is my father, and a man that loves me, and hath ever done so, is also at this day, one of the most careful and innocent men in the world'. Perhaps unfairly, I thought of those expensive Dutch visits! The next year Samuel told me 'I long to have him in town that I may see what can be done for him here: for I would fain do all I can, that I may have him live and take pleasure in my doing well in the world'. For good husbandry Samuel sent the old man six pairs of his old shoes 'which fit him, and are good, yet methought, it was a thing against my will to have him wear my old things'. Samuel once bought him a horse, and frequently sent him gifts of money. When Samuel's mother was ill, living in London, I took Pall with me to their house to prepare their meals for them. You can see that I did try!

Things changed after my in-laws went to Brampton. Samuel's mother was old, frail and querulous. She was very proud of Samuel, but did not like me. I do not believe either Samuel or I liked her at all. Samuel often described her to me as 'pettish', 'froward' 'unquiett' and 'so insufferably foolish and simple'. My visits there without Samuel were unhappy on both sides. What had an elderly retired couple in common with their young French daughter-in-law? Absolutely nothing! Samuel wanted his dear ones to like each other but it was impossible. I insisted that my people, Mary Mercer, or Deb Willett, sometimes Will Hewer, my safe admirer, should come there with me, so that we could amuse and interest one another. For Samuel's sake, on each visit to Brampton, I tried very hard indeed, by my standards anyway, to keep the peace there. I visited the Mountagu family on each occasion, and went riding in the countryside. But there were always rows and I know they wrote carping letters to Samuel after my return to London. Tant pis!

Margaret Kite, the old washerwoman, died at Brampton in the spring of '67. Her last words were 'God bless my poor Sam!' Samuel wept at the news and this message. I wept too. Not for that sour old baggage. I wept for my motherless Samuel. I once told him after a visit sad stories of the ill, improvident, disquiet and sluttish manner that his parents lived in at Brampton.

Samuel did not like his sister Pall nor his two brothers Tom and

John. A strange reaction for such a nice friendly man. Paulina, or Pall, was plain, and that was putting it politely. She was in fact ugly. Once she had a lover called Robert Ensum, but he died in '66. Samuel promised him a dowry of £500, but he still died! Pall came to us as a maid to our household. I wanted her as a companion, since as such she might have acquired a lover or husband in London. But Samuel was adamant that if she were to come, it would have to be on the basis of a waiting servant, or not at all. He once described her to me as 'cunning, ill-natured, that I have no greate love for her'. To do him justice Samuel tried hard to match her. In our daydreams we planned a wedding for her, with the beautiful Bateliers, Will Hewer and Mary Mercer as Bridesmen and Bridesmaid. Eventually after half a dozen or more matches for poor, ill favoured Pall, young John Jackson a plain young man, handsome enough for Pall, one of no education nor discourse, but of few words was discovered and 'en effet' bribed with a substantial dowry to take her off the Pepys family hands. He came from Huntingdonshire. After her marriage – she swiftly became pregnant – Samuel found her grown fat and almost comely but also pert and proud. But I was glad for her sake – she looked much happier and at long last she had a man of her own.

Little Tom, Samuel's younger brother, worked with his father in the tailor's shop. He was reputed to be so idle that his father wanted to turn him out into the wide world. He was cheerful, and we were of an age when we both enjoyed talking and looking at clothes and fabrics. We came to like each other. Samuel tried hard to make a marriage match for him. Poor Tom! He died in some disgrace in '64, leaving debts and worse behind him. When I heard of his death, I went to lay him out for his funeral. It was the least that I could do for him. Samuel can be very odd with his family. One day at "My Lord's" lodgings he found Tom and Dr Thomas Pepys, his cousin, there already waiting to speak to him. He was very angry with them both for going out of town without his knowledge. I believe he regarded the Mountagu family as *his* preserve and it was not for any member of the Pepys family to use the Wardrobe as a rendezvous! As it happened it was quite important that the meeting should take place, as it concerned a possible wife for his brother Tom.

Of his brother John we saw less. I thought him harmless and melancholy. He suffered from fits, perhaps epilepsy, and also from the stone disease, which runs in the family. Perhaps as a result of these illnesses he was a little unbalanced. He wrote some terrible letters about Samuel to brother Tom, full of foul words and crafty designs. But kind Samuel forgave him and helped him in his preparation for the Church. Samuel once wrote of John that he had little hope of him doing well a Cambridge since during his stay in London, John had given him great cause of dissatisfaction with his manner of life. However Samuel helped him when he was at Cambridge. He came to live with us in London, and eventually took orders and went into the Church.

So of his immediate nearest and dearest – his father, his mother, Pall, Tom and John, Samuel only cared for and loved his father. He was a dutiful son to his mother and a dutiful brother to the other three, but like them, he did not. As for me, I liked his father immensely when he was living in London, but less so in the country, when he had little to do except live with his memories. As for the others, I felt nothing, except for little Tom – the little rascal.

What of the huge motley crowd of relatives whom we usually met in their own houses? I certainly did not want them in *my* house!

It was interesting to hear Samuel's views about his own family. At the burial in '61 of Aunt Kite, his mother's sister, 'besides us and my uncle Fenners family there was none of any quality, but poor and rascally people'. It was unfortunate for them that they were poor but to call one's own family 'rascally' was a bit extreme! Even worse a few months later, we were both invited to Uncle Thomas Fenner's (the blacksmith family) and Samuel described his uncle's new wife as a 'pitiful, old, ugly, ill-bred woman, in a hat, a mid-wife. Here were many of his, and as many of her, relations, sorry mean people . . . it made me loathe my company'. Uncle Fenner had two daughters, Mary and Katherine, who married two brothers, Will and Anthony Joyce. Samuel hated Will Joyce and disliked Anthony Joyce, who was a tallowman. He liked his wife Kate. Why? because she was pretty.

Thomas Pepys the turner (Uncle Thomas' son) of St Paul's Churchyard, Samuel thought was both vulgar and obstinate. They wrote terse, almost rude letters to each other about the family Will litigation. In '58 they had been friends – now there was nothing but pointless legal squabbles.

The strangest and most bizarre incident occurred in the spring of '64. William Wight, Samuel's father's half brother, a staid, prosperous fishmonger, came to our house to see me. He told me what a pity it was that Samuel and I were still childless (which was not his business) and quite quickly came to the point. He wanted to sleep with me sufficiently often to produce a child, and to give me the huge sum of £500 either in money or jewels *beforehand* and then make the child his heir. I was very angry. At first I thought it was a curious sort of joke, but the old fool was in earnest. He tried to make advances to me, then and there, but I sent him packing, and in a state told Samuel everything that night when he returned. Why then did Aunt Wight send me a new scarf, laced, as a token of my many 'givings' to her? I just do not understand them, although she is undoubtedly fond of me, and he just lusts after me. Very difficult for Samuel – but we continued to see them frequently, just as though that lustful scene had never happened.

There were always funerals in the Pepys' and their relations' families. That was one reason why I needed two suits of black mourning. As Samuel once said 'A sad consideration how the Pepys decay and nobody in a way of encreasing them'. Perfectly true. He and I still show no signs of increasing the human race. His brothers are childless and likely to remain so. We are indeed decaying.

I attended most of the Pepys' funerals in London, sometimes alone, sometimes with Samuel.

In one month in '60 Samuel's cousin Scott, his Aunt Wight with whom I used to play cards, and his cousin Strudwick between them lost no less than five children. His uncle Talbot died at the same time. I have mentioned that Aunt Kite died in September and we went to her funeral, also to his Uncle Fenner's funeral. Aunt Bell died in the Plague year. His family was so large and widespread, that often the news came to me first, being at home. I would greet him by saying 'Aunt James is lately dead of the stone', and other sad tidings. They were always dying. Mr Edward Pepys, son of John Pepys of Ashtead – one of the grander Pepys, originally from Norfolk, married a new wife in June '62. 'The only pretty wife in the Pepys family (and she not a Pepys)' said Samuel rather sourly! I hoped he wasn't including me, but was not too sure of it. Anyway, a few months later, we both went to Edward's funeral in our new coach.

There were many isolated happy moments 'en famille'. On New Years Eve of '61 we entertained Samuel's father, his brother Thomas, his Uncle Fenner and his two sons, and Dr Thomas Pepys, and gave them a barrel of oysters, a dish of neat's-tongue and a dish of anchovies – with much mirth and happiness (perhaps it was only seasonal goodwill). In the afternoon Samuel and I went by coach to his cousin Thomas Pepys and met Samuel's father again, Dr Thomas Pepys and his cousins Hardwick and Scott – and *all* their wives. It was about then that Samuel borrowed £1000 from cousin Thomas to lend to the profligate "My Lord".

Another occasion arose in the spring of '69. Samuel and I and Betty Pepys (yet another cousin) and Will Hewer (now definitely part of the family) visited cousin Stradwick (Betty Pepys' husband) – our first visit there since Samuel's brother Tom died. The delay was caused by the family feud about cousin Scott. Samuel was glad to see them again 'they being good and substantial people, and kind'. There we met cousin Roger Pepys and his wife, and cousin Turner. Samuel drank a pint of the juice of oranges for the first time, of whose peel they make comfits, but he said he was doubtful whether it might not do him hurt!

As Samuel grew more famous and better-known, it was inevitable that he would meet more important people, not connected with his family – the Penns and Battens. Thus over a passage of time he gently shed the 'rascally' tradesmen members of his family from his life.

CHAPTER TEN

A LA MODE

"I know that a woman is a dish for the Gods, If the Devil dress her not" William Shakespeare

From my Anjou family I inherited a sense of fashion. I know which clothes suit me, and which colours and materials produce the effects I want. Luckily my dapper little tailor's son agrees with me. More than that, he positively encourages me to look my best – on a minimum and miniscule budget of course. I am his most valuable asset in the new exciting society world we are moving into. He knows it and I know that he knows it. His strong Puritan upbringing often clashes with what we both know is currently fashionable, and therefore rather daring. He is always torn between pride in 'owning' a handsome, well-dressed wife, and guilt that his money appears to be rapidly squandered on frivolities. I would call them essentials of course. Samuel's tailoring background makes him an absolute joy to have with me our expeditions to the shops on 'Change, where materials are sold. Little does he realise how hard I, and my maid sometimes as well, work as sempstresses, cutting and sewing at home. Not only practical household smocks, but clothes that might turn the Duke of York's head towards me at the Theatre.

Our friends often give me presents for my wardrobe, particularly as chosen Valentines. My French friends, such as the Bateliers, are just as interested in 'la mode' as I. Samuel's father encourages me in my sartorial tastes. I remember a most fine cloth at 26 shillings a yard, a rich lace for a petticoat – all costing £5. Samuel could not refuse to take his own father's advice!

Also 'en famille' I include Tom Pepys, Samuel's brother, a tailor, who comes to see my new mantle put on. I would go out with Tom to buy velvet for a new cloak for Samuel, and for me a velvet coat, also on another occasion a 'pair of boddice' for me. Tom is a delight to me, and his sure taste helps us in our respective choice.

Some of our early jealous quarrels were caused by my provocative clothes and fashions. For instance the black patches that I sometimes put on my face. A silly fashion I admit, but men do seem to appreciate the effect. As Samuel put it 'My wife seemed very pretty today it being the first time *I had given her leave* to weare a black patch'. If I ask Samuel for anything, very nicely, he usually gives it to me, even his 'permission'.

Early in the autumn of 1660 Samuel gave me £15 to buy mourning things – the Duke of Gloucester had just died, and very smart black clothes are essential for the 'haut monde'. Later I was to own two dark mourning suits – one for grand remembrances, the other for less memorable people.

Samuel is the first to admire my choice, and the first to condemn it if necessary. He said once 'My wife had on her new petticoat that she bought which indeed is a very fine cloth and a fine lace, but that being of a light colour, and the lace all silver, it makes *no great show*'. Do you see the clash of the Puritan and the Cavalier in Samuel?

With only slight reluctance Samuel will buy me jewelry, 'my wife being a little impatient I went along with her to buy her a necklace of pearl which will cost £4.10s. which I am willing to comply with her in for her encouragement, and because I have lately got money'. In our household the money comes in and goes out again as fast. Plus ça change, plus c'est la même chose.

My hair fashions too come in for his scrutiny 'my wife shewed me her head, which was very well dressed'. Our friend Surgeon Pierce's wife, Elisabeth, La Belle Pierce as Samuel calls her, came to see me and brought me a pair of peruques of hair as the fashion now is for ladies to wear which are pretty and are of 'my wifes *own hair or else I should not endure them*'. But the battle of the fair white locks was still to come.

On the Old Exchange we walked together and bought a white whiske and thence to Pater Noster Row where we bought some green-watered moire – lovely clouded silk – for a morning waist coat. This was for the very grand occasion when I was taken to the Queen's presence-chamber where I was placed behind the Queen's Chair. Afterwards Samuel said 'But my wife with two or three patches on and well dressed did seem to me much handsomer than she' (i.e. 'the Princess Henrietta who is very pretty, but much below my expectations'). Samuel the Courtier's compliments *are* welcome.

Often quite unexpectedly, he gives me sums of 'pin' money. Once he gave me £4 to lay out upon lace and other things for myself. One of my 'pettycoats' was later used to line Samuel's new grey cloth suit and faced white coat.

"Elizabeth Pepys in her new 'sac' dress" by Noble by permission of Mary Evans Picture Library

Our grand friends and cousins, the Mountagus at the Wardrobe, of course have much more money than the young struggling Pepys, but we have to put on a show. Samuel described the scene 'My wife put on her black silk gown which is now laced all over with black gimp lace, *as the fashion is,* in which she is very pretty. She and I walked to "My Lady's" at the Wardrobe, there dined and was exceedingly much made of'. I remember that evening I talked to "My Lord" in French, to our mutual satisfaction! Another occasion at the Wardrobe I showed the Mountagus my handsome new lace handkerchief. Lady Mountagu encouraged Samuel to lay out money on my clothes and as a result he bought me a lace which cost £6.

Samuel is constantly torn between our peacock pride and his income. He expressed his dilemma thus: 'I pray to God to keep me so to order myself and my wife's expenses that no inconvenience in purse *or honour* follow this my prodigality' . . . 'for now I am coming to lay out a great deal of money in clothes for my wife, I must forbear other expences'.

Going to church of a Sunday morning of necessity one shows one's Sunday best clothes, and Samuel and I are no exception. He noted once 'To church my wife with me whose black mourning costume is now grown so old that I am *ashamed* to go to church with her'. The colour black soon fades and looks shabby: so once again Samuel's pride and shame fought his purse. On another church visit with Samuel I was wearing my green petticoat of flowered satin with fine white and black gimp lace which I had sewn together and did look very pretty. Once we walked after church to Grays Inn 'to observe fashions of the ladies, because of my wife's making some clothes', commented my husband.

But outré fashion still worried Samuel. He took occasion to fall out with me very highly about my ribbons being ill-matched. Nor did he like the two colours! He resorted to very high words so that in a fit of passion he called me a whore, for which he was afterwards sorry. Notice that this time it was the tailor within Samuel arguing with the Puritan – the choice of colour being more important than the fact of wearing ribbons in the first place! But I did not look like a whore and he certainly should not have called me such an outrageous word. I certainly had not been behaving indiscreetly. Shortly afterwards he gave me £20 to lay out for Easter clothes – perhaps cause and effect? The effect was 'that we went by coach to the New Exchange to buy some new fashion petticoats of Sarcenett with a black broad lace printed round the bottom and in front'. 'Very handsome' was Samuel's opinion.

One day I put on my pretty new slashed waistcoat and Samuel started to sing French psalms at home with Mr Spong, his musical patent agent. Were the psalms sung as a reaction to my finery?

Sometimes my clothes become part of Samuel's extensive wardrobe. One winter's day he wore my last year's model of a muff for keeping cold hands warm, which serves him so well, that he has promptly purchased a new pair for me.

One of the hazards of London life was brought home to me one night. With me I had a new ferrandin, a silky poplin waistcoat, and as my coach was travelling along Cheapside a man stopped and asked me the way to the Tower of London. As I was telling him, from the other side of the way another man snatched my precious bundle out of my lap and ran away with it. I cried when I got home and Samuel comforted me. Another time Samuel and I between us managed to leave my scarf, waistcoat and nightdressings in the Westminster coach. I had asked Samuel to look after them for me! Adieu to 25 shillings.

One Christmas evening in bed I told Samuel that I was distressed at not having a new winter gown. He was ashamed that I should be seen out in a taffeta gown 'when all the world wears moyre', but we could not come to any resolution what to do, other than for me to appear as I was (*without* a new winter gown). That Easter he laid out 10 shilling upon pendants *and* painted leather gloves, 'very pretty and all the mode', as he described them.

One of the many reasons why Samuel does not always take me to the theatre with him is because the King and the Royal entourage might be there. My sweet darling little popinjay will be dressed 'comme il faut', but I might *not* be! One evening Samuel and I and my smart little baggage, Mary Ashwell, went to the Theatre Royal to see the 'Humerous Lieutenant'. He was ashamed that both of us were in such a pickle with all the other ladies being finer and better dressed in the pit than were were.

Each year I go to the countryside, usually Brampton, for 2 or 3 weeks, and there go horse riding in my riding-suit. As Samuel gads about in my absence from Town I often remind him of clothes I need on my return. I particularly wanted a new petticoat of the very pretty new silk striped stuff so he went to Pater Noster Row and bought me a very fine rich one – the best he could find, and much better than I had expected. My friend Lady Sandwich at Hinchingbroke had given me that advice, and Samuel, bless him, could refuse me, but not his Patron's lady!

John Creed, "My Lord's" Puritan secretary, once, very much out of character, sent me a very noble parti-coloured Indian gown.

Samuel himself priced it in Ludgate at £12 – £15, and caused it to be returned, because he thought that if Creed should choose to give me, or us, a present, it should be of at least £50 value! But when poor Mrs Russel, the waterman's wife, gave me a very fine St George in alabaster which adorns my closet that was acceptable as a present.

To get the scale of outlay in proportion, Samuel made a calculation in the winter of '63 that he was spending 55 pounds, and for me 12 pounds – solely on clothes. Our household expenses for servants, food and entertainment that same winter came to 110 pounds.

For care of my skin I have obtained some odd things. Samuel's ugly aunt Wight recommended to me puppy dog water, which I duly tried. It made poor aunt Wight no prettier. In the spring I go with our maids to the fields near the river and gather May-Dew, which is fun and might be helpful. It was Mrs Turner who taught me to wash my face in May-Dew.

Samuel's rising career has brought him some rich presents. Sir William Warren, the great timber merchant, gave me a pair of white gloves wrapped up in paper. He handed the parcel to Samuel, who felt it to be harder and heavier than it should be. He used every kind of excuse to get me out of the room, and I could see the reason for it. I knew he was on the horns of a dilemma – to tell or not to tell me what was the real present. To his surprise and mine he told me of the hard core of the present – 40 pieces in good gold! Shortly afterwards I acquired an expensive new laced gown and a pretty silk for a petticoat. Cause and effect again!

On Easter Day in '64 I dressed myself in my 'new best laced gown and new petticoat both brought for me by my husband'. But Samuel was not well and could not go out, so reluctantly I stayed at home reading with him Dr Fuller's book, and looking up my mother's ancestry to prove to him that the Cliffords were a notable family.

Court fashion dictates curious customs. Madame Mary Charette's, the French boutique in the Piazza, Covent Garden – sold me a mask on one occasion, and a vizard on another. Curious because they both conceal part of one's face – and why? So that every man of 'ton' will look at us . . . and speculate.

Samuel often surprises me. In the autumn of '64 he purchased a pair of gloves trimmed with yellow ribbon for 20 shillings to match my new petticoat, and paid me such a compliment, 'I could not think it too much which is a strange slavery that I stand in, to beauty, that I value nothing near it'. I remember the words of his own song 'Beauty, Retire', I know the depths of his feelings for that strange attribute which we call 'beauty'.

Once he gave me £15 for my new handsome winter suit of moyre *and* to buy a suit for poor plain Pall, which I did, not that it did very much for her.

On Whit Sunday, my husband noted that I looked 'very fine in a new yellow birds-eye hood as the fashion is now'. The Mountagues (both of them) admired my new lace whiske and new light-coloured flowered ash silk gown. They were both fashion-conscious and encouraged us to dress up to their high standards. But occasionally I went too far, for when it came to wearing my light-coloured almost white locks, Samuel was obdurate. Not because he thought them unattractive – indeed he thought them very pretty. It was because they were not made of my own hair which made him forbid me to wear them. They were he said 'not natural' and vexed him. The Puritan was fighting with the Cavalier streak in Samuel and the proud Cavalier was losing the battle. Another battle lost was when we quarrelled about my décolletage, Samuel described the scene like this 'my wife and I fell out I being displeased with her cutting away a lace handkercher so wide about the neck, down to her breasts almost, out of a belief, but without reason that it is the fashion. Here we did give one another the lie too much, but were presently friends'. William Batelier had been to see me beforehand and Samuel was jealous. Indeed he had cause to be.

Shortly afterwards another occasion arose for expensive presents. Samuel was escorting three beautiful ladies to the New Exchange; I and my two lovely friends, Mrs Elizabeth Pierce, the surgeon's wife, with the beautiful complexion, and the actress Mrs Elizabeth Knepp. Each of us received from Samuel a pair of white gloves and a pair of Jessamine perfumed flower gloves. The three of us were then the following night at the silly play 'Love in a Tub' by the Duke's company.

The battle of the hair locks was by no means over. Samuel and I went to see 'Heraclius' at the Duke's playhouse. The King's mistress, Mrs Stewart was there with her locks done up with 'puffes' and several other great ladies had their hair done so, Samuel then said 'although I do not like it, but my wife do mightily – but it is only because she sees it is the fashion' – I thought his reluctant approval of the fashion applied now to me, but I was mistaken. In May '67 I had dressed up with my new fair white hair locks and Samuel was almost apoplectic, swearing at me several times and bent his fist as though to strike me. What could I do but keep quiet, and sulk?

The following day I came down to see Samuel in my nightgown and we started with some marital bargaining. If I was given money to buy lace for my second black mourning gown I would promise *not* to wear white locks in Samuel's presence. Before we knew where we were 'we flew to very high terms' and I cried (but that is another story) . . . Eventually we made up our quarrel and became good friends again. A warm bed is a great soother. A few days later we met the Pierces and both remarked how 'very fine Elizabeth was in her *own* hair' so that tacitly I agreed to restrain myself with my 'white locks'.

A few days later I came back from Woolwich planning to go to Mrs Pierce's to meet our actor friends. I dressed in my new second mourning suit with black moyre waistcoat and short petticoat, laced with silver lace, with laced lining. Again Samuel lost his temper. He was horrid angry, and as a result I sulked upstairs. He wanted me to wear a cloth gown which I would not do. The point is that a party with the fashionable actors and actresses of the Town requires that one should dress appropriately for the occasion, not in a cloth gown in front of Elizabeth Knepp and the others. I tackled him again a few days later. He described it as 'a discourse about her clothes and my humours in not suffering her to wear them as she pleases . . . and grew to high words between us'! In the summer I had a very fine new suit of laced cuffs and perquisite, and Samuel bought me a nightgown for 24 shillings.

La Belle Pierce is now out of Samuel's favour because she paints her face. Samuel has admired her consistently for years, but at a fancy whim, he has abandoned her. I received a New Year's gift from Samuel of a lace handerchief, which cost him £3.

Over the years of our marriage Samuel (and others) have given me jewelry, which I showed him in the winter of '67/8. He had just given me a ring for a Valentine, a turky-stone (turquoise) set with diamonds. I suppose the total value of my collection is about £150, including a lovely necklace with 3 rows of pearls given me in '66 which cost £80.

In the spring of '68 Samuel described me as 'extraordinary fine in her flower tabby suit bought a year and more ago before my mothers death put her into mourning, everybody in love with it, and indeed she is very fine and handsome in it'.

At the end of the winter of '68/69 the battle of the hair locks was eventually won and lost. Samuel and I, and Mary Mercer and Deb. Willett went to see James Shirley's play 'The Gratefull Servant' at the Duke of York's. Afterwards we all repaired to Mrs Grotier's, the Queen's tire-woman, for a new pair of locks for myself. Mrs Grotier is an oldish French woman 'with a pretty hand as most I have seen' said Samuel. If the Queen can wear 'locks', so can Mrs Pepys, particularly if Mr Pepys is surrounded by his 'family' of three pretty girls.

For many years now – certainly from '59 or earlier – I have been buying my clothes from Unthankes, the Huguenot tailor at Charing Cross. I think he said his name was really Huguetan or Hercontaud. When we first moved to our house in Axe Street he used to dine with Samuel and myself. We were so poor that we could offer him only sheep's trotters. Samuel or I would buy the material – silk or ferrandin – and he would make it up, often by the next day. Later on he moved to the New Exchange. Recently I have been buying fine clothes from him for our forthcoming visit to Brussels and Paris with Samuel and Balty.

Some people think that I spend too much time and effort on replenishing my wardrobe – all at Samuel's expense. The facts are that he spends £5 on himself for every £1 on my back; that his own father and brother encourage him to buy clothes for me; that our cousins and patrons the Mountagus do likewise; that our 'milieu' of court, stage and churchgoing demand high standards, and finally, not only does Samuel like to see me in 'fine rags', but the guilt of his frequent forays after pretty ladies forces him to be nice to me afterwards. Poor Samuel, he is caught up in this everlasting fandango. But my French friends say to me with some truth – 'Elizabeth, qui s'excuse, s'accuse'.

CHAPTER ELEVEN

FRIENDS, NEIGHBOURS AND ENEMIES

"Dans l'adversité de nos meilleurs amis, nous trouvons quelque chose que ne nous déplait pas"
Rochefoucauld

Samuel first met Sir William Penn in June '60 at Trinity House in Stepney where we had great entertainment. "My Lord" was his host, and later that day came the first mention of the place of the Clerk of the Acts for Samuel. That same eventful week Samuel met a Mr William Coventry about his business. On the same day Samuel and I went to Dorset House to deliver a list of the names of the justices of the peace for Huntingdonshire.

Little did Samuel know at the time the important roles Penn and Coventry were going to play in his career, and therefore in our life. He bade farewell to Sir George Downing whose fifty pounds pay to Samuel had kept the Pepys family those last two years. Samuel thought Downing was a stingy fellow and did not care to see him again. The 29th June was the day when Samuel obtained his warrant from the Duke of York to be clerk of the Acts entirely through our patron "My Lord".

On the 4th July Samuel went to view the houses in Seething Lane belonging to the Navy – one of which was going to be ours – we hoped. Two days later Samuel's new salary of £350 was published and he immediately bought from brother Tom a new jackanapes silk coat with silver buttons. We celebrated our new fortune at Clodin's for a great wedding of our Dutch friends, the Hartlibs and Roders. 'But among all the beauties there, my wife' Samuel said proudly 'was thought the greatest'. We moved into the Navy office house in the middle of July and discovered that all our neighbours, inevitably, were Samuel's senior officials at the Office – Penns, Battens and Sir John Minnes.

The Penn family consisted of Sir William – a handsome, smooth, comely, fair man near forty, and therefore twelve years older than Samuel – his wife Martha, who was rather plain and dowdy, and their three children, Pegg, a daughter of my age, and two sons, the elder called William. These were our friends, neighbours, and enemies! Sir William, an Admiral, was said to be the ablest man in the Navy and had been General at Sea under the Commonwealth. Also he was a colleague of General Monk and my Lord Sandwich, so we had to be very careful! But Samuel hated Sir William. Unfortunately both of us had to put on a brave face and dissemble, and in fact act like hypocrites!

In August the trio of neighbours, Battens, Penns and Pepys went to the Navy Church of St Olave's in Hart Street to see the churchwardens, to demand that a large dignified wooden pew be built for the three families. Samuel reported that Mr Daniel Milles, the rector, was a very good minister. First impressions! Later on Samuel called the poor man 'a cunning fellow and knows where the good victuals and the good drink is . . .' Mr Milles always made lazy sermons in Samuel's view.

But back to Samuel and Sir William. By July '62 Samuel described him to me as 'one I hate with all my heart for his base treacherous tricks but yet I think it not policy to declare it yet'. When Sir William went to Ireland, he asked Samuel to look after his house, next to ours, which most reluctantly Samuel agreed to do. Lord Sandwich, then Admiral of the Fleet, admitted to Samuel that he too disliked Penn, 'a mean fellow', who was the Vice Admiral of the Fleet. When Samuel and Penn fell out one day at the Office about our friend Mr Turner, Samuel won the argument and told me 'Penn did take it like a base raskall, and so I shall remember him while I live'. Samuel describes Lady Martha Penn, as a 'well looked, fat, short, old Dutchwoman but one that hath been heretofore pretty handsome and is now very discreet and I believe hath more wit than her husband . . . very well pleased I was with the old woman'. Once she showed Samuel and me her beautiful red goldfish from China, kept in a large glass of water!

So we led a strange life with these neighbours. Samuel not only had to work with Admiral Penn, but went to the theatre, taverns (where Penn sang very bawdy songs) and other social occasions with him. He even joined with Admirals Penn and Batten in joint ownership of a Privateer. The three neighbours borrowed the 'Flying Greyhound' for a winter's legal 'piracy'. Samuel was lucky to get his money back. Those two Admirals were not to be trusted – in my opinion.

In the early days of our relationship with the Penns, Samuel and the two Sir Williams had a coach and chariot race in the Park. My husband's clothes were spoilt and there was dirt all over his velvet coat. He played bowls with Penn and sent him a joke counterfeit letter about a stolen tankard which Samuel called very good sport. Samuel loathed the man but was prepared to have many jolly adventures with him.

Young William Penn, who was a year or two older than me, visited us that same summer. He had the manners of a courtier and had just come from France specially, he said, to visit me! Samuel met him too and gave him the accolade of being 'a fine gentleman, most modish, well-grown, learned', but also thought he had acquired a 'vanity of the French garb and affected manner of speech and gait'. After leaving Oxford University he and his parents visited our house and had dinner with us. He sent us a copy of the book about the Quakers that he wrote, but Samuel dismissed it as nonsense, and was ashamed to have read it.

My favourite in this curious family was the Penn's daughter Margaret, or Peg as she was known. Unfortunately she was Samuel's favourite too, whom he tousled and kissed from time to time. He thought that I did not know, but walls have ears and servants have tongues. In '61 I went by coach to Clerkenwell to visit her at her school. She was then about 15 and a pretty, intelligent girl. Once, out of pure friendship for me, she sent us a delicious lobster for supper. 'Timeos Danaosque dona ferentes' . . . Samuel knew there must be a sinister motive 'there is plot or design in it for we have a little while carried ourselves pretty strange to them'. Meanwhile I enjoyed the lobster supper. On another occasion her father took her and us to the theatre to see 'The little Thief' by John Fletcher. We sat in the pits and the two men rather grandly sat in Penn's box. Little Peg could be great fun. One summer evening dancing and larking about, she and I put the men's solemn periwigs on our heads and went on dancing our heads off! I think Samuel was amused, but I was not sure!

When Peg married Anthony Lowther early in '67 we lent them many kitchen utensils 'for dressing their dinner', as Samuel put it. Because of Lent it was a private wedding so I did not go to it. That gossip Mrs Turner told Samuel that Sir William Penn gave his daughter £4000 on her wedding. I hope so, but doubt it.

Samuel does not gossip himself, but he does encourage it, and does like listening to it. Thomas Turner of the Navy Office, whose house borders on ours, and his wife and pretty daughter Betty (who Samuel and Will Hewer look at far too much), are *real* friends of ours. But Mrs Turner is a real, honest-to-goodness gossip. One evening in spring '67 she and Samuel sat up late talking about our neighbours. First she destroyed Lord Brouncker and his mistress – then Samuel heard about the Penns (and the

Turners have known them for far longer than we have). William Penn was a 'pityful fellow' when she first knew them, and his lady was one of the 'soured, dirty woman ever a dirty slattern' etc. but Penn was a turncoat – first a King's man, than a Roundhead, and now a King's man again. The only disquieting piece of gossip revealed was the close relationship by cypher between Sir William Coventry (whom Samuel admires) and Sir William Penn (whom he hates).

Despite Sir William's undoubted charm and ability, I have never felt comfortable with him, perhaps influenced by Samuel's secret hatred of him. Once he came with us to see our pictures being painted, another time in his coach to Moorefields. As good neighbours we visited him when he was ill one winter of gout, and sitting forlornly by his fireside.

In the winter of '67 after we had ostensibly become friends, but in fact were still enemies, the Penns gave a large dinner at their house for the Navy big-wigs. Lord Brouncker was there and that funny old cavalier Sir John Minnes, and the Battens and ourselves. We were given favours to wear to put in our hats, which Samuel found to be an absurd custom. At another party later that year given by us for the Battens and Penns, Meg, now married to Mr Lowther, was there. Samuel told me 'she is grown a fool, having not a word to say'. I know the feeling only too well. I thought of myself then as a sophisticate at 24 years of age, married 9 years. That poor shy recently married girl of 16 or 17 was out of her depth with the old roués round the table. Here I speak only of the two Sir Williams!

After Samuel's triumphant speech in the Commons in '68, Penn was impeached for corruption, although not directly as a result. Samuel made a point of being kind and helpful, sitting with him in the evening to console him.

My husband – as I find out the longer I know him – is a curious man. There are many reasons why he dislikes the Penns. They do not dress to his high standard but 'in palterly clothes'. Another is that they keep an indifferent table – 'a sorry dinner not anything handsome or clean, but some silver plates they borrowed of us'. After her marriage he thought Margaret Penn and her new husband 'a very sorry couple, methinks, though rich'.

So much for the Penns. The Battens, who lived next to the Penns, were heartily disliked by them. Our little Seething Lane was a hotbed of malice and fairly well concealed hatred. Admiral Sir William Batten was the Surveyor to the Navy. He was a strong barrel of a man, probably rising 60 when we first knew him. It is said that he taught William Penn the navy business and disliked him (or was envious of his success) ever since. He is a wealthy man even more so than Penn, with a country house in Walthamstow, to which we were later invited. Whenever I meet him he is merry and polite. He wife, Lady Batten, is a different kettle of fish. For a long time she played 'la grande dame' towards me. Martha is the unmarried daughter and another girl is married to Captain Browne of the 'Rosebush'. Their son Benjamin is married to a pretty girl whom Samuel kissed – fairly legitimately – at a forfeits party given by Sir William Penn. And there was black Mingo, their handsome African servant, always full of fun and a dancer of repute – 'Congo caperings' we called it.

One could well ask what on earth these grand Admirals, Knights and their Ladies, were doing talking, eating, drinking and making merry (lots of Valentines and other pretty frivolities) with the young, naive pair of Pepys. I think there were probably three reasons for it. They each knew the other's families and habits so well. After all, they had been living in each other's pockets in Seething Lane for a considerable time. 'En effet' they were bored stiff part of the time. Secondly, Samuel was a polite, interested, handsome young man – apparently no threat to either of them, and he responded affably to their Dolphin tavern roystering, little wagers and frolics. Thirdly, I was his very pretty wife, and those old rogues liked to see a pretty neighbour. Both their wives were plain, dowdy frumps, and I made a welcome change!

Quite early on after our arrival in Seething Lane we decided to give the gallant Admirals and their wives and Martha Batten a fine dinner. It was rather brave of us, particularly as the fire smoked during the meal, and it cost poor Samuel £5. After that we were launched in the local society. The Battens took us to visit the Navy dockyard at Chatham. Visiting a dockyard with an Admiral is rather different from visiting it with my dear little Clerk of the Acts. Sir William also lent Samuel £40 for the funeral and legal expenses incurred after Uncle Robert's death. It was the only time to my knowledge that Samuel borrowed money from anyone, except for the lute he pawned long ago. Again Samuel disliked this Sir William for his dishonesty and corruption. He was swindling the Chatham 'Chest' for disabled seamen at the time.

I had a curious relationship with Lady Batten (who was born Elizabeth Woodcock). She was Sir William's second wife, having married him in '59. She made a 'State' visit to see me in our new house in November '60, which pleased Samuel, who was not there, more than it pleased me. She and I used to go on expeditions together, including that horrible visit to see the Cromwell butchery, to Deptford and Woolwich to see various Navy ships, and Sir William once gave me a very daring Valentine. In the spring of '61 we dined with them once on a chine of beef, and later supped. Late at night stupidly I fell down there and hurt my knee, and Samuel implied that these young French girls cannot imbibe their wine 'comme il faut'. We seemed to be on good terms, but Samuel's grapevine reported to him (perhaps that gossip Mrs Turner again) ' that Lady Batten and her daughter do look something askew upon my wife because my wife do not buckle to them and is not solicitous for their acquaintance'. More than that, Lady B. actually spoke to Samuel of my having spoken unhandsomely of her, Samuel said he was sorry that this should be so, though he does not desire that there should be any acquaintance between me and her.

Friends, neighbours and enemies!

That winter however, things took a turn for the better. The Pepys and all three Battens met for dinner at the Dolphin Tavern, and Samuel commented 'the best musique and very good song and we were very merry and danced'. This did not refer to the Battens but to his old gaming friend Captain Cocke and *his* beautiful German wife, who were also at the Dolphin. On Boxing Day the Battens, Samuel and I went by coach to Moorfields to walk in foul winter weather and ended up of course in an alehouse eating cakes, drinking ale and singing Christmas wassails together. Although I liked the old besom, she and I had our Sunday ritual pitched battle at the Navy church about precedence. After the sermon we stayed behind the Battens in the Navy Pew and went out by ourselves a good while after them which we judged to be polite. Childish of course, but amusing at the time.

In July '63 when I was at Brampton, Samuel went to Martha Batten's wedding to a Mr Castle, at our parish church, then rode to Walthamstow for the grand reception, where he was given the customary two pairs of gloves. He made a point of being very nice to Lady B 'she mighty kind to me', he wrote to me 'with a good dinner and merry'. On my return to London, later on, he told me that the Castle-Batten wedding was purely for convenience 'but methinks none of the kindness nor bridall respect between the bridegroom and bride, that was between my wife and I', which is exactly what a happy married man should say to his young wife.

One evening in early winter of '65 Samuel dined at Trinity House. He had been sworn a Younger Brother of Trinity House in Deptford three years before. Afterwards Lady Batten appeared with a troop of a dozen women expecting to be made much of, wives of the Trinity House members. It was foul November weather and poor Lady Batten walked through the dirty street with new spick and span white shoes and dropped her galoshes in the mud where they stuck. What do you think my gallant husband did? He roared with laughter, thus vexing her, and left without offering to help her! He was still friends with Sir William; played him once or more at billiards and won an angel. Such a talented man!

During the Great Fire of 1666 our whole street was in a panic. Sir William Batten helped Samuel dig a deep pit in the Navy Office garden. Bon viveur Batten buried his valuable wine. My husband buried his papers, and for some curious reason, our expensive parmesan cheese! Sir William took the panic in his stride, sitting peacefully in his garden, melancholy but inactive!

In October '67 Sir William was ill. Samuel visited him and came back to tell me that he would not live much longer, which troubled both of us. We thought that he had been a good kind neighbour. He also owed Samuel some prize money. At his funeral at Walthamstow there were nearly 200 coaches of the gentry come to pay their last respects. Sir William Penn went to the funeral and reported that Lady Batten and her children-in-law were 'all broke in pieces' and that there was 'but £800 found in all the world, of money'. When Samuel and Sir W. Penn visited the widow, predictably she took it unkindly. Curiously enough a few days later Lady Batten sent for Samuel, and after finding fault with him, enlisted his support about the prize money in which Samuel and the two Sir Williams were involved.

In February '68 Samuel was now thoroughly master of his job at the Navy Office, and perfectly prepared to take on all comers. He accused Sir William Penn in front of the Board of neglect of duty, and gained the day. In March '69 Penn and Samuel were the only surviving members of the Navy Board from nine years back.

After Sir William Batten's death and Sir William Penn's impeachment, the tribal battlefields of the Seething Lane neighbourhood became more peaceful. Lady Batten moved away and our relationship with the Penns mellowed.

CHAPTER TWELVE

VALENTINES

"Saint Valentine's is past: Begin these Wood-pigeons but to couple now?" William Shakespeare

Once a year on Saint Valentine's Day there was an excuse for some ritual frolic. A 'sweetheart' would be chosen either by design or by chance for Samuel and myself, and our friends and neighbours. There was always an element of surprise, and the most unlikely partners turned up. Part of the ritual was the giving of a quite expensive present - depending on the relationship of the two people.

On the appropriate day in '60 I heard the sound of Mr Moore's voice in Samuel's dressing chamber. I got myself ready by putting on some frivolous clothes, came down and challenged Mr Moore for my Valentine. Henry Moore was a lawyer in Mr Crewe's house, who acted for "My Lord", and he and Samuel had interminable conversations apparently to the satisfaction of both! If I had challenged the wrong man I could pay a penalty!

The next year at Sir William Batten's we all chose our Valentines for the following day. I chose my dear Samuel, and Lady Batten chose Sir William Penn. In the morning Samuel went off early to the Battens and had some droll foolery with black Mingo before he was allowed in to give Martha Batten his Valentine, which he said he only did for 'complacent' good manners. Meanwhile Sir William Batten came to me as my second Valentine (which is not really allowed) and so we were very merry. A few days later Samuel and I and Martha Batten sallied forth to the Exchange and bought for her a 'payre of embroydered and six payre of plain white gloves' - all at a cost of 40 shillings. I went off to see her father who sent me half a dozen pair of gloves and a pair of silk stockings and *garters* for my Valentine.

The next year Samuel purposely refrained from visiting the William Battens house because the year before he had been embarassed by the choice of Martha Batten as Valentine and our previous friendship had faded. My Valentine was William Bowyer, the good humoured, slightly simple son of the kind family who looked after me when Samuel was at sea.

One year young Dickie Penn came to be my Valentine, and up to our bedroom, where we both were. Samuel coaxed Dickie to his side of the bed pretending coyly that Dickie should kiss him! Samuel's schoolboy sense of humour! He described my Valentine as a 'notable, stout, witty boy'!

The next year Samuel secured the beautiful Elizabeth Pierce, the surgeon's wife, as his Valentine. She had put Samuel's name on the bosom of her dress. Despite this, Samuel's reaction was not one of joy because her Valentine would cost him a lot of money. My Valentine was a bit mixed-up. Nice little Thomas Hill, the Huguenot merchant-musician, called up at the right place and the right time and I thought he came to be my Valentine as I thought I had drawn him, but not so. Anyway I called him up to my bedside and challenged him, thus forcing him to be my Valentine.

Mary Mercer's younger brother, little Will Mercer, a school boy, came next year to be my Valentine. He had written my name upon blue paper in gold letters done by himself. A promising lad. Samuel was also my Valentine and muttered that it would cost him £5. Indeed it did. That year there was a new custom of a drawing of a motto for one's unknown lover. James Pierce the surgeon was also my Valentine – the third that year – and the motto for me was 'Most courteous and most fair'. Samuel drew Elizabeth Pierce's little girl for a Valentine, at which he was relieved, because a smaller outlay on a present was involved – mean old thing!

Mary Mercer was Samuel's Valentine the next time, and he gave her a golden guinea. Roger Pepys was mine and again Samuel, as we had agreed that he should be my special Valentine each year for a ring worth £5.

Cousin Turner was Samuel's Valentine the next year. She is such a sweet favourite of ours that Samuel bought her a pair of green silk stockings and garters and shoestrings and two pairs of jessamine scented gloves, coming to 28 shillings.

And so it goes on, a pleasant custom towards the end of winter, which encourages people to be frivolous, sometimes kind, and enables the younger children to participate. Samuel and I certainly enjoy St Valentine's Day each year and much look forward to it.

CHAPTER THIRTEEN

MY LITTLE POPINJAY

"Il n'y a point de héros pour son valet de chambre"
Madame Cornuel

My husband's philosophy in relation to his wardrobe and personal clothes was made clear to me very early on in our marriage. The sartorial tradition in his family – his father a tailor for nearly 50 years, his brother Tom following in the same trade, and Samuel's own background in the cutting room and delivery of clothes to customers, meant to him simply that 'fine feathers do a gentleman make'. He said that in those early days 'for want of clothes, I was forced to sneak like a beggar'. Not really true of course because we were then not moving in high society from our little garret.

Samuel sometimes berates me for my untidiness with my clothes, but he admits to me the same problem 'I not being neat in clothes which I find a great fault in me, could not be so merry as otherwise, when I am in good habit, which makes me remember my father Osborne's [an early mentor] rule for a gentleman, to spare in all things rather than that'. On one occasion Samuel said to me 'I find that I must go handsomely whatever it costs me and the charge will be made up in the fruits it brings'. Another time he described our Sunday morning church-going – he in his new periwig, I in my handsome new mourning suit, as making 'a great showe'.

After three years of marriage our income was about £50 per annum. At that time Samuel's day by day wear was a suit of black stuff clothes – not very practical as a colour because it showed the dirt and needed constant cleaning. The Puritan upbringing of the family and constant mourning for dead brothers, sisters, and other relatives made black an essential colour. In addition our gay little spark had a grand suit for special occasions with great skirts at the back to nearly calf-level, a white suit with a silver *lace* coat, and a fine cloak to keep out the elements. All this in addition to the basic requirements of shirts, underclothes, nightgowns, shoes and stockings. For instance an Indian gown cost him 34 shillings, a scallop (a lace band in scallop-shell pattern) for his coat sleeves, £3, a hat from Mr Holden's 35 shillings, a belt the colour of his suit 55 shillings, a velvet cloak £8.10 shillings. His camelot (camel hair) suit cost more than £24 and, was, he said, 'the best that ever I wore in my life'. A 'common' riding cloak 'to save my best one' cost him 30 shillings. In October '63 Samuel reckoned his net worth was £717. (It had been £40 three years earlier). He had just spent £55 on a velvet cloak, two cloth shirts, black, both plain; a purple shagg gown trimmed with gold buttons and twist loop-lace, with a hat and silk tops for his legs; two periwigs costing £5 together and various other things 'being resolved henceforward to go like myself'! The next year he bought for £17 a fine coloured cloth suit, with plush lined cloak 'which is dear and noble'.

In our early days of marriage, Samuel's wardrobe was relatively modest and I washed and cleaned it all myself. With our increasing prosperity his wardrobe grew at a great rate. As a direct result our maid, or later, maids, kept busy washing and cleaning his clothes (and of course mine too), particularly his breeches, which were always getting torn or mud spattered. He needed the help of one or more maids to attire himself to brave the outside world. Since my maids were usually pretty, this little ritual often developed into more of a romp than I felt was seemly.

At certain times of year, in the spring or late autumn, there is the ceremonial changing over to lighter weight or heavier weight clothes. One May morning Samuel visited his tailor to try on a summer suit; not his fine one of flowered tabby vest and coloured tunic because he thought it *too fine* with the gold lace at the bands and was therefore afraid to be seen in it. Instead he put on the stuff suit made the previous year which had been repaired.

Quite soon some dashing outfits appeared. Brother Tom produced a Jackanapes coat with silver buttons and a new black baize waistcoat faced with silk. Samuel wore his first new *silk* suit in the summer of '60. But Tom was quickly berated in the cutting room for lying to Samuel about the quality of his new morning gown, and also for botching his new camlott coat. From Mr Pim, "My Lord's" tailor, Samuel bought a velvet coat down to his knees. When my father-in-law retired to the country and poor Tom had died, Samuel transferred his custom to Mr Langford who took over the trade and goodwill of the family business. Samuel described him as 'a very modest carefull young man'. He produced for him a new black cloth suit and cloak lined with silk moyre. Once I visited Mr Langford with Mary Mercer, looked at his wares and ordered two rich silk suits, which were produced in four days. Samuel usually trusted my eye for colour and fashion, which was a great compliment. Mr Burrows, the slopseller, sold Samuel two very large state-caps to wear at Court for £6 each. Sometimes Samuel would buy things from my French tailor Monsieur Unthancke. Early in '66 Mr Penny the tailor arrived on the scene and made a new plain velvet coat which my husband thought was very handsome. He also made a cloak and cassock for brother John's canonical dress. My brother-in-law was then studying for the church.

Samuel's mercer, Mrs Bennett in Paternoster Row, provided the material stuff for the camelot cloak for a cost of £6, and for the velvet coat above £8. We also bought velvet for another coat there and counterfeit damasks to hang in my closet in our house.

A well dressed man-about-town needs many accessories, such as lace from the 'laceman'. "My Lord" Mountagu's master-of-horse's mistress was a 'lacelady'. From her Samuel bought broad gold scallops for £6 a pair, to put round his coat sleeves. He bought buckles for his shoes. Mr Wotton, the shoemaker, provided a pair of new boots for 30 shillings, which were so tight that Samuel could hardly take them off after riding with Will Hewer to Brampton. He had to pay 4 shillings to his landlord en route for an old pair of shoes in which to finish the journey. Mr Wotton had a pretty wife and served free cider, so Samuel bought another pair of boots there a year later. Mr Wotton also blacked the sides of Samuel's shoes for poor Tom's funeral. Being a great walker, Samuel owns many pairs of shoes, never less than ten pairs in his closet. Once he was given a pair of light blue silk stockings by Captain Thomas Sparling of the "Assistance". He bought himself a pair of linen stockings in Holland on his visit there to meet the King. If he was in mourning he would wear short black stockings over the silk ones. Once at Biggleswade, riding to Hatfield in midwinter, his thread stockings were so cold under his boots, he had to stop and buy a pair of coarse woollen ones.

Samuel often wore a 'best' fur cap for important occasions. As he rose in the world so did his height! From Mr Holden he bought a beaver hat for £4.5 shillings, double the price of a cap or small hat. This added at least three inches to his height. He wore it to watch the Lord Mayor's show with his half cloth black stockings and a fashionable new coat. He bought a second hand beaver, from Sir William Batten, 'old but very good'. It is the fashion to keep one's hat on at dinner. Once Samuel caught a heavy cold by flinging off his hat at a dinner, and sitting with the draft on his neck. He usually wears his hat in Committe. He says that only clerks bare their heads at work. A handsome neat belt for second mourning cost him

Samuel Pepys by J. Hayls, by permission of National Portrait Gallery

24 shillings. A new slashed doublet and a false tabby waistcoat with gold lace, were also acquired by my little popinjay.

Naturally enough Samuel has a keen sense of fashion. One Sunday he put on his black cloth suit, with 'white lynings under all' as the fashion is, to appear under the breeches. At the end of '60 at his fathers tailor's shop he changed his long black cloak for a short one, 'long cloaks being now quite out'! Another Sunday (the Lord's Day and churchgoing habits requiring one's finery to be worn), my husband put on his new black bombazine stuff suit with a shoulder-belt according to the new fashion and the bands of his vest and tunic were laced with silk lace of the colour of his suit. And so, very handsome to Church!

At a family sartorial conference with brother Tom we decided Samuel needed to have a good cloak of cloth, lined with velvet and other modish things and a perruque. So Tom and I sallied forth to the family tailor shop together to buy the velvet and generally supervise my little master's 'modish garbe'. My husband also bought a velvet riding hat which was in the height of fashion.

After the victory over the Dutch navy on 3rd June '65, with our Lord Sandwich safe, Samuel was beside himself for 'joy of the good news which makes me willing to spare myself something extraordinary in clothes'. He was then 'worth £1900 for which the great God of Heaven and Earth be praised'. He sallied forth to his tailor's and havered between a black and a coloured silk ferrandin suit. The latter arrived two days later. He looked most peculiar in it, and I told him so as politely as I could. Nevertheless, he visited the Duke of Albermarle the next day wearing it. As he could not return the suit, he disguised some of its gaudy effects by immediately buying some good lace in gold for his sleeve bands. Shortly afterwards I left with my maid for Woolwich – to stay with Mrs Barbara Sheldon – it was the time of the plague.

For a long time Samuel flirted with the idea of wearing a large periwig on his head. He had bought a perruque – a smart little wig-from Tom his tailor brother. Many at Court wear them including the royal brothers, so they were fashionable. But there were several problems to contend with. In our society, keeping one's hair clean is difficult and periwigs harbour fleas and worse. Samuel needed to have his hair cut short in order to mount a periwig on his head. This in turn meant that in winter he caught cold – which he did frequently – if he was not wearing his periwig. Often I cut his hair for him. Mr Jervas, his original barber, stocked 'borders' and periwigs, but Samuel disliked one he saw there made of greasy old woman's hair. Samuel was reluctant though to let Mr Jervas cut his hair. There were several specialist shops about the Temple and new periwigs would cost between £2 and £3 each. His first purchase was from a Mr Chapman, Samuel told me 'there he cut off my hair which went a little to my heart at present to part with it'. He parted also with £3 – almost a young servant maid's wages for a year. The shorn Pepys hair was collected to form the basis of his next purchase, which cost 21s 6d more than the first and was to last two years.

One of the advantages of having a large ménage was that we also had a ready audience for our expensive frippery and foibles. Samuel's first act on the purchase of his startling new periwig was to show it off to his family. He had caused all the maids to look upon their master and his new wig and they concluded that it suited him (someone I know very well would have been most vexed if his choice had in any way been criticised), although Jane and Besse were mightily troubled because Samuel's own hair had been so shorn. Just to be sure, my little manikin showed it off at the Office to Sir William Batten and old Sir John Minnes, the Navy Comptroller and our neighbour. He reported back to me 'No great matter made of my periwig, as I was afraid there would be'. At church on the Lord's Day where he found that his arrival in a periwig did not prove so strange as he was afraid it would be for he thought that *all* the church would presently have cast their eyes *all* upon him, but he found no such thing! So Samuel and periwig were safely launched into society.

In the spring he allowed his own hair to grow again, but he found the convenience of wearing periwigs to be so great he cut if off and resumed wearing them.

During the Plague year of '66 it was rumoured that new periwigs were being made from hair of people who had died of the plague, but Samuel ensured that he only wore those made earlier. Nevertheless in March '67 he bought two more for £4. 10 shillings the pair. Thereafter he bought them each year from Monsieur Robins, William Batelier's friend in Covent Garden, who also kept an excellent little French restaurant – an 'ordinary'. Samuel's barber is now paid 20 shillings a year to keep his periwigs in good order. 'I am like to go very spruce, more than I used to do', said my man-about-town to me.

The haut monde all wear swords – such is the fashion. They probably do not care to use them and probably do not know how to wield them. But apparently it gives a devil-may-care swash-buckling appearance to the outside world. Of course if 'le bon ton' wear swords, so must my little hero.

I think it was the week when "My Lady" sent me two bottles of good red Tuscany wine from Florence, that Samuel first appeared wearing a sword. "My Lady" often coaxes him to spend more money; this time perhaps it was a result of the Tuscan wine they had been drinking together at the Wardrobe. His family, (as he used to call myself and maids and Will Hewer etc.) were all agog. Samuel is a fine rider and these days on the high roads one meets all kinds of rough and dangerous people, so a sword not only suits him, but might even deter footpads and others. Not content with that, in the spring of '63 he bought in Fleet Street a little sword with a gilt handle for 25 shillings, silk stockings to match his riding cloth suit for 15 shillings, plus a new belt for 15 shillings, on which to hang his sword. Once he went on foot to Greenwich, and was set upon by a large dog, who grabbed him by his garters and might have done him serious harm. That was bad enough, but he was wearing his sword and forgot to draw it to meet the dog. Then he admitted to me afterwards 'I had not the heart to use it for want of courage'. My husband may not be very brave but he is honest!

After the fire of London, when there were many homeless and desperate people in among the ruins of the city, Samuel would always carry his drawn sword in the hired coach taking him home. Later on, just after we had bought our own coach, Samuel bought from the cutler's a new sword for 12 shillings, and a belt to match. This was for our boy Tom Edwards to use in the coach, to help defend the opulent Pepys family from footpads. A new coach was indicative of filled purses within. Samuel sent his sword off to be re-gilt! Its primary purpose was for elegance, not in any way for self defence. His Easter Day parade would consist of his close-kneed coloured suit with new matching silk stockings, with belt *and* new gilt-handled sword, which I admit is very handsome. On another Sunday he would wear his best black cloth suit, trimmed with scarlet ribbons, very neat, with a velvet lined cloak, a very noble new beaver hat, and his black silk knit cannons (hose). He admitted, 'I like myself mightily in it and so does my wife'. I do indeed – Samuel looks magnificent.

For riding Samuel owns, as I do, a complete outfit of clothes – a camelot riding coat, which is warm and nearly rainproof, underneath which he wears a grey coloured cloth suit and also a faced white coat made of one of my old petticoats, with 'close' knees which are similar to riding breeches.

Apart from purchasing a hare's foot to keep on his person to ward off the colic, Samuel by trial and error started to dress more *sensibly*. He left off wearing a long gown within doors all day. He found that in the cold winter wind his legs in silk stockings only brought him daily pains. He refrained from wearing too many clothes, often only a doublet or a waistcoat cut open at the back under a coat. Outside he now wears a *long* cloak in the winter. One reason he gives me for what he calls his 'collique pain' is that he washes his feet too much in cold water. It was only after we had been married some years that I insisted we both used warm water to wash in. Often he went out in a thin silk waistcoat, open breasted, without any other coat over it. In hot weather he wears a cloth across his stomach to absorb his perspiration, which reduces the number of summer colds that he catches. Of course he admits that his daily dose of a turpentine pill each morning does help his colic! Although we always share a bed and keep each other warm in all the usual marital ways, we both of us wear long nightgowns. Samuel always wears in addition a nightcap and neckcloth in the winter, which often hampers his nocturnal activities, but at least keeps him warm. It also makes him snore noisily. There is nothing romantic 'of a midnight scene' in our house – although I make sure that I always look my best for Samuel.

Occasionally if Samuel had had too much 'drinking and roaring' the night before – usually with John Creed – he would lie in bed in his drawers, stockings and waistcoat till five o'clock in the morning. Sometimes he stayed the night with his boon companions for he was never allowed to go to sleep in our house fully clothed in a drunken state. He might return to his female ménage the worse for wear, but one way or another he would be made more sober, and so to bed – respectably.

Samuel is always generous. He gave Mr Shepley, "My Lord's" steward, a pair of buckskin gloves, admittedly five years old. He sent his father many pairs of shoes and old clothes. He looked over his old wardrobe and laid out things for his brother John and his father, even if it meant he would leave himself very short of clothes. He gave his brother Tom a suit of black stuff clothes, a hat and some shoes. He also makes sure our maids and young Tom are well dressed, partly I suspect because a brave face to the neighbours extends to all his 'family'. One Easter he had his old black suit refurbished and said to me rather smugly, 'I was pretty neat in clothes today.' He had young Will Hewer's old suit refurbished so that it looked as good as new. Court mourning say, for the death of the King of Spain, would need the use of one's best black mourning suit, if one had two suits. A death of a remote relation would only merit second best mourning! When his mother died Samuel had to spend a great deal of money on mourning clothes for his servants to wear, mainly for the Penn, Batten and Minnes households to see!

Although his friends John Creed and Thomas Povey pull Samuel's leg from time to time, he takes their jokes seriously – the former about the grandeur of our fine new horses and coach, and the latter about his gold laced sleeves in the Park. I tell him not to heed their jokes, made out of envy.

He spends large amounts of time, as I do, in planning his sartorial purchases. It is his hard earned money and he spends it lavishly. But he spends about five times as much a year on clothes for himself, including trimmings such as periwigs and swords, as he does on my clothes. I do not complain much. My little popinjay is a fine figure of a man, swaggering around Whitehall and St James with his useless sword and brave ribbons.

CHAPTER FOURTEEN

FAITH AND RELIGION

"Ah pour être devôt, je n'en suis pas moins Homme"
Molière

My father's family from Anjou were traditionally strict Roman Catholics. Converts to the Huguenot religion in France in the 16th century were numerous. The Huguenots, as they were called, were in their turn just as bigoted as the religion they had abjured. When Alexandre met and married his wife, my mother, we were initially brought up in Bideford, in the small Huguenot colony there. My mother flirted with the Catholic faith when she allowed Balty and I to be lured away in Paris to my Great Uncles' designated convents. But the nuns did not have long to work on me before our escape from Paris was engineered. Certainly my life would have been completely different if I had stayed there.

One ghost from the youthful past to reappear has been Father Fogourdy. He is an Irish Catholic priest, who knew my mother and I when we were living in Paris. He came to see me and my mother several times, out of friendship, in the spring of '64. Samuel met him too, and thinks him a sober and discreet person. I am sure that Samuel is worried in case Father Fogourdy tries to convert or abjure me to the other religion! The Father did try to persuade me to hear the famous Roulé preach at the French Ambassador's house in Westminster. The 'tempter' Samuel called him.

Samuel would often visit two or even three churches on the Lord's Day, mainly to hear the sermons, although he admits to sleeping through several. We know all the Huguenot pastors in London. Mr Wanley, our Axe Street house landlord, is one of them, so is my dentist Monsieur La Roche; Monsieur Brevin, whom we met at Sir George Carteret's, another. In the '60s Samuel and I would frequently go to the two French Huguenot churches in London – either together or separately. Charles II established our church of the Savoy and Edward VI founded the other French Protestant church of St Anthony's hospital in Threadneedle St, which was burned in the Great Fire, but afterwards rebuilt.

Once Samuel and Tom, the boy, went to the Savoy church. On their return Samuel described it to me 'a pretty place it is there they have the Common Prayer book read in French and the Minister do preach with his hat off, I suppose in further conformity with our church'. On another occasion he reported 'I to the French church here in the City – Threadneedle – and stood in the aisle all the sermon from a very young man upon the article in the Creed in order of Catechism upon the Resurrection'. The French church numbered many pretty ladies amongst the congregation. The Bateliers and Madame Lethulier, 'my fat brown beauty' was Samuel's unseemly description of her. We both knew and liked her. She was married to a merchant. One of the French pastors had three very pretty sisters. Samuel liked going to the French Huguenot churches, even though once he said to me 'I heard an old man make a tedious long sermon till they were fain to light candles to baptise the children by'.

Robert Frampton from Dorset became a Naval chaplain. At the end of '66 Samuel and I went to listen to his sermons in Westminster. He is now quite famous, and early in '67 he came to preach to us in our own church. His sermon was from Ecclesiastes XI verse 8 'But if a man live many years, and rejoice in them all, yet let him remember the days of darkness, for they shall be many. All that cometh is vanity'. Samuel described it to me 'I think the best sermon, for goodness and oratory without affection or study that ever I heard in my life. The truth is, he preaches the most like an apostle that ever I heard man, and it was much the best time that I ever spent in my life at church'.

I sometimes went to hear him preach by myself. When I compare him to poor, lazy Mr Milles, parson of our church, St Olave's, Hart Street, I wonder if we are talking of the same religion – the true Protestant religion.

Once, in '63 Samuel and I were invited by Mr Rawlinson our wine merchant to the Jewish synagogue 'But Lord to see the disorderly, laughing, sporting and no attention, but confusion in their service', was how Samuel described it afterwards. That visit was made out of curiosity.

In the winter of '68 at the height of our marital quarrels about Elizabeth Knepp and Deb. Willet, I hinted several times to Samuel, only to hurt him, that I was thinking of reverting to being a Catholic. He did not dare ask me to go to our usual Protestant churches in case I refused him and never went to church again. He thinks, and he ought to know by now, that I fear God and am truly and sincerely righteous. It was stupid of me to strike at Samuel's vulnerable spot, and now I regret it. But I quickly resumed going to Protestant churches with him, to his relief.

In the Pepys household on a Sunday night before bed, Samuel or I read a chapter out aloud from the Bible, and he reads prayers out of the Common Prayer Book. In September '61 Samuel had been gadding about on the Saturday, and was much the worse for wear on the Sunday. He came home and went to bed, without family prayers, for the first time ever. He dared not read prayers, for fear of the servants perceiving the state he was in. Sometimes we ask the maids to read extracts from the Bible, and then have prayers and so to bed. Samuel often sings psalms in English or in French for his and my enjoyment. On the face of it a most Godly household.

Samuel and I were chosen as godparents to many of our friends' children. Mrs Hunt's son John was one of my godsons. She is our friendly neighbour of Axe Lane, with whom I play cards. Samuel was godfather to his cousin Scott's boy (as also was Samuel Pepys of Ireland), to Mrs Martin's new daughter, and to Mrs Poole's daughter, heartily christened by Samuel as Elizabeth. Afterwards he kissed the mother *and* the two godmothers. I was godmother to Daniel Milles the Parson's young son of the same name. We gave him a gold basin which cost Samuel £10.14 shillings. I felt guilty when I remembered all Samuel's harsh verdicts on those 'lazy' sermons. I also went to Pegg Penn's child's christening, where the child made a flutter and noise. Christenings are made at short notice these days. Betty Mitchell went into labour at midnight on a Saturday; a girl child was born in the morning, and I, as godmother, attended the Christening in the afternoon. The child was called Betty after her mother.

Samuel naturally has several reasons for going to church every Sunday. For a start it was traditional in the Puritan family background in which he was brought up. It is quite essential for him to go and listen to the sermons and examine their content and delivery very closely, almost as an intellectual challenge. His own conduct to me, his family, his friends and his colleagues is at all times in the best of Christian traditions. He lies not, nor does he steal, but he often loves his neighbours, the pretty neighbours, in a way that our Maker hardly intended that he should.

"The Huguenot Church, London" by Hogarth, by permission of Mary Evans Picture Library

CHAPTER FIFTEEN

LA BONNE TABLE

"L'appetit vient en mangeant" Fr. Rabelais

When I married Samuel I had little experience of cuisine. My mother made vague attempts to interest me in some basic cooking, but at fifteen one has different ideas. The kitchen for me then had little interest! The old man of twenty two that I married, quite soon changed all that. Samuel then and now has always been fond and knowledgeable of 'la bonne table'.

Initially there were the inevitable disasters to which most young married women fall prone. Even five years after marriage I was dressing the remains of a turkey and burned my hand, which was a remarkably silly thing to do as Samuel was the first to point out. But I made tarts and marmalade and larded pullets for my master's table, often till 11 o'clock in the evening. In my young days I was squeamish about killing and plucking turkeys and chickens before I cooked them. There was no alternative. Even if Samuel had been there on the spot, which he was not, I could not have asked him to do it for me. As for cutting up chunks of red venison with which to make venison-pie (a great favourite of ours!) I had to force myself to be a butcher like all other London housewives who were working on a limited household budget. Sir Stephen Fox once sent us a whole buck, unskinned, uneverything – so generous, but bloody work for 'la bonne table'.

A typical meal for visitors in '60, when we were still poor, was a dish of marrow bones, a leg of mutton, a loin of veal, a dish of fowl, three pullets, two dozen little larks in one large dish, a great tart, neat's tongue, a dish of anchovies, a dish of prawns cooked with cheese – delicious, I can still remember it. To be fair it was a dinner for 12 people. It was for Samuel's family mainly, and I tried very hard. There was his father, his uncle Thomas Fenner the blacksmith and his two sons-in-law, Mr Pierce, the surgeon – and all their wives, and Samuel's brother Tom. It was a very fine dinner as Samuel later agreed. Possibly worth all the effort, but I am not quite sure.

Friends, thank goodness, sent us gifts of food. "My Lord" Mountagu sent me delicious brawn from his country estate. A pair of fine turtledoves, almost too pretty for the pot came from Samuel's clerk; gherkins from Captain Cocke, the gambler; crab and lobster from Peg Penn; a side of pork from Captain Grove; turkeys from Captain Anthony Deane; two cygnets from Mr Shepley, Lord Sandwich's steward. Mr Hosier in the Navy Yard sent us a whole doe. We had the umbles of it for dinner. Samuel also would bring back produce for the table, such as rabbits and lobsters. He had a catholic taste – occasionally red herrings for our breakfast. One needs to be a brave French lady to accept that!

In our Navy house in Seething Lane we had an oven with which I was not familiar. Samuel described the scene 'Making of pyes and tarts to try her oven with (which she hath never yet done) but not knowing the nature of it did heat it too hot and so did a little overbake her things'. Polite Samuel – the pies were nearly black, just edible 'but knows how to do better another time' said the schoolmaster in the family.

But he could be demanding too. Once he noted 'all alone to a leg of mutton, the sawce of which being made sweet, I was angry at it and eat none, but only dined upon the marrow bone that we had beside'. The French rarely have sweet sauces and I was not at my best that day. The master was often tetchy and angry at home at his family eating a fine pudding without *his* leave. On another occasion at Christmas he found that I and the maid with much ado had made shift to spit a great turkey . . . but not at all roasted, so Samuel was not fed till two o'clock. Spit-roasting is quite an art, which took me a long time to master. Two days later, on Christmas Day, we gave young brother Tom, the tailor, a good shoulder of mutton and a chicken. If we were alone we would make do with a boiled leg of mutton, rarely vegetables, and always many pies that I would make. A hashed pullet we considered a delicacy 'en famille'.

Fruits we had quite frequently. "My Lord" once sent me a hamper of 'millons' (melons) from Lisbon. We had the usual English countryside fruits of apples and pears, and were sometimes given grapes from Spain or Portugal by friends with overseas connections.

We ate cheeses each week, as different as possible. Once my two servants grumbled at some lovely Suffolk cheese, which made Samuel vexed when I told him. Servants! Baldock fair was a good place to buy cheese and other commodities.

We had a dreadful scene once, which was entirely my fault. Samuel came home to dinner, and left the table in a temper complaining of the blackness of the meat as it came out of the pot, blaming me and the maid for our sluttery. It was not particularly *old* meat, but the rich dark sauce had coloured it to some extent – I think! Another disaster was with some boiled great oysters (in March, so they should have been safe). Poor Samuel ate them with gusto, and was appallingly sick immediately afterwards, but mine were delicious.

Samuel's personal feast-day each year, the 26th March, was the anniversary of his operation for the cutting of his stone, and we usually indulged ourselves in a well spread table. I remember in '67 we asked the Turners, Samuel's cousins who were so good to him four years before, also their daughter Theophila, who was a great favourite with both of us, Joyce Norton, another cousin who lived with the Turners, and a jolly gentleman called Mr Lewin of the Kings Life-Guard, invited in order to keep young Theophila company. Samuel insisted that I should not work that day in the kitchen, so we had a man-cook in to dress and cook the dinner for the great occasion. The menu was a brace of stewed carps, six roasted chickens, and a hot jowl of salmon – all that for the first course, a 'tanzy' to follow and two neat's tongues and cheese for the second course. The 'tanzy' was made with many eggs and cream flavoured with the herb-juice of tansy – the whole dish a blend of an omelette and a soufflé – delicious. We were merry all the afternoon, talking and singing and Samuel piping on the flageolette. A day and a meal to remember.

My master's own discerning culinary taste was always present. We once dined à deux upon a most excellent dish of tripes 'of my own directing', as Samuel said proudly 'covered with mustard, of which we made a very great meal', and so we did.

Lord Brouncker, another important Navy Commissioner, and his mistress Mrs Williams, expressed an interest to meet me and see our new house. They suddenly arrived one evening without warning, and we made them welcome with wine and China oranges – a great rarity indeed. Luckily our house was clean and did us great honour, and they were mightily pleased with it.

My Lord Coventry rarely visited us, which was a pity as he was a good honest, capable man in the Navy, whom we both liked and respected. On one of his visits, I miscalculated, the leg of mutton and two capons were much underdone, and Samuel was rightly angry with me – 'mea culpa'. We were spending £7 a month on food at the time and living well, but that did not mean that each meal was perfect.

One day I was not feeling well, and Samuel dined by my bedside with great content on the most extraordinary mélange. A mess of 'brave' plum-porridge, a roasted pullet and a mince pie each, as it was Christmas Day. Next day I was up and about, busy making more mince pies.

It sounds easy, cooking for a small household, with money available, but often I would leave the house at five o'clock in the morning to go to market to buy fruit and other things for dinner. Samuel was pleased that I did try very hard to achieve 'la bonne table'.

Another sumptuous spread was partly prepared by a new cook-maid paid £4 per annum who had come from Lord Monk's house. She and I produced a fricassée of rabbits and chickens, a leg of mutton boiled, three carps in a dish, a great dish of a side of lamb, a dish of roasted pigeons, a dish of four lobsters, three tarts, a lamprey pie (a most rare pie, Samuel called it,) *and* a dish of anchovies. Samuel served good wine of several sorts and pronounced 'all things mighty noble and to my great content'. This was another 'Feast of the Stone' for the Turners, Mrs Wright (an Aunt) and Roger Pepys – so it was appropriate that we made a great effort.

Samuel favoured some strange dishes: once I procured a good hog's harslet which he described as 'a piece of meat I love, but have not eat of these seven years'. Also he was quite happy when we dined alone if I cooked him a simple meal of a good hen with eggs or a speciality of mine – a pleasant French fricassée of veal. On religious days such as Good Friday, we would have not a fast but a modest dish, for instance of sugar-sopps and fish – a Lenten dinner. If I had special commitments, for instance washing clothes day, we would have a simple pie baked of a leg of mutton. But at Christmas we would usually have traditional turkey and mince pies – often just the two of us, alone. I would stay up till 4 in the morning seeing my maids make mince pies; one Christmas we dined on some good ribs of beef roasted and of course mince pies . . . and plenty of good wine of our own. Samuel drank wine like a true Frenchman, or at least like someone married to a French wife. Over the New Year another traditional dish for the table was 'the best powdered goose that ever I eat'. Samuel's description of my meals was often appreciative.

Occasionally, not very often, I would procure for our table what *I* wanted! One April I had a mind to some fresh caught salmon and a *hundred* asparagus (Samuel calls them sparrowgrass and perhaps he is correct) . . . cost 18 pence. To myself I called it a pregnant urge, but alas, I was not pregnant.

At the height of the crisis with the Dutch fleet in the Medway I thought I might inspire Samuel to greater activity for our defence. I gave him a dinner which of course we ate in the middle of the day consisting of a ham of *French* bacon, boiled with pigeons. Our naval gentleman pronounced it to be an excellent dish. The Dutch ships still broke the boom and sank all of our ships.

My husband sets great store by his wine cellar. Since most of it is good honest red French wine – some Bataillhey – I of course approve wholeheartedly. But it is his responsibility and not mine to keep our little cellar stocked. One evening John Andrews and his wife dined with us. Mr Andrews is John Crewe's steward. John Crewe is son of Lord Crewe, who is "My Lady's" father! they were people that we rarely saw or cared about. Samuel however lost 'face'. He rather grandly said to the Andrews 'my people forgot to get the wine ready'. This was completely accurate, because Samuel's cellar was bare. Usually he has two or three different qualities of wine available but that night there was 'rien du tout'. I thought it was rather amusing, but kept a straight face whilst we were fain to stay a great while, while some could be fetched. If wives produce an overbaked pie there is trouble; if husbands cannot produce a bottle of wine there is – silence!

One day in '67 Samuel was at home on the Lord's Day, very busy on setting his books in order in his presses – his library in effect. I resolved to give my studious, intellectual husband an appropriate dinner, so we had powdered leg of pork and a loin of lamb (*not* mutton) roasted – a great delicacy,

Samuel once brought home for the table some English apples and pork. He told me that the butcher had commended it as the best in England 'for cloath and colour'. Of his beef the butcher said 'look how fat it is, the lean appears only here and there a speck, like beauty-spots'. Any good Parisienne housewife would have made short shrift of such a man. There lean meat is always in demand, not fat meat. So Samuel refrained from buying the English beef!

The Pepys ménage fared very well at the table. This was mainly because although, at first, I knew little about the method of preparation of good food, I had a father and a brother who demanded and received a high standard of cuisine. They also demanded a wide variety of dishes. I never knew for sure how my sweet impractical mother managed to satisfy the French blood in the family! My father regarded expenditure on good food and wine as essential, that is to say, requiring a high priority. Like all good Frenchmen he made sure that his, and our, mid-day repas was of the highest possible standard. Or else. This I inherited – all but the vital knowledge of exactly how to produce what was necessary. Luckily for me I married a man who had the same high standard, was prepared to spend household money to obtain it, and encouraged my successes although he occasionally discouraged me when I failed him.

CHAPTER SIXTEEN

LES PETITES OCCASIONS

"Le peuple a de la joie" Baron de Montesquieu

One of the advantages of being married to Samuel is his happy casual unpredictability. He suddenly says 'Let's go and see this, or go there, or visit somebody we have not seen for some time'. It is not just that he is restless, but his capacity for enjoyment, his abundant energy, and his questing mind – all working simultaneously – produce for me, anyway, dozens of happy 'petites occasions'.

We walk great distances for a variety of reasons. When we were poor we could not afford a coach unless it was essential and so became accustomed to walking. London is quite a small town and the green fields and parks are close by. Finally we are young, active and healthy, and actually like walking about! Oh and of course the dog always needs exercise.

Sometimes I visit Samuel in Whitehall and walk with him in St James Park to see the gallants and the fashionable ladies and the brave new alterations to the neighbouring houses.

My husband has his own barge or rowing boat on the Thames, which is oared by Mr Harry Russell, his boatman. He described one outing when 'we went to the water to spend the afternoon in pleasure and so we went to old Georges and there eat as much as we could of a hot shoulder of mutton and so to boat again and home'. That was one of our many summer pastorales.

Once we walked to the Spittle (Cockney rhyming slang for Christs Hospital). We waited for an hour or two for the Lord Mayor and the 'blewe-coate' boys to come. A 'fine sight of charity it is indeed', said Samuel. The young boys receive a good education quite free, but must wear their well-known blue uniform all the time in public. We stayed in the Hospital Chapel to hear a long-winded Presbyterian sermon, but slunk away after an hour.

Another expedition we made was to Hampton Court by barge down the Thames. We walked from Mortlake to Richmond and thence to the Palace. Mr Marriott the housekeeper, showed us the whole house which was nobly furnished.

In the spring I always need flowers for the house, so the Pepys family and their black dog, sally forth over the water to Halfway house and beyond into the fields gathering of yellow cow-slips to take back with us. We take cold lamb with us and sup on it lying in the long grass, singing, and it is a most pleasant walk back again.

Another early summer's day Samuel 'upon a suddaine motion' took me and Sarah and Will Hewer by water with some victuals with us as low as Gravesend intending to have gone into 'the Hope' to see the ship the "Royal James". On the way we met nice Mr Shepley "My Lords" country steward who sent us gifts for our table, in a small boat called a Hoy. We went on board at his invitation and sailed as far as Halfway Tree, a wellknown landmark near the river. There we saw a little Turkish boy and a negro boy who Mr Shepley was meeting, destined to become pages to the young Mountagu ladies. Then we returned home by our boat to a dish of mackerel fish and peas!

May was a good month for our expeditions. Samuel's family – that is me and the maids and Will Hewer took boat to Fox-Hall (Vauxhall) gardens on the south side of the Thames. We visited the old Spring Garden and walked for miles. The maids and I gathered pinks (not lilac) and then we all had delicious cakes and powdered beef and ale in the early summer sunshine. Such warm, innocent, carefree days. So home again by water with much pleasure, with Samuel usually singing his head off. In mid-summer in the long evenings after supper Samuel and I would walk to the boat and over the water to the halfway house. He described it as 'A pretty pleasant walk with the wind high'.

In the autumn we often visit puppet shows. At Charing Cross once we saw the 'Italian Motion'. Samuel thought their puppets were good, well made, but their puppet motions not as good as others we have seen at Bartholomew Fayre.

Occasionally Samuel would hire a coach and we would go for long trips around the outskirts of London: to places like Whitechapel, Bednell (Bethnal) Green, Hackney, Kingsland and Newington Green. The roads were rough, dusty and crowded, but it made a pleasant excursion. Samuel knows London well, much better than I do. As a child he was boarded in Hackney. He and brother Tom were kept at Kingsland as very young children by his old nurse Goody Lawrence. His Aunt Ellen and Mrs Herbert lived in Newington Green. Thence we went to Islington, to the Red Bull Inn at St John's and saw a rough and rude prize fight at fisticuffs. We had supper at the King's Head and drank a toast for 'remembrance of the old house sake'. We came back through Kingsland and Bishopsgate and returned home with great pleasure.

Another time it being very warm and pleasant we went by coach to take the air to Bow and Old Ford and thence to Hackney. There we stopped and played at shuffleboard, ate cherries and cream and so with good refreshment, returned home.

In Woolwich our walks were accompanied by the songs of the nightingales. During the plague year I spent a lot of time south of the river, and Samuel would visit me on his way to the dockyard.

Samuel keeps his barge near the Tower of London. Early one June morning, about 8 o'clock, well victualled with bottles of wine, beer and neat's-tongue, we met a large party of our friends, mainly the two Pierces and Mrs Clerke (Dr Clerke's handsome proud and fashionable lady) – a dozen altogether. We set off for the landmark called the Hope, all merrily playing at cards 'en route', and spending our time pretty merry. Samuel showed us all the Navy ships berthed there. Our collation was excellent, although I say it myself – anchovies and gammon and pasties and pies. Then we went on board the boat and Mr Russell rowed us down to Greenwich, where Samuel, Mrs Clerke and I landed to have a drink at an alehouse where we saw the King's pleasure boat on the river. We all sang and played cards on the way to London Bridge and Tower of London wharf, where we disembarked our large party. Samuel thought Mrs Clerke witty but conceited, 'making a great flutter with a few fine clothes'. Her husband could not come with us as the King was sick, and Dr Pierce was letting his blood!

The Beargarden was on Bankside near the Clinke Liberty. One day after dinner Mary Mercer, Samuel and I went there to watch, not the bears, but the bulls tossing the hunting dogs – one poor beast being thrown into one of the boxes. We both agreed that it is a rude and nasty pleasure. There were some rough gallants in the box with us ('Hectors' Samuel called them) who played their dogs for wagers against the bull. They flirted with Mary Mercer and drank her and our healths in wine. In the evening we went to a fireworks party – with serpents and rockets – organised by Mary Mercer's brother. The William Penns were there too. We stayed till midnight, flinging our fireworks and sparklers and burning one another, smutting ourselves with candlegrease and soot until we all looked like black devils out of Hell. William Batelier, my favourite Frenchman, was there too.

The Beargarden was a little bit similar to the Roman amphitheatre where spectators, mainly men, occasionally women, lusted after the blood either of other men or beasts, or both. John Creed, "My Lord's" crafty, gregarious secretary took Samuel and I there – to that horrible arena – to watch a prize fight. Samuel said that the sport was very good and that there were 'various humours to be seen among the rabble that is there'. He had sneaked into the bull house by a back way (perhaps that was appropriate). He was afraid that he was amongst the bears too. Eventually he got into the common pit and with his cloak about his face – ashamed to be with the rabble – he watched at very close quarters a brutal butcher beat savagely an equally brutal shoemaker. Creed and I watched too at a distance, which made the spectacle a little less degrading.

In mid summer '66 Samuel joined Jane Birch, our girl, and myself for a long walk in the evening. After his long day at the Navy Office it did Samuel good 'to take the ayre'. We went to Halfway house, our favourite rendezvous. It was a very good walk and all of us were happy. I had given young Jane a laced whiske dress of mine which makes her look a very graceful servant. We arrived and drank at the tavern. In the cool of the evening we came back again and sang in the boat on the river, all three of us, and passed a large boatful of Spaniards singing too! On Sunday of that week we went, with Mary Mercer this time, by water to Barne Elmes, where we walked by moonshine, called at Lambeth, drank there and ate cold meat in the boat and ate and sang, and returned home by almost twelve at night having had a very fine and pleasant day. Samuel had to restrain himself in his choice of songs – not because of his women folk – but because of the Lord's Day conventions.

During the summer I would sometimes take Jane, the maid, and Tom, the boy, to 'The Bottle of Hay' tavern in John's Street, on the way to Islington. There we would eat pasties and drink ale. It was a favourite place for a 'petite occasion' – simple and welcoming.

During Midsummer of '66, a month or so after the Medway naval disasters, Samuel and I decided upon a Sunday outing to Epsom in Surrey. We left at five in the morning with Mrs Turner in a hired coach with four horses, and faithful Will Hewer on horseback, victualled with wine, beer and cold fowl, gossiping inevitably 'en route', I think about Peg Lowther (Penn that was). It was hot and the roads were bumpy and dusty, but we reached Epsom by eight. Samuel drank four pints of the local Epsom water, which has healthy salts in it. We did not try it. Then we lodged at the King's Head. Gossip immediately informed us that Lord Buckhurst *and* Nelly Gwynn were lodged next door! My good handome friend Pembleton – the dancing master – *my* dancing master, happened to be in Epsom that day in the same tavern. We had a merry cheerful mid-day dinner, nevertheless. I was very pleased to have Samuel, sweet faithful Will Hewer and my Mr Pembleton with me. What more could a good girl want? We all had a nap after dinner and then went by coach in the afternoon to the Pepys' house in Ashtead. Will Hewer's horse broke loose and we were all unkindly cheerful to watch him recapture it. Samuel, mid-summer going to his head, plus the wine we had for dinner, frolicked in the woods and sprained his right foot. He should have been more careful at the age of thirty four, putting himself at risk. As far as I know he was pursuing no reluctant nymph. Mrs Turner is a good friend and comforted our wounded hero by putting her warm hand on the injured foot. I should have been more sympathetic. We arrived back in Seething Lane and Samuel needed to be helped from one end of the lane to our house. I put a Cere-cloth on his foot, but he still could not meet the Duke of York the next morning.

Undeterred by Samuel's grievous wounds, a few weeks later on another Sunday, we set off, this time for Barnet. We left with Mrs Turner by coach before five in the morning and reached the Wells by seven. For mid August it was remarkably cold. We met Joseph Batelier, William Hewer (whose lodgings then were in Barnet) and his uncle Steventon. Samuel drank three glasses with them. We then went to the Red Lion and we all drank something to keep the cold at bay and ate many delicious cheesecakes. We dined at Hatfield, having been to midday matins at the local church beforehand. In the afternoon we walked in Hatfield Park, visited the Vineyard, which Samuel described as 'a place of great delight . . . as much pleasure as could be desired in the world for country pleasure and good ayre'! I was wearing a straw hat, much worn in the countryside, which became me 'mightily' according to Samuel. We went from Hatfield back to Barnet, and William Hewer took us back to his lodging, which Samuel said with surprise was 'handsome'. He entertained us with cheesecakes, cream, tarts and other good things. Samuel then pilfered filberts in Will Hewer's garden. I think both of us are quite surprised how our 'boy' William has prospered and matured. With him we went several times to Bartholomew Fayre a great annual event with peculiar circus antics, mainly of poor wretched freak animals *and* humans. The rope dancing was usually superb. One visit there, wearing my dark vizard I was approached by the Dutchman Sam Hartlib, and bidden to his coach. Of course 'Incognito' or not, I refused to go, and Samuel seemed rather vexed.

Sometimes I would take Mary Mercer and Deb to see the gipsies at Lambeth and have our fortunes told. We never told Samuel of their prophecies – full of tall, dark, handsome men and mysterious journeys overseas. And death in the family.

In mid summer of '68 Samuel determined to make a grand tour of the West country. Both Lord Brouncker and Sir William Penn were ill, so when the cat's asleep, our mouse did play . . . We went from Barnet to Stevenage, thence to Huntingdon and briefly stopped at Brampton. My father-in-law had bad stories of my ill-words to him as usual. Then we went to Bedford and Newport where we went to church. Buckingham was 'a handsome old town'. Samuel was a determined traveller and complained of 'My people making me lose so much time'. He led and his family followed – in their own good time. We slept at Newport Pagnall and went next day to Oxford, the main objective. There we were shown the Colleges, particularly All Soul's, Christ Church, and Braze-Nose. My husband, a Master of Arts, I believe, of Cambridge, described Oxford as 'a mighty fine place, well seated and cheap entertainment'. He was remarkably good at damning people and things with faint praise. On the way home we called at Abingdon where there was a custard fair in progress and dined at Hungerford, where we had an excellent dinner of trout, eels and crayfish. Samuel thought it was a mean town. On our way to Salisbury we stopped at Old Sarum, where we spent the night in silken sheets at the George Inn. Will Hewer and Samuel explored the Minster in the morning which he thought was 'most admirable as big and handsomer than Westminster'. Both of us then explored the town and church, where the organ was much admired. The expedition consisted of Samuel, Will Hewer, Mr Murford (a navy office acquaintance), myself, Mrs Betty Turner and Deb Willett. We then went to Stonehenge. Samuel described the stones as being 'as prodigious as any tales I heard of them . . . God knows what their use was, they are hard to tell, but yet may be told'. We had many minor adventures, including lousy beds. The entourage moved on majestically via Philips-Norton towards Bath, where we stayed the night. On the morrow we went to the Cross Baths, though Samuel thought 'it cannot be clean to go so many bodies together in the *same* water'. The hot springs were exhilarating, although we all looked parboiled. From Bath we went to Bristol, where Samuel went to look at the docks. The other three went to see Deb's uncle Butts who lived in Bristol, while I chatted to the landlady of the Sun Inn. Deb is very well known and liked here. Her uncle pressed 'Bristol milk' from Spain on us before we returned to Bath. On the way back to Town we called at Marlborough which we thought was a pretty fair town. Samuel heard a new song in Newbury 'A Fine Old English Gentleman', and asked Will Hewer to copy it out for him. We stayed in Reading, and thence travelled to Maidenhead and Colnbrook. I was very angry with Samuel, for many serious reasons – but that is another story.

A few weeks later – friends again – we went, Samuel and his pretty harem, Deb, Mary Mercer, and myself, to the Spring Gardens. There we were disgusted by the behaviour of the young gallants or rakehells of the town, who forced their way into the little private arbours in the gardens and pestered the women with 'the confidence of the vice of the age' as Samuel said.

In August we sallied forth, Samuel and I and Deb, via Cobham to Guildford, where we saw Bishop Abbot's hospital, and to Liphook, where we stayed the night. Samuel was combining pleasure with business. At Petersfield he met three Navy Office colleagues on business, about the Turkish pirates he told me. We returned to Guildford and met there Samuel's aunt and uncle Wight, my benevolent old would-be seducer. We returned to London via Vauxhall.

When some exotic visitor from overseas comes to London we often go to gaze on him or her. Once we went to the Queen's Chapel at St James to see the Prince of Tuskany come out, a comely, dark and swarthy fat man in a smart black mourning suit. A few days later we saw him in the Park accompanied by many fine ladies.

There were skilled jugglers to be found in Islington, so incredible that I thought they must be guided and helped by the Devil himself! Samuel thought they performed 'so good tricks as I have never seen in my life of legerdemaine'.

Yes, London in the 17th century has all the exciting and interesting free sights – if one takes the trouble to find them and then enjoy them.

CHAPTER SEVENTEEN

MY MÉNAGE

"Je vis de bonne soupe et non de beau langage"
Molière

During our marriage we have made three homes for ourselves. Our first three years of marriage were spent in our little nest 'chez Mountagu' in Whitehall. It was only a small garret and I am sure that Samuel paid no rent for it – after all he was a servant in "My Lord's" establishment. I cannot say that we were particularly happy there. Our sexual life was like, I imagine, that of most newly-weds: ecstasy followed by a petty quarrel, caused by cold rooms, lack of food and Samuel's gallivanting abroad without me, followed by ecstasy again. Our 'period of differences' and subsequent separation was traumatic at the time, but much water has flowed under many bridges since then.

Our mutual happiness soared to heights undreamed of when we moved to the little house in Axe Yard. Ownership of our own house, the arrival of our little maid Jane Birch and Samuel's clumsy boy Eliezer, and above all such nice warm friendly neighbours around us. The Hunts, Major Greenlife and his wife, funny old Mrs Crisp with her harpsichon, even her pretty daughter Diana, with whom, predictably, the master had a fling. Axe yard and our small community was like a village – one of a hundred little London villages.

Jane Birch stayed with me for three years. She was a sweet, undemanding little thing. We have much in common, both of us untidy, both of us reluctant to kill poultry. I remember once 'My Lord' sent us turkeys brought back with him from Zealand on the voyage to bring the King home. We looked at one poor beast. Not only were we reluctant to kill it as it gobbled in Dutch to us, but we did not know *how* to do it. We both of us were squeamish about the fate of rabbits and fowls, but a large black turkey! Eventually we did what we had to. We paid little Jane three pounds a year for her services and she often worked nearly 18 hours a day. Samuel basted her with a broom for untidiness – possibly under the influence of the good bottle of Sack we had in the house by then. He appeased her with kind words – Puritan fashion – and she memded his breeches by our bedside. It was very Biblical.

With Samuel's promotion two years later, to Clerk of the Acts, we moved to the 'new' much larger Seething Lane house, where we are now. Samuel shrewdly negotiated to sell the lease of Axe Yard to Mr Dalton the wine merchant. He made a profit of £21 on the sale – sufficient to pay for two new suits *and* an addition to the household. In July '60 little Jane's rascally brother Wayneman joined us, at the time when Jane was ill – lame from a fall. Young Wayneman was described by Samuel as a 'pretty, well-looked young boy that would please us well'. In September I caught the lad out in petty thieving and a great deal more than we imagined at which Samuel and I were angry. A few days later Samuel tore up young Wayneman's 'prentice indentures and sent him packing. But his sister begged us to keep him on, and this rather reluctantly, we did. The shipyard workers often mistook him for Samuel's son on his visits of inspection – 'Young Pepys' he was called. I felt sad that I had failed to provide Samuel with a real son – or that *he* had failed to make me pregnant.

Wayneman stayed with us for three years: It was little Wayneman's duty to rouse Samuel in the morning to get up and dress for the Office. Sometimes the boy overslept and made Samuel late. On occasion Samuel beat him soundly with a rod.

Samuel does sound like a Puritan school master from time to time – 'this punishment is going to hurt me much more than you'. We treat our servants no better, but certainly no worse, than anyone else. Samuel chose Wayneman's livery for special occasions – of grey cloth trimmed with black and gold lace. It was much grander than our neighbours' boys at the Penns and Battens – Admiral's boys too! When they bought liveries for *their* boys Samuel bought a *sword* for our boy! I took him to Brampton on my visits – the little Cockney boy revelling in the green countryside. With no master to check them, he and Sarah, the new maid, ran rampant. My relationship with the elder Pepys was fragile at the best of times, and two rumbustious undisciplined London servants proved the last straw! On our return Sarah left and a new cook called Susan, recommended by brother Balty, arrived. Young Wayneman then ran away.

Jane Birch left in the summer of '61 to better herself – we were both sorry to see her go. Samuel and I agreed that we should employ his plain sister Pall, not as a companion to me, but as a maid. It may seem peculiar to employ one's sister-in-law as a servant. When Samuel first broached it to his father at the end of

'60 after we had been in the Seething Lane house for a few months, I was most upset at the thought because of her known ill-nature 'en famille'. However I thought, with the confidence of a young married woman of nearly twenty, we could accommodate ourselves to each other. When Samuel suggested the possibility to Pall that she should come 'not as a sister but as a servant ', which she promised she would, she 'with many thanks did weep for joy'. Poor Paulina, she was a drudge in her parent's home in the country; far better to be a drudge in her smart brother's new home in London, where she might meet a suitable suitor. So we took her and young Lady Jemimah Mountagu by water to London Bridge and showed them all the Navy ships and traders. We took her to the theatre and I treated her more as a sister-in-law than a servant maid. It was not satisfactory. 'I am resolved not to keep her' said her master and brother 'Troubled to hear how proud and idle Pall is grown'. She also stole my scissors. So she left in September '61. Samuel's mother came up to town from Brampton, and they left together in the country-waggon – Pall crying exceedingly. Poor wretched unloved girl. Her parents did not want her back with them, and we did not want her in London. She had not a penny in the world, so Samuel gave her 20 shillings and much helpful advice on her departure. Samuel envisaged several candidates for an arranged bethrothal, but they all came to nought. I felt so sorry for her that at the beginning of '63 I suggested to Samuel that we try again with Pall as my woman-companion. At the time she was making sad little paper baskets at Brampton. Nothing came of it. In a most heartless way, I suggested that dear loyal William Hewer should marry her. He showed no signs of marrying anybody, and Samuel would provide a handsome dowry. William Hewer hinted, in the most delicate of compliments, that he prefered Samuel's wife to his sister – so that was that.

The redecoration of the grand new Navy house of ours in Seething Lane taxed Samuel's resources in time, money and temper. The joiners were flooring the dining room so he was looking after the workmen whose laziness much troubled him. He dined at home to see that the painters did their job and did not skimp. Samuel described how he spent 'All the afternoon among my workmen and did give them drink and very merry with them, it being my luck to meet with a sort of drolling workmen on all occasions'. Samuel's very sensible views were that if you make the English working man mildly drunk and merry enough he might do a modicum of work.

He consulted his father about gilded leather for the dining room.

It was duly finished with green serge hanging and gilt leather which we think is very handsome. That week we were locked out of the use of the leads (roof walks) by our neighbour Mrs Davis, whose husband was 'someone' in the Navy Office, and with whom at that stage, we would not argue. "My Lord" Sandwich meanwhile was spending a fortune on redecorating and rebuilding his house, known as the Wardrobe. This stimulated Samuel to further endeavours. We bought some new pictures from Mr Cade's. He played his violin and lute in the dining room, thus attracting the neighbours into the yard to hear him. The carpenters made a new door at the other side of the house, going into the entry, . . . and so it went on.

The new parlour was gilded, but not before Samuel had spent all day at home supervising the work. The Victualler of the Navy sent us a great chine of beef and half a dozen 'toungs', so we had some good meals in the midst of the squalor of the house rebuilding. Sarah, the housekeeper at "my Lord's" presented me with a cat as we were much troubled with mice. My theory is that Samuel's music attracts them from all over Seething Lane. Besides the cat, the mice, and my dog, we have two cages of yellow canary birds. Samuel's aviary encouraged our singing lessons and musical evenings. The only discordant note in our animal farm was when our tame monkey escaped from its large cage. Samuel, instead of coaxing it with some food, attacked it with a broom and struck it insensible before it could be returned to the cage. He regretted his temper, but the poor brute of a monkey was never the same again.

We had three grand dinners in a matter of two weeks. Our cooks come and go under the strain of cooking meals in a house so disordered. A new pair of stairs out of the parlour were being installed. The old unsafe ones were duly ripped out. The new stairs broke apart once and we had to use a stepladder to go upstairs. I think Sir George Carteret, the Treasurer of the Navy, was there at the time. I like to think that he felt the Pepys family needed more money. He promised Samuel that on the negotiation of a large bill of exchange £60 commission would be earned.

During Samuel's absence in the country for his Uncle Robert's funeral and reading of the will, I asked "My Lady" Mountagu, who was lonely with her husband away at sea, to come and inspect our new house, which she did.

Samuel was carousing at night too often – this was the spring of '61 – and often with a head aching all day from last night's debauch, he was up among the workmen urging them on. Samuel had many boon companions. I could name a round dozen amongst his colleagues – John Creed and James Pierce, the surgeon, and his friends Will Howe, Captain Rolt, Captain Ferrers and neighbours the Penns and Battens, who all tacitly encouraged Samuel to drink too much. But John Creed was by far the worst.

At long last on 20th June '61 the workmen left and the house looked a palace to its new owners.

The two worst perils for London houses are fire and theft. We experienced the latter at the end of the summer of '61, when Samuel lost his silver tankard and Will Hewer his clock. The servants were always leaving doors open during the day, and worse still, during the night. However, once a new maid, Doll, was so fast asleep on our return from church that we had to coax Wayneman, the boy, in at a window to open the door for us. Often Samuel would keep gold or silver in the house before converting it into a money draft at Viner's. I would ask the maids to keep a lighted candle in the dining room to scare would-be thieves away. The constable and the watch would often knock on our backyard door at two or three in the morning to tell us our doors had been left open by careless maids.

Another town hazard was that of riots – either from the prentices or poor unpaid seamen. Once in '61 there was a rising of fanatiques in Barnet. Rumours flew around that they were marching on our part of the city. Citizen Pepys found everybody in arms at their doors. He returned to our house to collect his sword and pistol and equipped himself for the fray. The poor fanatiques knew not what was in store for them. Samuel does not know how to use his sword and had no powder for his pistol!

A fourth house hazard would occur during a high strong wind when tiles and 'brick battes' would be torn from the rooves and hurled in the streets, often severely wounding people.

At the end of '61 our household in Seething Lane consisted of Will Hewer, who had not yet left us for his own independence; Sarah, who combed her master's head and washed his feet in a bath of herbs; Nell Payne, with whom he secretly played the fool, and naughty little Wayneman.

Samuel's net worth he told me was about £500. One way and another he was now earning nearly that amount each year, perhaps a little less. He was always a little vague with me! The household food bill and servant's wages were less than £100 a year. Samuel, restless as ever, set to work on the cellar with various alterations, and stocked it with wines as our fortunes prospered. Later on he found his tierce barrel of claret half consumed as the cellar door had been left unlocked. Mr Rawlinson has had five or six dozen new bottles made for Samuel's wine, with his crest upon them. It makes the wine taste much nicer. By mid '65 he had in the cellar two tierces of claret, two quarter casks of Canary, and a smaller vessel of Sack, a vessel of Tent, another of Malaga, and another of white wine. Samuel believed that none of his family or friends had ever had so much wine of their own at one time. Rather incongruously, Samuel's wines shared equal space with coals in the same cellar.

On Valentine's Day '66 the painters were again at work gilding a new chimney piece and Samuel's picture frames, in the dining room. Some pewter sconces were bought and hung up the side of the stairs, the pictures had been hung, and the house with its human and animal population had become a real home.

One week I remember well. It started off auspiciously when Captain Teddiman, having recently come from the Straights of Gibralter presented us with some anchovies, some olives and muscatt. Samuel was ashamed at not knowing what the latter was. Sweet vin de muscatel is what we would drink at home in France. It is too sweet for me and certainly not as good as the pink Anjou wine. "My Lord" Sandwich had just brought a Queen back to England according to Samuel, 'an agreeable lady and paints well'. "My Lord" had met the King of Portugal and described him as 'a very foole almost and his mother do all, and he is a very poor Prince'. We went to see the 'Portugal ladys' the Queen had brought back in her retinue but they were not handsome and their farthingales are to us a strange dress. The Queen went to Hampton Court and bonfires were burned across London. It did Samuel good to have "My Lord" back in the country, even if he was knee-deep in debt!

In the summer of '62 we did our household accounts together. Or rather I did them first and Samuel then corrected them. Our kitchen expenses on food, wine, fire wood, candles, soap and many other household things for five people came to 30 shillings a week.

I thought that our house was now complete from top to bottom. Samuel had had the cellars done out to his satisfaction. But I was wrong. On midsummer day '62 workmen started to take down the top of the house to make new rooves and indeed an extra floor. Two evenings later it rained cats and dogs. Three mornings later Samuel complained that all his ceilings had been spoiled with rain the night before, so that he feared they must all be newly whited for the second time. I shrugged my shoulders with nonchalence . . . 'c'est la vie!' I exclaimed helpfully. Next week we had the dining room wainscoated which made it very pretty. In addition my own closet was refurbished. That summer the rainstorms were violent and noisy and besides ruining our top floor, scared our cat. It had been duly locked in the chamber and was scared by the noise and set up a great mewing and leaped on to our bed, where it stayed. We had a restless night but the cat was comfortable.

Samuel kept up intermittent warfare with our neighbours on all sides. One such skirmish was with old Sir John Minnes over the rooftops on the leads. Unfortunately we were impeding the Minnes' view with our new buildings. A closet of small bedchamber space was in dispute between us. Sir William Penn entered the fray to stir things up but Samuel's legal training won the day. I was down in the country at Brampton, with maid and black dog. Each day I talked to my cousin "My Lord", who himself drew me a plot or plan of some alterations Samuel might do to the Pepys house at Brampton. "My Lord" has been spending a fortune in London rebuilding the Wardrobe, and another fortune restoring Hinchingbrook House in the country. He now suggested to me that Samuel spend a small fortune at Brampton for his poor old father and mother.

By the autumn on Samuel's return to London – he had been to Brampton for the local Court, and back via Cambridge – he found a good chimney-piece installed in the upper dining-room chamber, and the wainscoating nearly finished in the same room.

The next battle with the neighbours was on my account. Lady Batten's maid was called 'Nan', and she had an affected manner of calling out for 'Nan', which our maid Jane Birch mimicked to perfection from our garden. I am afraid I rather encouraged her, or at least did not discourage her. Lady Batten was duly vexed with me. She complained bitterly to Samuel and we went through the motions of scolding Jane – but we all thought it quite amusing.

In December the tapestry hangings were put up in my chamber, which pleased us both. That winter there was much snow. Come the inevitable thaw, our street was flooded including our new cellar and parts of the ground floor. It happens every few years and there is nothing we can do except clean it up.

We bought a handsome new dining room table for 50 shillings which can seat ten people in comfort. As we were buying it there was a 'scare-fire' in the neighbouring alley, but it was quickly quenched. London fires can gut a house in a couple of hours. Luckily our Seething Lane house is mainly composed of brickworks.

Early in '63 Jane Birch left us, to our great regret. For three years she had been a sweet little member of our family. She was replaced by Susan. After a good dinner Samuel gave her sixpence, equivalent to two days wages. That was duck week. Mr Cole, one of Samuel's timber merchants, had given us five couple of ducks as a present. I even tried my hand at duck pâté à la francais. It was timber week as well. Sir William Warren, who made a fortune out of supplies of wood to Samuel's Navy, left a box at our house – gloves for both of us and a state dish of silver, a silver cup, and both engraved with Samuel's 'arms'. Samuel described it as 'a very noble present and the best I ever had yet', and it was valued at £18 – the equivalent to me of three months household budget for four maids for a year.

The local ironmonger supplied fire dogs, tongues and shovels for the fireplace in my closet. Mr Sympson then came to set up my new chimney piece.

If drama was around the corner, as it is inevitably, in mid-17th century London – so was farce. Samuel has had a long standing legal case against a scoundrel called Mr Field, who had been committed to prison for libelling the Navy Office. Mr Field complained to the King from prison that he had evidence of embezzlement in the dockyards, which Samuel and I knew was almost certainly true. Out of the blue in February a bailiff arrived with a writ for Samuel from the Exchequer. I did not understand the legal complexities, but for twenty-four hours Samuel was hiding in Seething Lane, partly in our house, partly in the Batten's, and partly in the Minnes' lodgings. In and out of parlour windows, up and down ladders. Every time the five bailiffs, now reinforced by a constable, knocked on our door demanding to see Samuel, I would answer, more or less truthfully, that he was not there. Once we let them into our yard which was empty, and locked *them* in it. We have never seen anything so funny in all our lives. Samuel was partly scared and partly amused. Eventually Mr Clerke, the lawyer, obtained a Court note to 'free' Samuel and all was well again. It was the day before the Clerk of the Acts' 30th birthday, so we celebrated by going to two plays in one day; 'The Slighted Mayde' at the Duke's with a pretty actress in boy's apparel described by Samuel as 'having very fine legs only bends in the hams, as I perceive all women do'! Then to Court and saw 'The Wild Gallant' by Dryden. Neither the King nor the Pepys family enjoyed it. But my Lady Castlemaine, the royal mistress, was worth looking at, and so was little Mrs Stewart – the next in line.

In the spring of '63 a new cookmaid called Hannah arrived, to be paid at £4 per annum, the first time we ever paid so much. With my new mathematical lessons I worked that out to be less than 1½d per meal, excluding breakfast.

A fine singing blackbird was sent us by Mr Rendall, the Deptford house carpenter. It knows many tunes but none completely. The canaries now have singing company.

Captain Shales sent me a pretty cabinet and Mr Lever sent a pair of fine silver candlesticks – both for my closet. Samuel also bought silver spoons, forks and sugarbox for £23.

At the end of '63 Samuel reckoned his net worth to be £800, excluding the silver plate and house furnishings. In our household Will Hewer had grown up and left us; Jane Gentleman was then my maid; Besse was our excellent good natured cookmaid, and then there was little Susan described by the master as 'a most admirable slut and pleases us mightily doing more services than both the others, and deserves better wages'. We had had no boy since Wayneman had run away. My little black dog having died, a naval surgeon sent us an excellent mastiff called Towser, who helped to keep thieves away from the house.

In midsummer, I was at Brampton, and Samuel and the two maids were alone in the house. At eleven o'clock at night Samuel was woken by a noise. He wrote to me 'Knowing what money I have in the house, I began to sweat worse and worse till I melted almost to water. I rung the bell and could not for half an hour make either wench hear me: this made me fear the more lest they might be gagged'. Poor gallant Samuel lay there terrified. Towser needed to be let out, and had whined plaintively until Jane had risen sleepily and let him out for a run in the street!

In the winter we dined at "My Lady" Sandwich's by no means an unusual event. But for the first time Samuel looked around and on our return said to me that our little establishment produced as good or better a meal than that of his Patron served as neatly, and that our meat was as good and as well-dressed. I do not believe that he meant to pay *me* a compliment.

The same week poor little 'slut' Susan fell sick of the measles or scarlet fever. She recovered quickly and the next week – shades of King Arthur and his sword – showed us all how to lift a new iron chest from one side of the room to another. Neither Samuel, nor I, nor little Tom Edwards, could lift it up, let alone carry it away.

Shortly afterwards we sat up all night to see the Star or Comet pass overhead. Samuel wrote how it 'whether worn away or no, appears not with a tail but only is larger and duller than any other star and is come to rise betimes and to make a great arch and is quite gone to a new place in the heavens than it was before'. It reappeared after Christmas, but at dusk. Samuel told me that at

Gresham College Mr Hooke gave a curious lecture about the Comet, proving that it had appeared before in 1618, and probably it will appear again.

At the beginning of '65 our household consisted of Mary Mercer, Besse, the chamber maid, Jane Birch the cook maid, little girl Susan, and singing Tom Edwards. Poor little Tom once had his ears boxed so hard by his master that the latter's thumb was put out of joint and he suffered great pain for the next few days.

One night during February I was in bed. Samuel was late working at the office, when I heard strange noises over my head on the roof-leads. Not knowing what it was, and remembering that Samuel as usual had a lot of money hidden in the house, I sent Mary Mercer hot-foot to bring Samuel back to investigate the noises. Samuel told me that he dithered for two hours, or more, before he returned at almost two o'clock in the morning, 'in great fear to bed thinking every running of a mouse really a thief'. It is true our house has many exits and entries, but all was well! He said 'but if I escape tonight I will remedy it. God preserve us this night safe'. My gallant little man should have called the watch from his office and bidden them search our grounds. That is what I would have done!

Samuel has many loves in his life – his family, his wife, his women friends 'abroad', his money, his silver, his music – but also his books. As his income rises so does his expenditure on books. He showed me with great pride his whole study now full of books recently acquired, almost all with a similar binding. He had them bound at St Paul's Churchyard bookbinders and he was much pleased with his study, 'it being methinks a beautiful sight', as he said to me, and indeed it was.

One morning Samuel was not aroused as usual in order to dress for the office. Besse was found downstairs at six a.m. asleep with her clothes on close by the fireside and a candle which had been burning all night. So she has now left us. In mid-summer besides Mary Mercer and little Tom, the family consisted of another Mary, Alice and little Susan, altogether three maids and a boy.

In the beginning of '66 Samuel paid me a compliment which I shall always treasure. 'She works all day at home', he said, 'like a horse at the making of her hangings for our chamber and the bed'. I liked the graceful eloquent simile. I often wonder what he *really* studied at Magdalene College. At the same time he was fondling little Susan's breasts.

In the spring we were delighted by Jane Birch's return to the fold. The master was much pleased and soon 'poor Jane, my old, little Jane come to us again to my wifes and my great content and we hope to take mighty pleasure in her she having all the marks and qualities of a good and loving and honest servant'. But the next day Alice our cook-maid left in umbrage at the welcome we made to Jane. She was 'a good girl whom we loved and did well by her; she was an excellent servant but would not bear being told of any fault even in the fewest and kindest words'. The next cook-maid to join us was called Lucy. Samuel said that she was ugly. Be that as it may, she nearly killed herself in her first few days with us by falling down the stairs in the dark and might have broken her neck. She was a good, drudging servant but she would get herself drunk. My only fear is fire, if she leaves candles guttering at night.

Before the Sandwiches were asked to dinner we bought new drinking glasses, and a case of knives. Samuel had paid £40 for a new set of chairs and couch for the main living room. We also had to bring the bricklayers in to mend the dining room chimney and prevent it from smoking. At the end of the year, besides John Pepys, Samuel's brother, staying in the house, there was Tom Edwards, little no longer, but promoted to be a clerk in the Office. In addition we had no less than four maids. Over the New Year we invited all the Penn family and Lord Brouncker to dinner, but Sir John Minnes and Sir William Batten could not come. We sat down ten for the meal, but the main purpose of the evening was to show off all our large collection of silver plate. I secretly calculated that very little of it had been *purchased* by the Pepys family.

Next, the Batten house caught on fire through a faulty chimney piece, always a hazard, but with a great many helping hands and work it was soon stopped.

I taught our maids how to make tea. It is a new drink which Mr Pelling the Potticary (apothecary) tells me is good for my, and for Samuel's colds and 'defluxions'.

Jane Birch's brother died, leaving a wife and two small children. Samuel, always kind, gave her 20 shillings and what wine she needed for the funeral. He then bought a copper cistern for the table for £6 or £7, so that one could rinse the plates in it during the meal. Seven courses might require as many as 70 plates!

We always have a major comedy each year. Just before Christmas '67, we were woken at 7 a.m. by a mysterious knocking noise near, but not in, our bedchamber. Samuel and I lay there in bed listening to noisy ghosts going up and down our stairs. They broke down windows, removed stools and chairs. We lay, both of us, afraid. I restrained Samuel from rising from our warm, snug, safe bed! We were sure it was a gang of thieves in the house and we wondered what our people were doing below, thinking them either killed, or as afraid as we were. At eight o'clock and daylight, Samuel arose, removed his nightgown and night slippers, (it was mid-winter) and put on his house-gown and breeches. With a firebrand in hand, my hero safely opened the door, looked out, but neither saw nor heard anything! A detailed and very methodical investigation, as befitted the Clerk of the Acts, took place throughout the household. The master found nothing amiss. Our young gibb-cat leaped down the stair case from top to bottom in two great leaps and so frighted us, that we could not tell whether it was a cat or a spirit. The master decided that the house might be haunted! Our neighbours at Sir John Minnes' house had just had their chimney stacks cleaned. Even Samuel likened the episode – well-read man that he is – to Don Quixote's tilting at imaginary windmills.

Our increasing affluence led to the purchase of a new coach. Samuel thought that we might create a stable at the head of the little house by our garden where old 'goodman' Taylors puts his brooms and dirt. A most inventive plan.

Almost the happiest event of '68 was the strange wooing, betrothal, and marriage of our dear Jane Birch and Tom Edwards, the singing clerk in our household. In midsummer Jane had a hysterical crying fit. I was over the water at the Whitsters, where all our linen, etc. was laundered. Samuel and four others were needed to hold Jane down. A committee of enquiry was formed on my return, myself, Samuel and Will Hewer. Jane was in love. Tom had promised to marry her. Tom then grew cold and jilted her. The old, eternal story. That little bit of mid-summer madness was resolved the following spring when they got married in great style at Islington. Theophila Turner and Mary Batelier were bridesmaids and Talbot Pepys and Will Hewer were bridesmen. I supervised the whole affair. Little Jane and little Tom were part of my family. My dearest friends had known the pair since they were practically babes in arms. We wanted to make sure their life together in the very adult world of matrimony would be encouraged by our real love and care. It was one of the most moving moments of my life. My two little children grown up and now married. I was just twenty nine. Samuel was on the road to Dartford drinking a little buttered ale. He could have come to their wedding if he had so wished. At least he made Tom a handsome settlement of £40, and both Samuel and I gave £20 to Tom's new wife. Who knows what their future will be? As Samuel said of himself 'From so mean a beginning is matter of wonder to me. But it is Gods mercy to me and his blessing upon my taking pains and being punctual in my dealings'. But he should have been there.

A few months later we sailed for the Low Countries and France.

CHAPTER EIGHTEEN

MY FAIR COMPANIONS

''Elle flotte, elle hésite: En un mot, elle est femme''
Jean Racine

During our stay in our first little house in Axe Yard, Samuel had agreed – en principe – that I should have a female companion who would live with us and be part of 'our family'. Someone, a gentlewoman of course, who could become a good friend, certainly to me and possibly to Samuel as well, without in his case a friendship becoming too personal! She would be a companion for me to go with to the theatre, to market at the shops on the Exchange, and to make social calls on the Mountagus, Penns, Pierces etc. This paragon – if she could be found – would have to be young, about my age, be reasonably pretty (but preferably not too beautiful, for the reasons which had become apparent ever since I married Samuel in '55), and be socially acceptable to us and our friends. Of course if she could sing or play a musical instrument well, then the master would be beside himself with joy. If she could speak to me in French, that would then make me happier still. Samuel of course demurred about the probable cost of harbouring our paragon. It meant that he might have to sacrifice a new suit during the course of the year in order to pay her a small wage (between £10 and £20 for a year) plus board.

We had told our friends and acquaintances about our intentions, and almost immediately, dashing brother Balty came up with an equally dashing young lady, or to be more accurate, two dashing young ladies! One or both of them was probably his mistress.

Their name was Gosnell. They were attractive and vivacious. Both of them could sing and dance. Samuel inspected them and pronounced 'The youngest indeed hath a good voice and sings very well, besides other good qualitys, but I fear hath been bred up with too great libertys for my family and I fear greater inconvenience of expenses and my wife's liberty will follow, though I confess the gentlewoman, being pretty handsome and singing makes me have a good mind to her'.

So far so good. Balty of course had promised whichever sister that came to us a life of high society, with constant song and dance and a theatre show each day. He possibly gave them the impression that we had more money than was actually the case. What the sisters had not told us was that a stay with the Pepys was a temporary perch before they fluttered their wings on to the London stage as actresses.

In November 1662 the young 'Mrs' Gosnells came to midday dinner with Samuel and myself. After a singing audition, we took them to Whitehall by boat. 'I am mightily pleased with her humour and singing' said Samuel, and we agreed that the younger sister would join us the following week. In anticipation Samuel bought her a book of country dances since the paragon dances so well. We both liked her and christened her 'our Marmotte'. Samuel was still uncertain about the possible cost to his pocket that might be involved 'My wife promises it shall cost me nothing but her meat and wages and shall not be attended with *any* other expenses'. Clever Samuel also counted on the fact that these extra costs would be balanced by reduced expenditure and would save him money in having his wife go abroad on fewer visits and other delights. Samuel calculated his net worth that week at not less the £679: His *total* housekeeping bill being £7 per month!

She arrived on a Saturday and all seemed to be well. On the following day the three of us went to the French church since Balty had told me that the Gosnells had French blood. The service that day was in Dutch Walloon language, so we returned to our usual church. In the afternoon we took our 'petite Marmotte' to Samuel's aunt Wight's family. I think she was bored there, because an ultimatum arrived from her the next day. Her Uncle Justice Jiggins required her to come three times a week to him, and unless he was granted that he would not allow her to come to us! The next day she left, and we both went melancholy to bed. The following spring we saw her several times on the stage – a rather silent part in 'Hamlet' with Mr Thomas Betterton, and an excellent part as Pyramena in the 'Slighted Mayde' at the Duke's House. She was a determined young lady, and had achieved her ambition to act on the London Stage.

I am not sure what lessons, if any, we learned from Gosnell's three day stay with us, but I was determined to try our luck again. Samuel put it rather differently: 'My wife began to speak again of the necessity of our keeping somebody to bear her company, for her familiarity with the other servants is it that spoils them all and other company she hath none, which is too true'.

On the 12th March '63 Mary Ashwell joined our household as

my maid-companion from a young ladies school in Chelsea. Her father was a Clerk of the Exchequer – a friend of Samuel's. I took her to our neighbours the Hunts, and then by coach to Hyde Park to see and be seen. On Sunday she came to church with us although the Minnes family almost jostled us from the Navy pew. The next day we both went to "My Lords" lodgings where she played well on their harpsichon. Samuel heard, and liking what he heard, promptly purchased for her at the Temple a printed virginall-book. At home she played on Samuel's own 'tryangle' which pleased him. She could also dance very well with a fine carriage and deportment. So good was she that I determined to take lessons and perhaps coax Samuel to learn as well. That spring we had many pleasant walks in the countryside to Rotherhithe with Mary and Samuel, who was impressed with her prodigious memory of her Chelsea school days. We took her to the new Theatre Royal in Drury Lane to see Lacy act, to Woolwich to hear the nightingales, and introduced her to all our friends. She asked me if one of her French relations could join her on a visit to the Pierce's.

Samuel's comments were that she was 'a pretty girl, humble and active, ingenious at all sorts of fine works which pleases me very well and I hope will be very good entertainment for my wife without much cost'. But the merry jade encouraged us to play cards with her, persuaded Samuel to buy a bass viol, and our daily jaunts with her became part of a more exciting life – at least for me. One evening, we went by water to the Half Way house for a game of ninepins where Samuel thought that I was greatly taken up with Mr Pembleton, my dancing-master. I thought that he was greatly attracted to Mary Ashwell. In mid-June she and I went to Brampton by coach. Samuel kissed me 'au revoir' many times. He also kissed Ashwell. I hoped that she would be an amusing companion to while away the pastoral 'longueurs' of the evenings with my in-laws. It was not to be so. For the rest of June and all July it was reasonably agreeable – but very dull after our London activities. Mary and I got on each other's nerves and there was never any love lost between my mother-in-law and myself. The result one warm evening in August was that we all lost our tempers, and in a most undignified and childish way we slapped each other's faces. That destroyed our friendship completely. I thought that Samuel had been making advances to her, and she had been encouraging them. She left us on the 15th August having been with us five months. She also stole several yards of silk ribbons! Later I missed the little jade.

Curiously enough, that was not quite the end. Later that winter

Samuel called to see her at her Uncle's house in Ludgate, in order that she might come again to us to help dress me for the grand party we were planning for "My Lord" and Lady's first visit to our house. Mary Ashwell knew Chelsea well, as she had been to school and had friends there. Thus she knew about "My Lord" Mountagu's mistress whom he kept there – Mrs Becke. When "My Lord" crossexamined poor Samuel about the sources of his knowledge of Mrs Becke, he included Mary Ashwell as one of them not that in the event it caused her any harm.

I thought to myself that we had learned some lessons from 'la petite Marmotte's' short stay and from Mary Ashwell's much longer sojourn. The third time would be lucky if Samuel, I and the newcomer were sensible! Faithful Will Hewer provided us with Mary Mercer, who arrived in September 1664. Will had been lodging in great comfort and style in the Mercer household. There was no doubt that he admired and liked Mary, the 'decayed merchants daughter' he called her. We also liked her mother very much, and she was often included in our social activities during the next few years.

At the same time as she joined us, Samuel brought into the household sweet little Tom Edwards, recommended by Captain Cocke, the court musician. Little Tom, a freshfaced cherub from the Chapel Royal choir, sang like an angel. So could Mary Mercer, and my own voice was now much better trained. Samuel was in transports of delight. On the 9th September Mary Mercer dined with us at *table*, this being her first dinner in our house. After dinner Samuel and Mary Mercer, Tom and I, sat till eleven at night singing and fiddling. A great joy it is to Samuel to see himself master of so much pleasure in his own house. The girl played pretty well upon the harpsichon, but only ordinary tunes, but had a good hand, she sang a little, and had a good voice and an ear for music. From that first evening Mary Mercer was one of the family and treated as such. Samuel then described her as a pretty, modest, quiet maid, which was quite accurate. We took her frequently to the theatre with us – picture Samuel and his two beauties at 'The Rivalls' with Harris *and* Betterton!

By Christmas I was allowing Mary to comb Samuel's hair and wash his ears. Looking back on it I should have discouraged such intimacy. That was my first great mistake, but what could I have done to discourage such intimacy? At the end of January I sent her quickly to Samuel at the office because of strange noises above us at night in the house (but that is another story). I also took her with me to the new hothouse where we can bathe ourselves in plenty of very hot water, instead of just a little warm water at home.

She was a serious religious girl. I noticed that she would take the Sacrament in church, whilst Samuel and I made our way outside to talk to the fashionables amongst the congregation; or for me to talk to the dowdy wives (Penn and Batten), and for Samuel to look at the beauties (Mrs Letheuillier, Mary Batelier and others). We took her to the Whitehall Chapel to hear the famous young Stillingfleet, Samuel's friend, preach a good sermon. Once we went with her and John Creed by coach to take the air to Hackney, to play at shuffleboard and eat the pullets we had cooked ourselves. Whenever possible I persuaded Will Hewer to join us as I knew his 'tendresse' for Mary. Once we took her to the Park by coach to see the King. She came with me to Thomas Pepy's wife's christening of their first child. To Langford's the tailors, to order new suits for the master, with Samuel's mother and ourselves down to Woolwich by boat and the next day to Islington, where my mother-in-law regaled us with stories of Samuel's childhood there. We made another day trip by boat to Gravesend with Mary and Will Hewer. We went to dinner with her at William Joyce's . . . and so on.

During the summer of the Plague year, Mary Mercer, Mary the cook-maid and I left Seething Lane on 5th July, to stay for an indefinite period at Woolwich with William Sheldon, the Clerk of the Cheque, and his wife. William Hewer, Alice and little Susan stayed to look after Samuel in the City, although he came to see our little 'Court' as often as he could. Once "My Lord" Sandwich came to visit me at the Sheldons' in September '55, and Captain Herbert of his staff was much taken with Mary Mercer in her black dress. She and I and John Creed visited Lord and Lady Rutherford, who were staying at the King's Head, Deptford and had a very merry dinner and some music. Mary Mercer danced superbly. One night she danced a jig with Barbara Sheldon, our landlord's daughter, and myself. Samuel described it as 'Mercers dancing a jigg which she does the best I ever did see, having the most natural way of it and keeps time the most perfectly I ever did see'. It was a happy party to celebrate our ten years of marriage! In addition to Samuel, Will Hewer was there, little Tom Edwards and many others.

The plague abated a little and we decided at the beginning of December to return to London. Soon I was introducing Mary Mercer to the musical groups – the Pierces, the Colemans, Thomas Hill, Captain Rolt and the stage couple Mrs Knepp and Mr Harris, where her singing was received enthusiastically. About Christmas time Mary hinted to me that now she was part of the family, and not a maid any longer, she too ought to have a maid to look after her! Whatever next!

She came with me to the merry painting sessions at John Hayls' in the New Year of '66, and with us to Windsor to meet the Mountagu family. That was at the end of February, when she and I had a serious quarrel for the first time in the one and a half years she had been with us. It was the usual reason. She, like Mary Ashwell before her, was letting Samuel caress her in secret, and not showing enough reluctance in the matter.

In April, whilst I was in the country at Brampton for a few days, Mary's mother Mrs Mercer and a friend visited Samuel – her first visit to the Pepys house. Soon after my return the two of us, Mary and I, went by coach to Greenwich to be gossip (godmother) to Mrs Daniel's child. Mary introduced a tame sparrow into the household, which made Samuel laugh. As we had a dog and a cat already, I was not sure how long the sparrow would survive. In June Samuel was so busy at the Office that he set us to work at home to help him. Mercer and I were ruling paper for the Office to earn some pin money which made us work mighty hard! Mary Mercer knew the Batelier family well, as did her mother. During May and June they came often to see us for a good venison pasty supper. We took Mary with us to see the Lord Chancellor's house, that looks down over all London. Apart from Samuel taking an inordinate amount of trouble teaching Mercer how to sing – she *already* sings extremely well – our relationship appeared to be that of a genuine family. She could have been my favourite sister, such was the way I felt about her. At the end of July, I pointed this out forcibly to Samuel. I did not want our precious friendship disrupted. We took her to Bow to meet Lady Pooly, where all the Bateliers were spending the evening. Three days later we went to the awful Bear Garden, which was redeemed by a riotous firework party that night at Mrs Mercer's where Mary put on a boy's suit of Tom Edwards and danced a jig in a periwig! Next week we went to Moorfields to see Polichinello and the three of us went to Mr Longracke's wedding in Philpott Lane. So it went on.

During the midst of the terrible London Fire in September, I gave dear Mary Mercer notice. Her relationship with Samuel was becoming too dangerous; he had been fondling her breasts – that I was fairly sure of – since early summer, as she helped the little popinjay to get dressed in the early morning. I was rather cowardly, and chose a different reason. Without warning she had left our house to help her mother move her clothes and furniture, as the Mercer's house was being threatened by the fire. I worked myself up into a fine temper, met William Hewer, who still lodged with the Mercers, and then berated both mother and daughter. I am ashamed to say that I hit Mary in front of her mother and Will, and behaved like a common little harridan. Even Samuel had cause to agree with my decision (but for quite different reasons), when I told her to stay away from our house. What I did not care to say was 'stay away from my Samuel'! Meanwhile the Fire raged.

At the end of the month, with the Fire over, I hinted to Samuel that I would like to have Mercer back again, on condition that he behaved himself. His injured innocence would have done Harris the actor credit. A few days later, on Sunday, she came as usual to our church but she avoided looking up at us. A week later I mentioned to Samuel that I had found another 'fair Companion' recommended by Lady Penn, for £20 per annum, who sings, dances and plays on many instruments. We talked to her, but Samuel regarded her as a 'tawdry wench, and sings basely and would not take her for £7 per annum'. There's the rub as always. A pretty young girl with all the qualities we want will inevitably be seduced by Samuel sooner or later.

In mid-October a girl called Barker came to us from Lord Falconbridge's. She was so poor that we immediately spent £7 – £8 to re-clothe her. She was by no means pretty and her voice was out of use, but Samuel saw 'some fortune in her'. She stayed with us until May '67. She had mysterious absences and told lies to both Samuel and I. We sent her away with clothes worth £10 more than she came with, and 20 shillings in her purse.

At the end of June I tried to ger Mercer to come back to me again, but she made an excuse that she had friends at home who took up her time. In August she came to dinner with us in a 'paysan' dress and looking very pretty – still friends but reluctant to come back. She stayed with us in September on an informal basis and it was *almost* like old times – dinner with the Pierces, and going with her to see the 'Scornful Lady' at the Kings and 'Tu Quoque'. But she refused to stay with us. We continued to see her and her mother, off and on, for the next year or so.

My very dear friend William Batelier brought to me at the end of September a woman called Deborah Willett, who had spent 7 years at the school at Bow. She is extraordinarily handsome, and as Samuel says 'if we *must* have one, she should be handsome'. Deb is small, smaller than me, with excellent demure manners, and from a good family. Her aunt came some time later to inspect us, to make sure that we were suitable guardians for her pretty little niece.

Plus ça change, plus c'est la même chose.

Deb immediately became part of the family. We all adored her childlike innocence – in age she was little more than a child, as indeed I was when I first met Samuel. Mary Mercer I regarded, and still regard, as a sister of the same age. Little Deb is the younger sister that I have never had, and my protective instinct is thus much stronger. Mary Mercer could look after herself in our polite civilised jungle. I doubt whether Deborah could do that. She needed to come to a household that would protect her. William Batelier is a shrewd, intelligent young man. He knows Samuel and I extremely well. He trusts me to protect his little protegée Deb in every way I can.

So inevitably Samuel spent more time at home talking to us, more time taking us three to the theatre – often joined however either by Mary Mercer or by Will Hewer, at my request.

Early in October with Deb and Will Hewer we set off by coach on the famous expedition to recover Samuel's gold, that his father and I had buried on a dark night in the gardens at Brampton. The first night 'en route' the three of us slept in the same room, Deb in a separate bed. Thence we went to Audley End and Cambridge. The next night I slept with Deb and Samuel had the other bed. All very proper and chaste! We walked to Hinchingbroke, where we introduced little Deb to my Lady Mountagu. At Brampton that night Deb slept in the trundle bed, on wheels, which she herself requested. She did not help to dig up Samuel's gold, but she did carry up a bag of it every time we stopped at an inn on our way back. Back in London Samuel encouraged her to comb his hair by the fireside whilst I read aloud. We took her to see 'Macbeth', 'The Tempest', where she saw the King and Court present, the 'Indian Emperor' with Nell, 'The Mayden Queen' with Becke Marshall, 'Mustapha' with Betterton and Harris. We went to the actor's Nursery for young players and saw 'The Faithful Shepherd'. She went everywhere with us. She played cards with us when the Bateliers came to see us. We went shopping together to buy presents for Pall's wedding to Mr Jackson. Early in April Samuel gave her 10 shillings, as he did also to little Jane, so I thought nothing of it. We were on our way to Brampton to spend a few weeks there with my in-laws again.

I soon learned that in my absence Mary Mercer and young Tom Edwards were heard singing in our garden at Seething Lane, and that Samuel was taking her to plays and the Spring Gardens which worried me tremendously. When Samuel came to visit us at the end of May we made love on every possible occasion he was there – despite the rumours!

In the middle of June, Samuel, Will Hewer and Betty Turner came to collect our entourage at Brampton, and we set off to the West Country. In Bristol Deb's reception was heartwarming. Samuel described her mother as being 'a brave woman and mightily beloved'. Her Uncle Butts was kind to us and lavish with his hospitality.

On our return I had the most serious angry scene, or series of scenes, with Samuel that ever happened in our 13 years of marriage. But more of that later.

The next week everything seemed a little better and happier. We went to buy some linen for sheets together and took Deb to see Nan Marshall in the 'Indian Queens'. We went to the Mile End with Deb and ate a jowl of salmon at the Rose and Crown, where Samuel once lodged as a boy. We went to see Betterton at the Duke's in 'Henry the Fifth' and ate a lobster in Spring Gardens.

Can you imagine such lovely innocent mid-summer pleasures?

Samuel Cooper was painting me in miniature. At his studio I was chaperoned by Deb and Will Hewer. Afterwards we went in a glass hackney coach to the Park and drank pints of milk at the lodge. We saw Becke Marshall at the King's in a new play called 'Hyde Park' with live horses brought on to the stage.

All this must have seemed like fairyland to the little girl from Bristol. Once upon a time I had been a little fifteen year old from Bideford, Devon, looking at London for the first time.

Later on in the summer, with Deb and Mercer, we went to see the gypsies and to see Bartholomew Fayre 'in situ', and later separately as a puppet play. Mary Mercer came with the three of us to 'The Spanish Gipsys' with Joseph Haynes acting well in it. To an onlooker it must have been a fine sight – handsome Samuel aged 28 squiring his three lovely womenfolk. Certainly we always caused a stir amongst the audience.

In mid-March, after she had been with us six months, Samuel found little Deb Willett crying when he returned in the evening. I had been telling her as kindly and discreetly as I could that she must politely and *firmly* discourage my husband's advances. She simply did not seem to realise that his tender, skilful fondlings were not only wrong, but were a prelude to more serious love-making. She was such an innocent little baby that I do not think she comprehended what was wrong with the fumbles, and no idea at all what 'much worse' could be. In her dreamlike childish purity, she could not envisage anything wrong or unhappy happening in the Pepys household. She cried, not out of sadness, but out of puzzlement.

Our usual social whirl continued with the Pierces, Mrs Corbet the actress, and Mr Harris the actor. There was always good food and wines and always good dancing with a violin and theorbo. Samuel often urged the captive audience to sing his own songs. I once took little Deb on her own to a play appropriately entitled 'The Man is the Master'. We saw it a second time with Samuel and our usual friends, going afterwards to the Blue Balls tavern near the Duke of York's playhouse. Elizabeth Knepp and Harris brought Mr Bannister with them, the great music master, and we sang and danced until midnight.

It was a difficult time in the City – prentice riots on a large scale, the naval Press gangs out, and the wretched unpaid seamen of the fleet threatening to burn or pull down the Treasury Office. I thought to myself that Samuel was my little Nero fiddling on his flageolet whilst Rome threatened to be burnt over his head. The Militia and the watches were, thank goodness, very strict at night, ensuring law and order.

My strictures to Deb seemed to have passed over her head. I am fairly sure that Samuel had his way with her at the end of March. Our little old wooden London houses carry every sound, and my maids tell me everything (as far as I know).

This relationship continued unchanged for several months. Samuel was happy. Little Deborah was happy. I was happy but suspicious. After the evening of the 25th October all my worst suspicions were realised. I found them in an intimate compromising situation that shocked me to the core.

CHAPTER NINETEEN

MY FRIENDS THE GOLDEN BATELIERS

"Give me books, fruit, French wine and fine weather and a little music out of doors played by somebody I do not know" J. Keats

My friends the Bateliers have been wine shippers of Bordeaux for many generations. Of course their real name is Batailley, but that is too difficult for the English, and Samuel always calls them the 'Bateliers'.

From their two chateaux in the Medoc they have been sending their Bordeaux wine – 'claret' the English call it, to England for many years, although Samuel says it is not as good as what he calls 'Ho Brian'.

They are Huguenots of course. Joseph Batailley, the father, was naturalised in 1648, although he was born in Bordeaux, but he tells me there were members of his family, a Nicholas, a Peter and a Louis living in London early last century. Joseph was originally a factor in London for Mr Leachland, the King's wine merchant, and on his death Joseph served wines to the King by order of the Committee for the Revenue and held a clerkship in the English Customs service. Joseph's wife Susanna is English and they have four children – two sons called Joseph and William, and two daughters Mary, and Susan whom Samuel calls 'black' which means that she has dark hair and skin.

In 1665 the family were living on the north side of Crutched Friars, next door to Thomas Andrews and opposite our house, so that of course I saw a lot of them. Then Samuel and the Pepys family and faithful Will Hewer all became friends with the Bateliers (for that is what I will call them now) – they were such an easy family to make friends with!

Joseph, the son, is about my age, and he and Mary keep a small linen draper's shop in the Royal Exchange. Besides wine they import fine linen and silks from Bordeaux and Marseilles. Samuel calls Mary 'my beauty Mrs Batelier who is indeed one of the finest women I ever saw in my life' and buys linen from her at the old Exchange. In January 1666 both sisters came to visit me, and

Samuel was there and described the scene. 'We sat and talked together an houre with infinite pleasure to me and so the fair creature (Mary) went away and proves one of the modestest women and pretty that ever I saw in my life and my wife judges her so too'. That summer Susan, the dark pretty brunette came back from France and visited me. Samuel made her sing a French song and we gave them – for Mary was there too – sweetmeats and then we all sang. They had brought some fat cage birds called Ortalans over from France, which they are going to give, or perhaps sell, to the King to eat. We are a strange race, eating caged birds!

That summer they all came to our house many times for venison pasty and a good supper and always talk, talk, talk, and of course songs and dancing and much fine red wine from Bordeaux. In July Samuel met Joseph for the first time. He described him as 'a pretty man, understanding and well discoursed, much pleased with his company'. But I liked handsome William – not madly, not to distraction – I just liked him immensely. And he liked me. Samuel was never quite sure about us! He wrote 'and home where I met Mr Batelier and my wife – but Lord to see how soon I could conceive evil fears and thoughts concerning them'.

Once we went to Bow to Lady Pooly's with all the Bateliers and Susanna their mother, who was a dog breeder. She was distressed by the loss of a dog borrowed from the Duke of Albermarle's son to line a pretty bitch of hers. Luckily the dog returned, so all was well.

In mid-August we had another venison pasty, not only for William and Mary Batelier, but also for Christian Le Brun, who lived in St. Olaves, and of course Will Hewer. We had a very merry supper and Samuel remarked how well William Batelier dances. At three or four in the morning, Samuel and William were still dancing, dressed as women. Dear Samuel, what a little devil he can be!

Later that month – it was a marvellous long, hot, merry summer – William and Mary over supper told us stories of witches and spirits. Once in Bordeaux William was making a bargain or contract for some young claret wines with another grower at a tavern. William had surreptitiously hired a fellow to thunder upon a deal board to simulate the noise of rain and hail. At once William claimed that the thunder outside would spoil and turn the other merchants' grapes and vines and thus reduce their value. William claims that the other merchants abated their price by two pistoles per tun for their wine. What a marvellous story – I suppose it was really true?

We often went to the theatre with William.

We introduced him and his sister to all the family, Samuel's Aunt Wight, the Talbot Pepys, Samuel's father and mother, Pall, and Balty of course. Occasionally we went to the Wells' at Barnet to see old Joseph Batelier the father.

In September '66 there was a great fire in Fish Street and friends and relatives of the Bateliers called Woolfe and Stanes had their houses burned down. The son Joseph lost his draper's shop too where he used to pay £100 rent a year, although now at the Exchange he pays only £3. I hope Samuel has got his figures right. The Bateliers persuaded me to take on a cook-maid called Nell. Samuel called her an old, tall maid, but he always prefers pretty young servants. William went off to Marseilles with lots of commissions to execute as a factor. Samuel was bored by him and said that 'he grew troublesome in his talking so much of his going to France'. But before he went William produced Deborah Willett for us, or rather for me.

In the autumn William brought me a lovely spaniel puppy bred by his mother and stayed and supped with us and played a game of cards afterwards.

He also brought us on another occasion some oysters and some bottles of the 1666 Bordeaux red wine which Samuel found mighty good. William produced an absurd story about the King of France now wearing vests and that the noblemen of France have to do the like, which is the greatest indignity ever done by any Prince to others! William and Samuel were agreed on that.

We asked all the Bateliers to supper in December, including old Joseph. As usual we gave them venison pasties and other good cheer, and we had a merry evening, although Joseph was very gloomy that wines laden by him in France before the late proclamation was out, cannot now be brought into England, which will cause much loss to the Bateliers.

On Boxing Day young Joseph and his new, very pregnant wife dined with us. Samuel rather rudely said that her great belly had spoiled her looks already. But it was a lovely evening. Thomas Andrews brought his viol and played most excellently. I had invited Pembleton and a fiddler and we all danced until midnight and then had supper and played at 'cross-purposes', and mighty merry we were, and so to bed.

In the New Year the Bateliers and the Mercers came to supper and cards and we ate a great cake given us by Mr Russell, the waterman. Samuel certainly liked it. Also in January we had another party with the two Mercer sisters, William Batelier *and* Pembleton (now *that* was a bit difficult), old Lady Penn and Pegg

Penn and Mr Lowther, her new husband. Samuel was rather taken with Peg, but I supposes he was jealous with two of my admirers being present, and such good dancers too!

In the autumn of that year old Joseph Batelier died in the night, and Samuel and I were mightily troubled for he had been a very good man. I knew that Samuel was seeing too much of some of his 'young women', but we all put a brave face on and pretended nothing was amiss. At the end of October we had a dancing party with Betty Turner, both Mercers, 'ugly' Mrs Parker, and of course William Batelier and 'my' Mr Pembleton. Samuel enjoyed it, although his dancing is not as good as it might be.

In the New Year of 1667/8 we had a musical dancing party. It was cold and we had good fires and candles all ready. Betty Turner and my two admirers and I fell to dancing. Samuel had arranged with Mr Greeting, 'some extraordinary music, with two viollins and a base viollin and theorbo, four hands, the Duke of Buckinghams musicians and the best in town' as he described them. We danced all night and Samuel paid the four fiddlers £3, and it was well worth it too. But William, who has taken over the wine business after his father's death, was much worried about the business of an Impost on wine, although Samuel says the House of Lords have reason for it, being a matter wherein money might be saved to his Majesty.

The next night Samuel and I were in bed and talking about poor Pall, his unmarried sister, for whom Samuel takes such pains. The Pepys family had been talking about suitors and dowries for her for years. Anyway we agreed that when she got married, she would be married from our house and Will Hewer and my William Batelier would be the Bridesmen, and Mary Mercer and Deb Willett the bridesmaids. We wanted it to be a gay, merry affair and decided to do all we could with our best friends to make it so.

In the autumn of '68 we went one day to the Temple by water to see at the Duke's playhouse 'The Maid in the Mill' revived. After that I went with Deborah to Unthanke's and the Exchange and bought a few small things leaving Mary Mercer and Samuel in the coach, where in quarter of an hour or so he had taught her to sing the 'Lark's Song' perfectly because she had such a good ear and voice. We walked to Whitehall but I was angry with Samuel. I know what he thinks of my voice, certainly by comparison with Mary Mercer's, but I was so furious with him for his smug triumph at teaching Mercer so quickly and so easily when he finds it so difficult to teach me. I was very rude to him, unfortunately in front of William Batelier, which was embarrassing for everyone.

Samuel was obviously rather vexed with me.

Samuel, despite some unfounded suspicions of handsome William, often meets him socially and on business outside our home. I remember one night they came back in a coach via London Wall where they were stopped many times by the watch because of the prentice and student riots in the City. Every stop meant 'much time and some trouble and more money to every watch to them to drink'. Anyway that was Samuel's story. I think they both enjoyed the journey home and joined the watch in their late night drinking.

In the summer of '68 William went to Impington, the Talbot Pepys' home, where he was nobly used by Samuel's cousin, but Samuel is still suspicious of him. In late August William and Mary, his sister, and Deb and Mary Mercer, Samuel and I met at the Bateliers' home. Also there were the Pierce family, Elizabeth Knepp the actress, Joseph Harris the actor and fat young Mr. Gumbleton. We danced all night long with a noble supper, and about two in the morning the table was spread again for such a noble breakfast that even Samuel was taken aback. We stayed there till almost three in the morning. The next day with William and Deborah we went to Bartholomew Fayre and saw the rope dancing, by Jacob Hall, also a rather nasty little stage play called 'Merry Andrew'. That day I remember old Mrs Batelier gave me another pretty spaniel bitch called Flora which I adore, but Samuel is less enthusiastic!

In the autumn William went off to France on business, not however before he had introduced a French periwig maker to Samuel, who made him a handsome new wig in the latest fashion.

Early in the New Year of '69 old Mrs Batelier, Mary and Susan came to dinner with us together with Will Hewer, his mother, and Mr Spong, Samuel's patent agent and musician friend. But Samuel was a little bored with the endless stories about William as recounted by his fond mother. Mr Spong and Samuel then tried out a new measuring instrument which they call a Parallelogram or 'Protractor'.

William came back from France quite suddenly and Samuel met him at Whitehall, his boots all dirty from the journey. He brought letters to the King from France, probably about the French army or navy. I think he is an agent for the British government. There had been a rumour that William had been drowned, and I was desolate, but the first day he was back in town he came to sup with us and told us many pretty things of France and the greatness of the present King, Louis Quatorze. Secretly he had brought some excellent prints of Robert Nantueills', the engraver from Rheims, for Samuel. They were of the French King and Minister J-B Colbert and others, which Samuel pronounced 'Most excellent to my great content'. Just as well too, because my handsome William also brought me a great many perfumed gloves of various kinds. Most of them were much too large but I accepted very gratefully two or three dozen of them, which vexed Samuel and made him angry! So angry that I returned most of the gloves to William. But more was to come. The next day William came round to see me, with French books mainly for Samuel but some for me. There was 'L'Estat de France' by Jean de Maraix and others and also two printed music books of French songs for both of us. He is a kind thoughtful, lovely friend to have.

At the end of January Balty and William dined with us and Samuel made us read in French – bien sûr – out aloud, and also Mr Boyle's 'Book of Formes'. Samuel's eyes are troubling him again. William then read a French discourse which he had particularly brought over with him from France for Samuel. It was an

The Bataillhey Chateau, Bordeaux, by permission of the owners

invitation to the people of France to apply themselves to the study of Navigation. If the King of France really equips their Navy and increases its size and encourages their sea trade as he has already started to, then in Samuel's opinion, they will be a great competitor to the English 'and that will undo us in a few years'.

I remember an evening in February when Thomas Povey, Samuel's friend on the Tangier Committee, and William Batelier met to talk in our house about some merchandise of wine and linen. I think William hoped to supply Tangier with his goods, but Samuel told me he did not like the fact that two of his friends should use his house as a rendezvous to discuss their commercial problems. Perhaps as a result of Samuel's obvious displeasure, the next week William came to see us again. He brought some lovely new clothes for me, but Samuel appeared not so much jealous as calculating, 'she is likely to lead me to much expence' so he seemed so vexed only to prevent me taking *too* much. But clever William had brought Samuel yet another Nanteuill print of the King of France's head even bigger than the previous one! The next evening Samuel and William settled up. My French clothes cost £22, which I do agree was rather a lot, but there were gloves, shoes, hoods and other clothes, and Samuel's prints etc. cost £5.

William was friendly not only with Will Hewer but also, rather surprisingly, with Talbot Pepys. One evening after the theatre at Whitehall, the three men followed up in a hackney coach and we all stopped at Hercules Pillars in Fleet Street, and Samuel gave us the very best supper and we had a pretty merry evening. But Samuel's eyes trouble him more and more. He was obviously in some pain at the theatre trying to see, despite the candle lights. The next night we went out to the Batelier's house, where was my Mr Pembleton, my 'pretty neat black man'. as Samuel described him. I thought John Pembleton – a dark well dressed handsome man – almost as attractive – but not quite – as William Batelier. After supper some fiddles and so to dance – another merry evening.

In the autumn of '68 after that golden summer, William told Samuel that he was going to Cambridge to see the Talbot Pepys family and to see the Fair. He told me that he had seen Samuel with beautiful Mrs Elizabeth Knepp at dinner the same day. Roger Pepys at Impington had been entertaining Will Hewer and myself, and we both wrote to Samuel in London to tell him of the noble entertainment Roger had afforded us. But William came to Impington mainly to see me.

In October Samuel met old Mrs Batelier, who was giving a housewarming party for William and many of their friends. We had a gay, lively evening and Samuel thought that Mrs Batelier was not only a merry person but a gentlewoman of some understanding. The next day Samuel bought yet another wig from William's French periwig maker.

William continued to come and see me – to see us – during the following spring, often with Mary, sometimes with Talbot Pepys – once to supper at the Mulberry garden. And William recommended a new cook-maid for us, a blackamore girl called Doll, who dressed our meat very well, and we are both pleased with her.

Samuel's cousin Theophila Turner and the Talbot Pepys and I dined several times at William's house when Samuel was busy on Admiralty work. Often his nose was a little out of joint that we did not send for him to enjoy our dancing and suppers. One evening we all dined at the Povy's and William and Mary were there too. The Bateliers were liked by everyone. I know Samuel found it sometimes hard to believe but it was a long, beautiful, innocent relationship we all had together.

In early March of '69 Samuel organised a great party with the Turners, the Roger Pepys family and others. Samuel thought that Betty Turner was looking very pretty. William and his sister Susan were there. In the evening there was music organised by Mr Greeting with violins and theorbos – the best in town according to Samuel. And we all danced with mighty mirth and jigs, and William danced the 'Blackmore and Blackmore Mad', and then we fell to country dances again, and such a splendid supper during the evening. I wore a French gown called a "Sac" which William had brought over from France. Samuel said to me that it was one of the days and nights of his life which he spent with the greatest content, and that which he can but hope to repeat again a few times in his whole life.

Samuel wrote in his diary (he never showed it to me but he sometimes told me what he had written) – the last entry before his eyes forced him to give up the close writing in May of '69, just before we went to France – 'With my wife to the Park with Mary Batelier and a Dutch gentleman friend of hers to the 'Worlds End' a drinking house nearby and there merry, and so home late'.

For over five years – marvellous years – the handsome, kind and generous Bateliers were part of my life and Samuel's too. We were never happier than in their golden company.

CHAPTER TWENTY

'SO MUCH IN LOVE OF PLAYS'

''Le dernier acte est sanglant. Quelque belle que soit le comedie en toute la reste'' Pascal

The stage has always been in Samuel's blood, ever since he was a lad when he was offered a part as a woman by Sir Robert Cooke. With his pretty treble voice and pink cheeks he would have made an admirable stage woman. He was not much amused when I made that point to him. The 'Red Bull' at Clerkenwell has staged bloodthirsty melodramas for many years. Samuel as a young boy used to sneak in frequently when he was lodged in the East end of London. He grew up with the excitement of the theatre being actually on his doorstep.

His education at St Paul's and Cambridge enabled him to read for pleasure many works and plays that subsequently appeared on the London stage. Having read the original work he felt that he knew what the author intended for the role. Woe betide the actor who strayed too far from the text. Thus he was able to explain to me why Thomas Betterton was so good, perhaps unique, in a particular role, or equally how the great Betterton was lamentable as Romeo in Will Shakespeare's play. He could, with his clear mind, distinguish a poor plot but excellent singing and dancing, or occasionally vice versa.

So the first thing Samuel taught me was the ability to detect the best features in every production – assuming there were some! In the summer of '61 we went to see a French comedy at Drury Lane 'which was so ill done and the scenes and company and everything so nasty and out of order and poor that we were sick all the while in our minds to be there . . . nothing but the foolery of the farce' was how Samuel described it. When I went in the middle of the afternoon without Samuel, often with Will Hewer and usually with Mary Mercer, Ashwell, or Deb Willett, after Samuel's guidance, I was confident that I could obtain the greatest pleasure from the performance. I saw James Shirley's new play 'The Court Secret' and told Samuel how badly performed it was, so that he did not go to see it.

Later on in our married life we met socially several of the leading actors and actresses: they would dine or sup at our house, or we would meet them at Mrs Elizabeth Pierce's, whose sister was an actress. They would tell us the stage gossip, and give us their views of the roles then being played. London is a small city compared to Paris, with only a very few theatres, so that both of us, as inveterate theatre-goers, often visited the same productions several times. Thomas Killigrew, whom Samuel met and talked to quite often, was the proprietor of the King's Company in Brydges Street, Drury Lane. The main rival theatre was the Duke of York's company in Portugal St, Lincolns Inn Fields, under Sir William Davenant, who engaged Thomas Betterton.

Both of us agreed that Thomas Betterton was the best actor in London. At Whitefriars we saw Massinger's 'Bondman' several times, described by my husband as 'an excellent play and well done . . . But above all that I ever saw Betterton do the Bondman the best . . . which we both so doate on and do still but for Betterton he is called by us both the best actor in the world'. He was two years younger than Samuel and said to be the son of King Charles I's under-cook. Betterton has three disadvantages for an actor. His voice is low and he is incapable of the ranting and roaring that some parts might demand. He is ungainly which is unusual for a notable actor, but makes me study his actions the more. Finally from a woman's point of view he has small eyes – all in all not a particularly attractive man. He usually acted with Davenant's company at the Duke of York's theatre. We saw him act with much imagination the main role in 'Hamlet, Prince of Denmark'. On the other hand we saw him as Romeo and his wife as Juliet in Will Shakespeare's play at the Opera on a first night when most of the cast did not know their lines. Betterton and his wife as Ianthe performed John Webster's 'Duchess of Malfi' to admiration. One of Samuel's friends, Mr Benier, tells us that Betterton is not married to the actress Mrs Mary Saunderson, as is rumoured. Betterton is said to be a very sober serious man, studious and humble, very hard working and studies his part carefully and is rich already at 27 with what he earns and saves.

In July '60 Samuel met Edward Kynaston, the young actor who was already famous for acting ladies' parts. As the Duke's sister Olympia in 'The Loyall Subject', Samuel thought he was 'the loveliest lady that ever I saw in my life', which is high praise. That was our first acquaintance with the players. Then a little later, Balty's young lady, and briefly my companion 'our little Marmotte' Gosnell went on the stage, and we saw her act on several occasions.

In the 'Rivals' by Davenant she sang and danced finely, but fell out of key in a song with Harris, who cleverly altered his own pitch to agree with hers.

We first met Mrs Knepp at the end of '65. She had been acting at the King's House for nearly two years, and had already started to make her name. She was married to a small unattractive, melancholy, jealous jockey, whom neither Samuel nor I cared for. It did not appear that Mrs Knepp cared for him either. On the other hand her husband's jealousy was well-founded.

We were swiftly drawn into a network of glamorous intrigue that nearly ruined our marriage. Through Elizabeth Knepp we met Joseph Harris the actor, pretty Nelly Gwynn, and other famous stage names. Samuel had just finished composing a song based on Solyman's words to Roxalana in the 'Siege of Rhodes', which begins 'Beauty Retire, thou dost my pity move, Relieve my pity, and then trust my love'. Very appropriate words for what later happened to us all.

We, that is Samuel and I and Mary Mercer, walked on a cold December afternoon to a musical soirée at Mrs Pierce's. I was then confident and able to sing in public, whatever Samuel may have secretly thought. There by arrangement were most of our musical friends. Mrs Coleman, an actress who has played Ianthe in the 'Siege of Rhodes', her husband Edward, Nicholas Lanier, of the famous composer-musicians family of that name, Mrs Clerke's sister Mrs Worshipp, a diplomat called Captain Rolt – and Mrs Elizabeth Knepp 'Here the best company for musique I ever was in' said Samuel afterwards.

During '66 we both of us saw a certain amount of beautiful Mrs Elizabeth Knepp. Not only did she like – perhaps more than like – Samuel, but she also liked me, and this was warmly reciprocated. She was a beautiful, intelligent and kind woman in my opinion.

The Plague year and the Great Fire of London meant that we were pre-occupied with many serious events, so that theatre going was considerably reduced. On the 25th October Samuel talked to Mrs Knepp who said that both the main theatres were re-opening. Lord Brouncker's mistress, Mrs Williams, told Samuel that the Duke's house will be more popular because of their women actresses, the King's having but men! All three of us, Samuel and I and Mrs Knepp, went to the theatre together when she was not on stage; she had an excellent part in the 'Indian Emperor' by John Dryden. Sometimes Samuel hid himself and pretended (to himself anyway) that he was not there at the play 'Here I was in pain to be seen and hid myself', so that his colleagues at the Navy Office would not see him!

We first met little pretty Nelly Gwynn at the King's House for a performance of 'The Humerous Lieutenant'. Mrs Elizabeth Knepp, who sang well in that production, introduced us to her. Samuel and I both kissed her 'and a mighty pretty soul she is, too' said Samuel. We saw her several times backstage, and Samuel sometimes saw her without me, but usually with Mrs Knepp.

There were many excellent reasons for going to the theatre. It was relatively inexpensive; once Samuel sat in the one shilling seats, and four of the Navy Office clerks sat in the half crown box at the same performance. Oh the shame of it! Seats were also available at 18 pence each. The most expensive upper boxes were 4 shillings a seat, but opening nights were at doubled prices. At one stage in Samuel's life he was gadding to the theatre *twice* a day although he rarely informed me of the second visit. As far as I could tell, he would take me on about half of his visits! In '61 he swore solemnly to me that he would never go to a play without me. I looked at him and smiled. He really meant it!

The Theatre is a very social occasion. The King and his brother go several times a week, usually with the mistress of the moment, leaving their plain wives at home. The Court gallants are there, and the riff-raff in the pits are fairly well restrained in their criticisms. So my little popinjay and I dress up to the nines. If the Duke of York ogles me, as he does, I want to be seen at my best. To see and be seen in fact.

Samuel always attracted strange adventures at the theatre. I am not talking about amatory adventures with Mrs Elizabeth Knepp, and cosy little talks with Nelly. Once at the 'Lost Lady' he was spat upon backward by mistake by a lady. All was well however, since she was a very pretty lady and he told me that he was not troubled at it at all!

At the 'Red Bull' theatre, which was less reputable, the young boy actor did not know his song so his master fell about his ears and beat him so, that it put the whole house into an uproar. Melodrama hangs in the balance, and is easily tipped into farce!

At Sir William Davenant's Opera 'The Siege of Rhodes' we both stayed to see the King and Elizabeth Queen of Bohemia, King James I's daughter. Additional free drama was provided when part of the wooden theatre collapsed by the breaking of a wooden board over our heads. We had a great deal of dust that fell onto the ladies' necks and on the men's hair which made good sport for everyone else. Other people's misfortunes unfortunately can be uproarious! We were not always so lucky. In midsummer of '64 we were at the

King's House watching the 'Silent Woman', when a heavy hailstorm emptied most of the theatre. We were in the middle of the pit, open to the elements. Only the Blackfriars theatre has a roof over the pit as well as the boxes. So exeunt two wet, bedraggled Pepys in their sodden finery, and back home.

Another hazard was the rabble of young blades usually led by young Thomas Killigrew, causing an affray in the pit, but we would hide ourselves so they did not see us. If one avoided the pit, one then sat so high and far off, that one missed most of the words and sat with a wind coming into ones back and neck.

Once a gentleman in the audience eating of fruit in the midst of the play, did drop down dead, seemingly choked, but with much ado Orange Moll, the actress, thrust her finger down his throat and brought him to life again. Real life drama in addition to Will Shakespeare's 'Henry IV' on stage. It was a custom to eat fruit at the theatre – Samuel once bought a dozen oranges at 6 pence a piece for me and Deb or Mary Mercer. Occasionally the peel was used to pelt an unappreciated player!

Mr Joseph Harris was very nearly Mr Thomas Betterton's equal. In the summer of '63 he demanded more money from his patron Sir William Davenant than even Betterton was getting. The problem was that the King and the Court were so taken with Harris, and praised him as much – or *more* – than Betterton, that he grew very proud . . . But yet the critics all say that Betterton acts some parts that none but himself can do. We started to admire Harris in '64, and first met him at Elizabeth Pierce's with Mrs Knepp in early '66. Dear pretty Mrs Knepp and her friend, my friend Elizabeth Pierce, brought him one evening from his performance at the Duke's playhouse. Mrs Knepp was dressed like a country maid, with a straw hat, straight from the set of the 'Goblins'. At first Samuel could not identify her in her stage attire. We had four fiddlers that night at the Navy Office – Samuel was feeling munificent 'only the musique did not please me, they not being contented with less than 30s' was his complaint. It was a wonderful evening – despite all the cross-currents – Harris sang his famous Irish song which Samuel praised as 'the strangest in itself and the prettiest sung by him ever heard'. Mrs Knepp felt unwell so I went back to her house with her to put her to bed. Remember, I liked her and she liked me. Harris stayed a long time with us; a very curious and understanding person and a man of fine conversation.

Thomas Killigrew, patron of the King's company, told Samuel that the audiences were but half of what they were before the Great

Fire, and that Mrs Knepp is likely to make the best actor that ever come upon the stage she understanding so well her roles that they are going to give her £30 a-year more. He also told Samuel of the recent improvements he has made at his theatre: the stage he said 'is much better and more glorious than before now he has many wax candles in place, previously not above 3 lbs of tallow now, all things civil, no rudeness anywhere: then as in a beargarden, then two or three fiddlers, now nine or ten of the best; then nothing on the ground but rushes and everything else mean: now, all otherwise'.

Joseph Harris, and Mrs Elizabeth Knepp of course, came and dined with us in early January '67. The more we met, the more we liked him. Samuel said of him 'we discourse of many things, do find him an excellent person, such as in my whole acquaintance I do not know another better qualified for converse . . . of his own trade or of other kind, a man of great understanding and observation . . .' We took him back to his theatre, the Duke's house, where we was acting in the 'Tempest'. Then after the play was over we went back to the office to dance with Mr Pembleton and William Batelier. The following day Samuel – bit between his teeth – first went to the Actors' Nursery or training school in Golden Lane, then to the Duke of York's, and then to the King's house, and liking neither of the plays, returned home! Later he took me and Deb to the Nursery to see a pastoral comedy called the 'Faithful Shepherd', but we thought that the young actors were not ready yet to appear in the main theatres.

From time to time my husband would make vows. Rash vows such as the reduction of this theatre going. This was not because of economy but because if young Samuel Pepys, up and coming Clerk of the Acts, was seen to be *always* theatre-going, he might be regarded as under-employed, or even as my compatriots would say 'un homme pas serieux'.

In November '67 he promised to give £10 to the poor charity if he went to the theatre before Christmas. By the end of the month we were watching 'The Mistaken Beauty' at the King's Playhouse!

My dear husband is a snob – a nice snob – but still a snob. His views on theatre audiences I think reveal this. 'Not so well pleased with the company at the house (theatre) today which was full of *citizens*, there hardly being a gallant man or woman in the house', he said. But what if the gallants happen to be young Thomas Killigrew's riotous sparks?

His puritanical spirit wages war perpetually with the cavalier in him. He visited Mesdames Knepp and Nelly Gwynn in their tiring-rooms at the King's House and complained that 'they were both so painted that he decided abruptly to dislike them'. He also eventually loathed pretty Mrs Pierce because she painted herself too. I know – or I think I know – the limits I can go to with Samuel, and I do not risk painting myself.

We became knowledgeable about theatre design – after all Samuel knew his way to all the tiring-rooms in London! When the Theatre Royal in Drury Lane was near completion, we both visited it and agreed that the house is made with extra-ordinary good convenience, yet it has some faults. For instance the narrowness of the passages is dangerous. Our London theatres are built of wood and do catch fire from time to time. The distance from the stage to the boxes is too great and thus it is difficult to hear the actors. Lastly the musicians play below the stage and the noise of the bass and treble musicians will be difficult to hear.

In the spring of '66 we both of us walked to inspect the King's playhouse, where the stage was being ripped out to make it wider but all rather dirty. We saw the inside of the stage and all the tiring-rooms and machines and indeed it is a sight worthy of seeing. Samuel thus described it 'But to see their clothes and the various sorts and what a mixture of things there was: here a wooden leg, there a ruff, here a hobby-horse, there a crown, would make a man split himself to see with laughing and particularly Lacys wardrobe and Robert and William Shotterell's. But then again to think how fine they show on the stage by candle-light and how poor things look at too near hand. The machines are fine and the paintings very pretty'.

We saw all of London's best actors and actresses on the boards in one production or another; poor Mr Clun, murdered by an Irishman on his way home after playing in the 'Alchemist' in the summer of '64; Major Mohun in the 'Beggers Bush' in Killigrew's King's House who was said to be the best actor in the world, lately come over with the King from Holland; poor Mr Young, a bad actor at best; Mr Nicholas Burt, who acted the Moor so well in the 'Moor of Venice', but broke his leg dancing in John Suckling's 'Aglaura'; Mr Hart, that fine actor, hopelessly in love with sweet Nelly, and she in love either with the King or Lord Buckhurst or both; William Smith of the Duke's who killed a man in a brawl; and Lacy, the dancing master actor in 'Love in a Maze' as a country fellow clown which he did to admiration, (His part in the 'French Dancing Master' was considered the best in the world), and as the Irish footman in 'The Committee' quite beyond imagination. We saw him too in John Fletcher's 'The Faithful Shepherdess'. He is almost in the same class as Betterton and Harris. When the latter two rivals acted together in 'Henry the Fifth' their parts were incomparably written and performed and the whole play was full of depth, raptures of wit and sense. We saw Lacy as 'Jawny' in 'The Taming of the Shrew' and as the country gentleman in 'The Change of Crowns'. Lacy had a terrible quarrel with Ned Howards of the King's House, which almost came to a duel!

As for actresses, Mrs Elizabeth Knepp once brought Mrs Corbet with her to meet us. We saw Mrs Covey acting as Doll Common in the 'Scornful Lady'. Nelly and Becke Marshall, the two sisters, daughters of a Puritan minister, both acted frequently at the King's House. We also saw Mary Davis known as Orange Moll who danced a jig in 'Richard the Third', such a sad and melancholy play.

Mrs Betty Hall, the darkhaired actress with a little Roman nose, was one of our favourites – she was in the 'Humerous Lover' with Mrs Knepp. The famous Nelly Gwynn acted the great part of Coelia in the 'Humerous Lieutenant', and we both saw her as Florimell in the 'Maiden Queen'. Samuel described her 'both as a mad girle, then most and best of all when she comes in like a young gallant and hath the motions and carriage of a young spark, the most that ever any man have'. Oh and I must not forget Mrs Knepp! As the widow in the 'Scornful Lady', and in the 'Custom of the Country' she was the only actor to sing her parts admirably. Her great role as Mrs Weaver in the 'Indian Emperor' shows that she is coming on to be a great actor. She sang admirably the song 'All night I weepe' in 'The Chance' at the King's.

Yes, I will never forget my friend, beautiful, talented, treacherous Mrs Elizabeth Knepp – nor I imagine will Samuel.

CHAPTER TWENTY ONE

SAMUEL'S GADDING ABOUT

"Le coeur a ses raisons, que la raison ne connait pas"
B. Pascal

During the course of our brief courtship, it was quite clear to me that not only did Samuel have a roving eye for the women, but given half a chance, a roving hand as well.

He dallies with, and sometimes kisses, every pretty or even moderately pretty wench he comes across. On the Exchange, at the taverns, at other people's houses, and unfortunately even in *our* houses.

He always assumed that I knew nothing of his furtive little amours with Betty Lane and Betty Howlett. *We* bought linens from Betty Lane of Westminster Hall in the early days! The little Howlett girl, he called his 'little sweetheart', and his 'second wife' because she looked somewhat like me – a most dubious compliment. They were both sweet pretty things, and Rebecca Allen even prettier still. When gossips told me about the wretched Mrs Bagwell, the Deptford carpenter's wife, I started to grow worried. His adventures were becoming more frequent, more indiscriminate and totally pointless.

I realised that he was incapable of keeping his hands off *any* reasonably pretty woman, unless I did something positive about it. Curiously enough I believe that that is usually as far as it goes, but I cannot be sure.

To an outsider Samuel might have given the impression that not all was well at home. But apart from my regular heavy 'monthlies' we sleep together practically every night of our marriage, except during the alarums and excursions during the Plague Year, the Fire of London, and periodic visits to Brampton. We are warm responsive lovers, and not only does Samuel want me in bed, but my French blood – thank goodness – more than reciprocates his own desires. Despite minor tiffs or differences during the day, inevitable in any marriage, we are together at night – 'and so to bed'. My basic philosophy about Samuel's known and unknown amours developed quite clearly and strongly. I would make no protest or even hint at a protest at his often daily peccadilloes in the outside world: that would have meant scenes *every* day!

One arena into which I would launch myself with violent feminine jealous rage would be if he tried to seduce *my* friends – for instance, the two beautiful French Batelier sisters whom he admires immensely (and admiration from Samuel is often closely followed by lust). I protect them and chaperone them very, very closely. My good friend William, their brother, tacitly helps me. It is in all our interests to make sure that Samuel, whom we all love, behaves sensibly and discreetly with this lovely family.

The same applies to my friend Mrs Elizabeth Pierce, 'La Belle Pierce'. Her husband, James Pierce, surgeon of the Navy ship 'Naseby', and I have an arrangement to protect that friendship. He is quite often at sea and he and Samuel like each other. His wife is not only beautiful, with a lovely complexion, but she is a smart, sophisticated woman, a few years older than I am. She has some money of her own, and has more friends of the 'haut monde' than we have. She knows the female fashions and newest styles at Court, and shows me how best they can suit me. Moreover she is cheerful, gay, dashing and convivial. It was through her that we met the stage people, Harris, Corbet and of course Mrs Knepp.

I need our friendship with the Bateliers and the Pierces and will retain it at all costs. I enlisted their support and have received it. We keep Samuel in his correct place as a loving, intelligent husband. Elizabeth Pierce told me all about the 'Dapper Dicky' episode between Samuel and Elizabeth Knepp. When they exchanged silly little lovers notes signed with aliases. Over the years we have had scores of lovely days and evenings with these two families, and Samuel has not been allowed to stray from my side!

The second arena in which I will fight Samuel *almost* to the death is the field of expenditure and presents. Although like most men he is quite secretive about his sources of income and the amounts that he receives, I know all his major revenues such as the interest on his great loan to "My Lord" Sandwich for example. Also I think I know most of his expenditures! Obviously I control as best I can the basic household expenditure on food and so on. Samuel pays the boys and maids each week. I know accurately what he spends on clothes for himself, and for myself. I guess at his heavy outgoings on books. Our silverware has been mostly given to him or to me by grateful Navy suppliers. We usually purchase together things for the house: furnishings, painting, pots and pans etc. I am confident that he is not spending a *great* deal of money 'abroad' on his wenches. What he spends in the taverns roystering with John Creed and the neighbouring Admirals is of course none of my business. What he lays out on entertaining his wenches at the theatre when I am in the countryside, I never *know* for certain, although my friends in town are perfectly happy to give me their estimates! But more anon.

The final arena in which I fight Samuel, literally to the finish – no 'ifs' and 'buts' to it – is seduction by the master within our own household. The French have a vulgar phrase for it, and doubtless the English have the equivalent. Something to do with dogs and doorsteps.

Over the years of our marriage we must have had a round dozen of little girl maids, and counting Gosnell, Barker, Mercer and Willett, four companion-maids for myself. Samuel may technically own the house; he may call the inhabitants of it 'his family' – which I like and much approve of. But like all wives and housewives I run it from six in the morning, often till midnight. My master can dally with *me* and fondle *me* when and where he likes, but not the members of my household once they are inside my doors!

I suspect, knowing Samuel's amatory habits very well indeed, that he has fondled some of my little maids – perhaps Nell and Susan? By that I do not mean harmless, almost paternal 'busses' on the cheeks. Several of them were pretty enough and I am fairly sure that he handled them in intimate ways from time to time – but not to my certain knowledge. Of course they all adored him. He is the most attractive and fascinating man that I know, and his worldly charm unleashed on a little 13 year old is overwhelming. Combing his hair by the fireside and helping him to dress and undress however are dangerous manoeuvers.

With my companion-ladies it was a different matter. I think that he honestly thought that there was an element of 'droit de Seigneur' – perhaps even that they were substitute wives, if for any reason I was 'hors de combat'.

Mary Mercer he liked and admired, and she was our close companion for several years. When she left at my instigation, it was because Samuel's course of seduction was well under way, and I wanted to prevent the irrevocable clash. I am fairly sure that after she left us – and we remained friends – she did succumb to Samuel's fatal charms. But *outside* our household.

Little Deb Willett was another matter. On the 25th October '68 I discovered them in as compromising a situation as is possible. Either they had been already intimate, or undoubtedly they would be very soon, and that was the last straw. My husband and my little girl in our bedroom!

Samuel's loving nature can be explained in many ways. I, who know him best of all, am still amazed at his capacity for creating an amorous interlude. This he then imagines is more serious and much deeper than it is. He deceives himself most of the time. He believes that it is his love of beauty that drives him to his excesses. Undoubtedly he has an eye and an ear for beauty – paintings, buildings, music, books, and of course, women. He may have an ailment that compels him to chase after so many women, although since his successful operation for the stone, he suffers little other than the usual run of colds and coughs in the winter season. I often wonder to myself as he is kissing me at midnight in our matrimonial bed, who else he has been kissing during the day. For, knowing my Samuel, I cannot imagine any day passing without a casual little encounter – most of them, thank goodness, completely forgettable. It cannot be lack of confidence in himself, because he has that in plenty. With his ability he has risen from the ranks of the fishmongers, the butchers and the bakers, to be a notable – indeed powerful – servant of the King. He has no need to bolster his self-esteem with casual adventures. He has now made a name for himself; has a household, a career, many friends at Court, a widespread loving family – and certainly a handsome loving wife! What more does he want?

Samuel and I have had some horrifying quarrels – inevitably about women or servants. He may suspect I have admirers or even lovers, but he does not know. His character is such that he needs to have proof of something before he will act. The memory of some of those fights still lingers . . .

In November '62 I wrote him a letter at the office telling the reasons why I wanted and needed to have a woman companion to live with us. I knew he was now worth nearly £700, and that a gentlewoman would cost us less than £20 per annum. He was not as interested in my loneliness and my feeling of frustration, having no one to talk to during the day and much of the evening, as he was in his pocket. I told him that if he denied me this request I would leave him, and he could replace me with one of the Bowyer girls. This ultimatum, which I fully meant, carried the day: shortly afterwards Gosnell appeared. But the quarrel had lasted a long time and was very bitter on my part.

On the 9th March '63 we had the same quarrel on the same subject. I quoted to him a letter I had written him previously, for I kept copies of some of my letters to him on important subjects. He seized it from me, tore it and *all my other letters,* including loving ones he had written to me. He also destroyed the will in which he had left everything to me. I cried and cried and begged him to stop, but his passionate rage would not allow him to. It was a terrible, dangerous, pointless row. I determined to teach him a lesson – better still two lessons at once.

Mary Ashwell joined me two weeks later as my companion. At the same time I began an ostentatious affair with John Pembleton, my dancing master that 'pretty, neat black man'. I made sure that Samuel was beside himself with terrible jealousy. The Bible says 'an eye for an eye, a tooth for a tooth' – so be it.

In the spring of '63 Ashwell had just come, and John Pembleton was giving me dancing lessons twice a day. I had not really forgotten Samuel's humiliating cruelty when he destroyed all my letters. It was the day after he had given his father and brother Tom a long lecture in our home on 'good husbandry', at which all three had fallen to weeping! He criticised the cleanliness of the house a few hours after I had been cooking and entertaining *his* family. We fell to an exchange of angry *words* – this time. He called me a 'lazy beggar' and I retaliated – the first time ever in a most childish way – by calling him the worst word that I could think of – a 'pricklouse', which vexed him! Pricklouse is London slang for a poor tailor!

On the 2nd October '64 Samuel went off by himself on a lovely autumnal Sunday to visit various churches, and to sit next to the pretty Butler sisters if possible, then to gossip at the Wardrobe with "My Lady", and came back after the sun had set. It had not occurred to him to ask me to go with him, so I was very angry with him for not coming home and for gadding abroad to look for and at the beauties of the town.

A week before Christmas 1664 Samuel ordered me rather crossly to dismiss my good natured maid Besse, because she had forgotten to put out her master's clothes that morning. He was in an evil mood; his health in midwinter is often poorly with wind and spots; he was wenching away with Mrs Bagwell and Betty Martin, so my local gossips told me. I told Samuel quite nicely that it was not up to me 'to *command*' our servants, and that in any case, Besse's misdemeanour was slight and did not warrant dismissal. To my surprise he at once hit me hard over my left eye. We are much the same height and in some ways I have as much physical courage as he has – perhaps more. So I attacked him and scratched and bit him like an angry cat defending a kitten. Everyone in the house heard our fight, some saw it. All saw my bruised face and poulticed black eye, the following day. But Besse stayed. I made sure all the household had a happy riotous Christmas week but

Samuel commented, 'Then home to bed, leaving my wife and people up to more sports, but without any great satisfaction to myself'. We have a proverb from my native Anjou 'Cet animal est tres méchant, quand on l'attaque il se defend'.

In the spring of '67 a furious row had blown up with Samuel when he threatened to hit me over my wearing the new fashionable hair locks in the Park when walking there with him and John Creed . . . The following morning, a Sunday, I bearded my master in his den; he was busy on his accounts or counting the silver spoils. We had a rather sterile debate about my need for a second mourning gown, and the possibility that I might not wear my white-locks in *his* presence. Samuel lost his temper and then so did I: all our deep dark suspicions came tumbling out. I accused him of having an affair with Mrs Knepp, and he accused me of having one with Mr Pembleton. It went on for some hours and was most upsetting to both of us – but we made friends again in our usual way! Of course within a few days I obtained my second mourning suit, and Samuel continued to see Elizabeth Knepp!

That summer our love-hate relationship continued. The 12th July I was cross with Samuel for not dining at home, and the little brute pulled my nose sharply. Our row continued most of the day, alternating between our house and the office although he persuaded me into the garden so that our noisy quarrel could not be overheard. Eventually we ended pretty good friends and so to bed. Our rows always end up in bed, which is just as well.

But it was in the autumn of that ill-fated year that the 'Deborah affaire' started. She arrived in September: the following month at the theatre I had to remonstrate with Samuel about his close attentions to her. He perceived I was already jealous of his kindness to her so that he began to fear the girl was not likely to stay long with us. The amazing fact is that by one means or another, the uneasy truce between the three of us lasted for another year. Samuel tried most of his paternal wiles of seduction on the poor little girl, and I used my maternal guile to protect her. But I lost the battle in the end.

On one occasion in the summer of '68 I broke down and cried and threatened to leave him and go and live with my parents in Paris. That night I left Samuel's bed and slept in Deborah's with her. Later that year after I found them both 'in flagrante' I had no alternative other than to give the poor girl notice, but not until weeks of grief and anguished negotiations had gone by.

Since by now Samuel's promises were worth nothing, I enlisted poor Will Hewer's services as personal bloodhound. I ordered him to follow and stay with his master and friend every hour of the day, and to make sure Samuel kept his promise to keep away from poor little Deborah. She left on the 14th November, three weeks after the horrible discovery. I tried to find a solution whereby she could stay with us, but in vain.

Silly besotted Samuel, who could not keep his amorous hands from my little Deborah. I told him that if I left him now he would be the laughing stock of Whitehall. I would make all the world know of his perfidy. Imagine the Duke of York saying to him 'I miss seeing your pretty wife, Sandwich's cousin, at Court. Where is she now?'

I humiliated Samuel in every way that an outraged wife can; several times after Deb left, I attacked and hit him at night without response. But since I love the little demon, I could not keep my rage going. By the end of November, on a Sunday, he noted that 'My wife and I lay long with mighty content'. My clever little husband seduced me too – with the most beautiful new coach and horses, and fine clothes, and love.

In January '69 I thought that he was up to his tricks again, gadding about. I accused him of seeing Deb, after his vows to me that he never would. Moreover dear Will Hewer may love me, but he is Samuel's erstwhile boy, and colleague and close friend. He just might connive as man to man to let Samuel see Deb again. I pretended one night – or was it pretence – to attack him in bed with red hot fire tongs, much to his dismay. Much to my dismay too, that I was capable of showing my sweet wretched husband such intended violence.

I keep an eye on beautiful Mrs Knepp. I will not allow her in my house. Samuel knows that I will leave him if he sees either her or little Deb. On the other hand I will see what I want of my good friends William Batelier and Henry Sheres. And Samuel will just have to make of it what he will.

There was one terrible humiliating week in the middle of November after Deborah had left. Samuel, despite his vows and promises, was clearly still doting on her, and Will Hewer was trying to keep the peace between the two people he loved. At home I caused poor Samuel to weep practically every night. He wrote in his diary 'weeping to myself for grief, which she discerning, come to bed and mighty kind'.

That just about sums up our marriage at the moment. Anger, bitterness, grief, love and kindness.

MY LORD SANDWICH'S STORY

"Men that hazard all, do it in hope of fair advantage" W. Shakespeare

When I was seventeen my father Sir Sydney, an ardent Royalist, was expelled from the country and died two years later. I was his only surviving son, and his death in '44 was a bitter blow to me. Before I was 20 I had fought, usually on horseback, at the battles of Lincoln, Marston Moor and Naseby, and was active with the troops that stormed Bristol. I had become by then a close personal friend of my cousin Oliver Cromwell. I became a Member of Parliament for Huntingdonshire, a Member of the Council of State in '53, and Commissioner of the Treasury the year after. Oliver made me joint Admiral at sea in '56 and as General at Sea together with Admiral Blake I commanded the fleet off Cadiz. Oliver expected me to rid the Navy of the 'disconcerting radicals', but I made little effort to do this. When he was invested as Protector on 26th June 1657 (two years after my young protegés, Samuel and Elizabeth Pepys, were married), as one of his closest friends I attended him with drawn sword, together with Richard Cromwell and Whitelocke. As the Heralds cried out 'God Save the Protector' there was every possible panoply of power except a royal crown. Indeed I urged him strongly in private to accept – or perhaps even take – the Crown of England. Yet a few incredible, strange and dangerous years later I carried the Sceptre at King Charles II's coronation. 'The King is dead', I said, 'Long live the King'. King Charles gave me the Order of the Garter, and later wrote on 9 June 1665 'My Lord Sandwich, Though you have already done me very eminent services, yet the great part you have had in this happy victory (at sea) which it hath pleased God to send us, adds very much to the former obligations I have to you'. Veritably I was made to be another King-Maker

The Mountagus have had a distinctly feudal relationship with the Pepys family for many generations. In 1631 John Pepys (Samuel's father) was one of the Clerks to my father Sir Sydney, and was entrusted by him with letters of State to and from the

King. Lord Dorchester and powerful Windebank, Clerk of the Signet then, and Secretary of State later, often used Samuel's father as a trusted intermediary. The relationship has lasted well over the years. I use Samuel now as my father used his father. Although we are a secretive family – at least the Mountagu men are – my wife and I have always had a soft spot for Samuel. In the summer of '61 when there was a great smallpox scare, my eldest, young Hinchingbroke, (I was at sea at the time) developed symptoms of the 'pox, and my wife with my agreement, sent three of our sons, Sydney, Oliver (named after the Protector of course) and John, at short notice to live for a few days at Samuel and Elizabeth's house until the 'pox scare died down and Hinchingbroke recovered.

It must have been about '53 that our cousin Walter Mountagu (Sir Henry's younger boy) who was the Queen's confessor in Paris, asked me to help the young St. Michels who were known to him. Apparently their father had been the Queen's Gentleman-Carver and Captain of her Horse. I believe that young Elizabeth subsequently met my servant Samuel Pepys as a result of my interest. I know too that my young friend Robin Holmes, who subsequently became a distinguished naval captain under my command and was knighted, was also a suitor for Elizabeth's hand, either in marriage or outside it! A few years later when I was at sea off Dover harbour destined to bring the King back, I met young Balthazar St. Michel again on board ship. He was a handsome young scoundrel wishing to become a Reformado – a volunteer officer without an official (paid for) commission. He was a lad of great charm, and Samuel seemed to care for him as a younger brother. Samuel had then been married to Elizabeth for about five years. I treated young Balty very civilly at table. Afterwards I believe he went for a commission in Albermarle's Guards.

My family maintained a small house in Whitehall, called the Wardrobe, in addition to our estate at Hinchingbroke, near Brampton, where my cousins, the Pepys, lived. My father had married a Jemimah Pepys, and we had much affection for that family. In 1655 young Samuel Pepys, fresh down from Cambridge, married Elizabeth, another remote cousin of mine through the Cliffords; a pretty little Huguenot child. It was suggested to me that Samuel might help run my small London establishment whilst I was at sea with the Fleet. Slightly to my surprise he not only did all my fetching and carrying, paying bills and collecting monies, but he was also most acceptable to my wife, who spent most of her time in the country with our young children, Jemimah,

Edward, Sydney, Oliver and John.

Samuel and Elizabeth would call me "My Lord" and my wife "My Lady" which of course was not necessary. My title of Lord Sandwich was not warranted until the summer of 1660.

To the dismay of our family, cousin Oliver Cromwell died in September '58, and in April of the next year Richard Cromwell fell from power, and the Rump Parliament was restored. The Mountagu fortunes were inextricably linked to the Cromwell's. Although I thought I had a trump card by control of the fleet, this turned out not to be the case, and I was lucky to escape the scaffold and hide in the country at Hinchingbroke. My able secretary, John Creed, and young Samuel kept me posted of events in London. I then helped Samuel secure a small Navy appointment, as a clerk under George Downing, who spent much time in Holland.

Early in 1660 Samuel informed me to my amazement that I had been made a Member of the Council of State. I had expected worse things. It seemed that my naval experience still meant something, and the new appointment was called 'General-at-Sea'. I still had my secret contacts with the King in exile and I sailed with the fleet in April with the intention of collecting him and bringing him back to the English throne. Samuel was now with me as my confidential secretary. We were only a few years apart in age, and I quickly devloped a respect for his dedication to honest work, and for his love of music, which we both shared. The return of Charles II is recorded in the history books, so I will not repeat it, other than to say Samuel was of much help to me, drafting the royal resolution, signing passes, discussing choice of captains for promotion, ordering silk flags, barges etc.

On the 23rd May the King made his brother, the Duke of York, Lord High Admiral, and made Mr William Coventry his secretary, and confirmed my appointment as Admiral. I was so pleased with the successful outcome of the King's return that I said to Samuel 'We must have a little patience and we will rise together. In the meantime I will do yet all the good jobs for you I can'.

Pretty little Elizabeth often came to the Wardrobe to see my wife and our children and they all liked her. One of them gave her a cat and often small presents of food for their table. We knew full well that they were, by our standards, quite poor. Now I must confess that I too was much taken with her. Several times I caused Captain William Ferrers, my rather loudmouthed master of horse, to solicit Elizabeth on my behalf, discreetly unbeknown to Samuel – which in a courteous way she declined. More than that, my eldest son, later Lord Hinchingbroke, did exactly the same thing and sought her favours – with the same lack of success! Neither father nor son behaved particularly well – perhaps we hoped for 'droits de Seigneur'. One evening in June '63 at Trinity House we were all talking about handsome women and I asked Sir John Minnes at dinner 'Sir John, what do you think of your neighbour's wife?' looking at Samuel. 'Do you not think he hath a great beauty to his wife? 'Upon my word he hath', he replied.

All this time I was spending far too much money. I even had to start borrowing money from Samuel – £1000 it was. My expenses were enormous. We had refurbished the Wardrobe, and were doing much building work in the country. Thus we had two large establishments. My children were growing up fast. We all lived very well. I had my portrait painted by Peter Lely and others.

Early in 1660 my fleet took the Queen to France and in November I went to sea again to fetch her from Lisbon, and afterwards went with the fleet to take Tangier and chase the Barbary pirates. I was at sea most of '61. In September of that year I made Samuel my legal Deputy whilst I was away. He was left without his patron for some considerable time.

In the autumn of '62 I secured a warrant from the King for Samuel to search the Tower of London for a hidden treasure trove. A Mr Wade of Axe Yard, known to Samuel, reported to me that £7000 in coin, hidden in butter-firkins, was buried in the Tower grounds. The King was to receive £3000, Mr Wade £2000 and I would receive the balance. Samuel most methodically mounted four thorough searches over a period of a month – but they found nothing.

Samuel and Elizabeth used to spend a night or two at the Wardrobe in Whitehall each week, whilst their new house at the Navy Office was being made ready for them. So my family saw a great deal of them, and respected their help and advice.

During '63 I had acquired a married mistress – little Betty Becke – who lived in Chelsea. She was an expensive lady to maintain, but well worth it – and quite discreet too. Imagine my surprise when young Samuel, out of the blue, wrote me a long letter dated November 18th, which he sent by hand of his man Will Hewer. After a long preamble about every bit of bread he eats telling him that he owes it to me and how he now feels that it is his duty to me 'to expose the safety of your honour, etc. etc.' he referred to my declining Court attendances, remarked upon by the King. But what made me angry was that he more than hinted about my wench in Chelsea. First of all, he showed me little respect in referring to her. Secondly, it was, and is the fashion in the Haut Monde to

Edward Montague, by Sir Peter Lely, by permission of the National Portrait Gallery

acquire a mistress, and the King and his brother do encourage it shamefully. Finally, my friend Samuel was getting quite well-known for his own fancies, so my people tell me – a Betty Lane and handsome Mrs Pierce.

For a few days I thought that Samuel's letter was the sign to end not only our friendship – for that is what it is – but also my future patronage, which could have been serious for him. Then on the 22nd I confronted Samuel at the Wardrobe and asked for the sources for his discovery of my little amour, which he rather haltingly disclosed, and then he fell to weeping in front of me. I did not know whether to laugh or to cry myself! So I changed the subject. On the 25th, Samuel brought me a little peace-offering – a Terella by Sir Christopher Wren. But I valued Samuel's advice. He met so many people in the City of London, and was aware of many cross-currents before other people. So I thought to shed little Becky and promised myself to go no more to Chelsea. I was angry with Will Howe, my boy (a friend of Samuel's) as I was now sure that he was the prime source of Samuel's information. But on the 30th December and again on the 10th January when I met him I asked pointedly after Elizabeth, his wife, my cousin, to keep Samuel in his place. However in my heart I admire his impudence and courage in so writing to me.

During 1664 our relationship gradually mended. My wife and children of course knew little (or so I hoped) of my temporary break with Samuel. His father, the little tailor, now in retirement at Brampton, was kind to my daughters Jem and Paulina. Elizabeth, by herself, came to dinner with us several times when my wife was sick of the measles. My wife was pregnant again as a result of our reconciliation (she guessed at my Chelsea wench). My debts were now nearly £10,000, but I was going to sea again and did not care too much.

Naturally I was still seeing little Becky. I little realised that my man John Creed, my private secretary, was gossiping to Samuel about my mistress, and that in June '64 Samuel had actually met her (and considered her 'with not one goode feature in her face, yet is a fine lady, of a fine taille, very well couraged and mighty discreet . . . and wonders less of my favour to her and I dare warrant she hath brains enough to entangle him').

I had put waterworks in at Hinchingbroke and was much in debt, of which I still owed £1000 to Samuel. Our little daughter Katherine was born about then, with a scarred face, which I felt should not be tampered with. Meanwhile I had problems about Prince Rupert's command at sea, but if he fails against the Dutch, I cannot be blamed. Elizabeth came to dine with us alone in

November – we all like her so much, especially the Mountagu men! My son Hinchingbroke had the smallpox again and Jem was married.

During most of the Plague year I was at sea with my fleet. Samuel came to see me in his little yacht, the "Bezan", when I was on the 'Prince' at Gravesend in September. I told him how concerned I was for him being in London during the Plague. Later in the month I was at sea again with our fleet of over 100 ships to try to catch the Dutch East India ships rounding the North Cape. We failed completely at Bergen (where my cousin Edward was killed) and Copenhagen, but captured some East India ships with their booty, from which I benefited. I entrusted Samuel with the sale and disposal of the prize goods. Naval politics are even more difficult than usual. There are factions at Court between the King and his brother the Duke, but the King approves of what I am doing and the Duke of York is still titular Head of the Navy. I am at loggerheads with Coventry, but friendly with Prince Rupert. And Samuel respects Coventry for his fairness and efficiency and the Duke of York approved Samuel to be Surveyor General of the Tangier committee! What did I do? I played my guitar which I commend above all music in the world.

In response the King has made me the Ambassador in Spain and his brother the Duke of York has been made General of both sea and land forces. The disposal of the sea prizes has caused me many problems and for some reason I am in some disgrace, possibly because my wife and I are parting. But the King is still my friend. At the end of February, just before I sailed for Spain, I had a long talk with Samuel at Cranborne. I told him who my most reliable friends are at Court.

I was out of the country in 1667 when the Dutch Fleet sailed the Medway and burnt our Navy. I like to think that if I had had the fleet then, things would have turned out better.

It was not until September '68 that I returned from Spain, arriving at Mounts Bay, in Cornwall, where Sydney, my son, met me. Heavily in debt as usual, I asked my trusty Samuel to lend me £500 which he did. On return to London I was greeted kindly by the King. Samuel and I met again in October. He is mighty grand and a favourite of the Duke of York and of Albermarle, but not of Buckingham, which is no surprise. I dined with Samuel several times and discussed my many problems with him. My daughter Pauline died in February, and then I retired from Court to Hinchingbroke for several months. I saw Samuel again but the old spark of friendship had diminished. I no longer had connections with the Navy, and his star was still ascending.

WILL HEWER'S STORY

"As the master is, so is the servant" Petronius

I was two years younger than my pretty little mistress Elizabeth Pepys and thus nine years younger than my new master, Mr Samuel Pepys when I joined their small household in Seething Lane in July 1660. They had been married five years already, and had only just moved into their new house.

My father, Thomas Hewer, was a printer and stationer living at St. Sepulchre's parish in Holborn, London. His main business was to supply the Navy Office with anything that needed to be printed. My mother was called Anne Blackburne before her marriage to my father in 1639 and I was born three years later.

My family were of Huguenot stock. Originally John Hewé, a bookbinder, came to London from France in 1562 and was naturalised in 1571. He and his wife lived with a Noell Gobert. His name was also spelled as John Hué, and their home was then in St. Giles Cripplegate. There were four children, Richard, Mary, Anne and the youngest, Thomas, who was my grandfather. All the family were originally members of the French church in London and later joined St. Sepulchre's.

My kind uncle, Robert Blackburne, was then Secretary to the Admiralty and frequently met my new master, and in March at Westminster had presented him with his Warrant to the two Generals of the Fleet, of whom Lord Mountagu was one. My uncle Robert it was, that suggested I join the Pepys household.

Since I was 17 and though I say it myself, full grown, I quickly made myself quite indispensable to Mr Pepys, whom my uncle wrote to now as 'Esquire' – a sure sign that Mr Pepys was on his way up in the world, because I shortly found out that his father, whom I later came to know full well, was a small tailor, and his mother, so it was said, a washerwoman.

I would have done anything for those two. I fetched money from the Privy Seal Office at Worcester House. I collected my master's new velvet coat and cap from Mr Pims. I visited the Mountagu household at the Wardrobe on many occasions. I went to many Protestant churches with my master, and I enjoyed every moment

W. Hewer by Sir Godfrey Kneller by permission of Mary Evans Picture Gallery

of my life with the Pepys.

But after a year with them things started to go wrong. One summer there was a burglary in the house and my master lost a silver tankard, which was bad enough, but the thief took my clock, which was worse. A few months later I was severely reprimanded for keeping my hat on in the house, and for being too proud and lazy. Also for not giving my master and mistress enough respect. Mr Pepys told me that I wore my cloak like a ruffian and wore immodest garb and to my surprise he even boxed both my ears, which really disturbed me. Of course like most young lads I drank a lot. I liked a quart or two of sack at the Dolphin. At the Office one day, making up the books at Deptford with the other clerks, I was at ease for a moment in the master's study, whereupon he struck me. But I did not complain: I was paid well – £30 per annum as office clerk, to fetch and to carry and to do everything they asked of me.

In mid summer of '60 I was eighteen and, as my horseracing friends would say, feeling my oats. I had been a-roystering on the Town and came home late, well after dark, the worse for wear. Elizabeth was still up and about. Mr Pepys was abroad, gadding about, as he would put it. She warned me that if he heard about my late homecoming he would be very angry with me, at which point I sat down and wept sorely. I wept, not because of my master's probable displeasure, but for my mistress' sake, in case *she* was blamed for my thoughtless habits. And Mr Pepys had a fierce temper when he was roused. 'I'd expect his being at home' is what he would have said of me . . . and he who pays the piper . . .

It was a strange relationship we had, the three of us – Mr Pepys, Elizabeth and I. My master encouraged me to bring my Aunt, Mrs Blackburne, back to the Pepys house on social visits. Samuel Pepys found her 'a very high dame and a costly one'! On the other hand my Uncle was a man of consequence in the Admiralty Office and his good opinions were still solicited. At times I hinted to my mother of my true feelings for Elizabeth and my mother would chaperone us abroad in the park and on other social occasions. On the Spring mornings I would accompany Elizabeth to the green countryside to collect 'May-dew' for her complexion. I told her she needed it not, but she just smiled at me. At the time the master's sister Paulina – Pall they called her – an ill-favoured, sour young lady, I thought, was in the household as a servant, not as companion, to my mistress. Also there was young Jane Birch, whom everyone liked, and her rascally brother Wayneman, whose indentures were later torn up by my master. But servants come and servants go. I didn't think of myself as one! For instance I remember in February '62 I was told off for not going to church on the Lord's Day with the maids, and also I'm afraid that I told the mistress rather impudently that 'I will not be made a slave of'.

In the autumn of '62 I went on horseback for a journey in the country with my master to Ware and Puckeridge and so to Cambridge (where my master had been at college). Then on to Impington where I met more members of the Pepys family, Dr John and Mr Roger, and then met my master's father, mother and two brothers. We also visited Lady Mountagu at Hinchingbroke, and her young daughter. We returned to London on horseback in one day, very weary.

In December '62 Mr Chetwind died. He was one of the senior clerks at the Office – a pale and sallow old man, well liked by my master, who described him as 'my old and most ingenious acquaintance'. I had been kind and useful to him. To everyone's surprise he died with £3000 and made me his executor. I think that was the day when I felt that I had grown up. The day that an old friend had died. But it also meant that I was now financially independent of the Pepys, although that did not stop my master trying, and succeeding, in improving my education. He made me construe Latin verses and chided me for my indifferent grammar. My Uncle Blackburne went to see my master on my behalf. I used to complain about their usage of me, particularly by my mistress. So the result was that I went to lodge at Mrs Mercer's with a deduction of £15 per year of my salary, because I had been getting free board and keep at the Pepys.

Occasionally I would take a day off to see my parents and to take some physic over the holidays. But every summer I would accompany my master and mistress on horseback on their many expeditions to the country outside London, to Kingsland, Hackney, Mile End and other places.

After I left the Pepys' service in November '63 I wept again. A strong, sturdy lad weeping like a child, and Samuel gave me good healthy bracing advice. Elizabeth gave me nothing. But it was that winter that Samuel became so jealous of me, on account of my many visits to his household, usually when he was out. 'Now God forgive me how apt I am to be jealous of her as to this fellow Will . . . but this cursed humour I cannot cool in myself by all the reason I have, which God forgive me of the folly of it and the disgrace it brings me'. I am sure that is what Mr Pepys – no longer my master – was saying of me.

In the autumn of '64, after I had known the Pepys family for four years, I introduced Mary Mercer to them, or as my master put it 'a decayed merchant's daughter'. Mary's mother was my landlady. Mary is a good looking girl. The Pepys liked their friends and servants to be good looking, and more to the point she had a good musical ear and voice *and* played well on the harpsicord, which again meant a great deal to my master.

But I must concentrate my thoughts – these events happened a long time ago. As I write this I believe that man and boy, friend and colleague, I have been with Samuel Pepys for over 40 years. In those faraway days of our youth there are still three or four incidents which stand out clearly. I am talking of the golden days before Elizabeth's death, which happened when I was twenty seven. Ever since then I have been by the side of my friend Samuel Pepys. When my father Thomas died in the Plague Year, I inherited more money. My Uncle Blackburne became Secretary to the East India Company in '67 and then I started to trade on my own account. In '74 I backed the building of three new warships for the Navy. I was later Treasurer of Tangier – that was in '80–84 – on the special Navy Commission which replaced the Navy Board. And of course my Directorship and Deputy Chairmanship of the East India Company made me a rich man. Samuel Pepys came to live with me in Clapham, and we have grown old together in great happiness. He and I were Masters of the Clothworkers Company. I was made Member of Parliament for Yarmouth, Isle of Wight in '85–87 and Samuel Pepys too could have stood there if he so wished. I travelled to the Continent, and once went to Tangier and Spain with Samuel, helped by the Houblon brothers. Samuel Pepys had a great career at the Navy Office. My friends tell me that I had a career of some note there too.

But I digress – old men ramble on.

What I remember best of my early life with Pepys can best be called the times of drama.

Drama at the Navy Office, the perilous years of the Plague, the Great Fire, and when the Dutch warships were in the Medway. Now I have to be careful how I write this as my old friend is still very much alive. Very simply, this was my long secret (fairly secret anyway) love for Elizabeth Pepys, and my part in the devastating quarrels they had towards the end of their lives together. Samuel never married again. I never married. Both I suspect for the same reason – our love of the same woman.

By the year '64 I was accepted as a member of the Pepys family, in the sense that I went with them on most of their social occasions and met their friends and their patrons, the Mountagus. We went to the theatre together from time to time – (the Pepys went practically every day, so much so that I told Elizabeth frankly that people were gossiping about Samuel's mania for playgoing). We went to the launch of 'the Royal Catherine' at Woolwich. Sometimes I stayed with them in their fine new house, or went to Brampton with them to see their family there. During the height of the plague I rode out alone with Elizabeth, at Samuel's request, to take her away to the countryside. My father died in April that year of the plague, as did the father of Tom Edwards, Samuel's boy – both in St. Sepulchres, and the next year my widowed mother's house at Pye Corner was burned in the Fire, and I helped her move to Islington. I also helped move Samuel's secret store of gold to Woolwich, where Elizabeth and I guarded it night and day with our lives!

Shortly after that Elizabeth suggested to Samuel, and separately to me, that I should marry Samuel's sister Paulina, Now I tried never to show my true feelings to Elizabeth. We were frequently alone, and most women, I am told can sense the other person's attitude to them. Perhaps she wanted to bind me closer to the family. Perhaps she felt genuinely sorry for Pall, who was plain, even ugly and hitherto quite unloved. Perhaps she felt that Pall's dowry, of which Samuel had promised £600 as a share, was an inducement for me. She did not know quite how independent my own means were. I thanked her warmly for the honour and politely declined, saying that I preferred to stay a bachelor. In '69 when Pall married young John Jackson, Talbot Pepys and I were both her Bridesmen.

I must here record (because I fear no one else will) Samuel's bravery during the long drawn out Plague Year, and later during the Great Fire of London. Although not a physically brave man, nor was I for that, he made a point of us all working normally when the Court had fled town – a good example to the rest of us. I was ill for a time that long, sad summer, but luckily not of the plague, although it was all over King Street and the Axe. Samuel sent Elizabeth to Deptford and Woolwich and I often stayed with him in town, but it was business as usual at the Navy Office, and Samuel set a good example to all of us.

Samuel was in the midst of the London Fire late in '66. He personally told the King and Duke of York to command houses to be pulled down before the fire arrived, otherwise nothing could stop it. They commanded Samuel to order the Lord Mayor to do just that. The Duke of York offered Samuel whatever soldiers he needed to get the work done: he also wrote strongly to Mr

Coventry likewise. Samuel then met the King and his brother on their barge and went to Queenhithe with them to supervise the checking of the fire.

My point is that Samuel was a London citizen – no more, no less. He chose deliberately to intervene in both catastrophes, and by his brave example alleviate the sad and grievous situation in the City.

Back to Samuel's gold again. In '67 when the Dutch fleet were in the Medway, the whole of London – everyone – was in a panic. We all felt that the Dutch would invade and take or burn the capital. On the 8th June eighty sail were spotted off Harwich, and the noise of the gunfire could be heard in Bednall-greene, as it was then called. Soon Chatham was threatened and I advised Samuel that I should collect £400 of wage money, which I did. Despite fireships sent towards the Dutch and a boom and chain across the river around the 'Hope', the Dutch evaded the first and broke the second and captured the great 'Royal Charles'. We sank our own ships at Barking creek to try and stop the Dutch. They burnt the 'Royal James', 'The Royal Oake' and the 'London'. I drew out £500 of my own money from Backewells the goldsmiths, and Samuel sent £1000 more by Mr Gibson to Caxton. The panic continued but eventually the Dutch withdrew. Samuel investigated closely all our erstwhile defences. It is clear that nobody in England came out of the Medway disaster with any credit.

But Samuel's gold was still underground at Brampton! It was only in October that he deemed it prudent to retrieve his treasure, and enlisted my help. The great expedition set forth, Samuel and Elizabeth and pretty young Deborah Willett, both very handsome in their morning gowns, in a hired coach with four horses since the return load was likely to be rather heavy. I rode on horseback from Allgate to Enfield, and we all stayed very merrily at the Rein-Deer Inn on the way. On the morrow we visited Audley-End House and then Cambridge, where Samuel showed us all Trinity College and St. John's library and King's College Chapel. We duly arrived at Brampton where all the Pepys family and myself went off to a good plain country dinner with Lady Mountagu at Hinchingbroke. That night Samuel, his father and Elizabeth dug up the buried gold with the aid of a darkened lantern. Initially they could not find it, and Samuel was out of his wits. Eventually they did find it, but the bags had rotted and the gold had scattered. Samuel carried them up – all that he could find – to his brother's room and locked them up. After a little supper I was conscripted to help Samuel wash the dirt off every individual piece and count them. The reckoning was 100 pieces short. Samuel thought that the neighbours close by would have taken them, which made him even more angry! There was nothing for it, and so I helped Samuel from midnight with another search by candlelight, which revealed a further 45 pieces; and so in to cleanse them. It was past two in the morning before we crept off to bed. Was that enough? Early in the morning Samuel and I with pails and a sieve locked ourselves into the garden and sifted and resifted all the earth into pails and eventually found another 34 pieces! At ten in the morning we set off for London in convoy, as before, Samuel, Elizabeth and Deborah in the coach sitting on top of the gold. Brother John Pepys and I and two other men on horseback acted as guards to the convoy. We stayed the night at Stevenage. Elizabeth and Deb each carried one bag of gold up to their chamber and I carried the rest in a basket, whilst Samuel assumed the role of guardian angel. The following day we followed the same procedure in reverse and all went well, with the gold back safely in the Pepys household by noon.

Later that year naval affairs took precedence in our lives. In November I remember that I was giving Samuel good advice about his report concerning seamen's tickets. We were then very nearly equal in our knowledge of the business. But it was on the 5th March of '68 that Samuel started to make his name. He and I went by boat to Westminster, but on the way, to fortify himself for the ordeal ahead, we went to the Dog tavern and drank some mulled sack, and at Mrs Howlett's in the Hall a dram of brandy. Before 'a mighty full House' of Parliament, the members of the Navy Office were called to give an account of themselves: Lord Brouncker, Sir John Minnes, Sir T. Harvey and Samuel. The other member, Sir W. Penn, who was also a member of parliament, rather cowardly elected to stay on the floor of the house. Samuel was their spokesman and he spoke without interruption for three hours. It was a great moment for him, and everybody congratulated him, apart from his three enemies, Littleton, Lee and Wiles. Whilst Samuel enjoyed a celebratory dinner at Lord Brouncker's and went to the theatre afterward, I went back to see Elizabeth and tell her of her husband's triumph. The next day, I recall, both the King and his brother the Duke of York personally congratulated Samuel on his fine speech. That night we – that is my family, Samuel, Elizabeth and Deb had dinner together, talking and playing at cards happily.

My personal trouble had started long before. One way or another I had been delegated to watch over Samuel's household, and if necessary to squire Elizabeth to the theatre and other places.

I realised now I must have been in love with her all the time. In January '68 I foolishly bought her a handsome and expensive locket of diamonds worth about £40. As I told her, and meant it, it was out of gratitude for their kindnesses to me. She and I knew it was more than that. But Samuel interceded and asked her to return it to me, which reluctantly she did. Samuel thought that it was a matter of honour that she should not accept such an expensive present, at which I was very sad and troubled. That summer however, I commissioned Abraham Bosse, the Huguenot painter, to paint not only Elizabeth, but also a portrait of Samuel – so that he could not complain – although he did not like me doing it. Elizabeth preferred Bosse to her own painter teacher, Mr Alexander Browne.

Sometimes I asked the Pepys to dinner with me in my own lodgings. Samuel later described them as 'two best chambers so finely furnished, and all so rich and neat that I was mightily pleased with him and them, and here only my wife and I and the two girls and had a mighty neat dish of custards and tarts and good drink and talk. And so away home to bed with infinite content at this his treat: for it was mighty pretty and everything rich'. They came there to see me several times. Sometimes Elizabeth came alone.

In June '66 after the great news of the sea-victory over the Dutch fleet (the day *before* we learnt that we were sadly beaten), I remember I had asked the Pepys family to supper, including his nice old father, at my lodgings. Samuel said that be found my chamber 'mighty fine with pictures and everything else, *very curious*'. It was curious because he could not believe that his young boy Will Hewer had come of age and was living well and had considerable taste of his own. Samuel was most knowledgeable about paintings and prints, so my taste was indeed 'curious'.

Occasionally in the evening my mother and I, by invitation, dined with the Pepys, sometimes with dear Mr Spong, who taught us both the use of a parallelogram and how to draw maps. Samuel always believes in combining education with pleasure. The three of us, Samuel, Elizabeth and I, often talked of the business of the Office and its future and of course, our future. In December '68 another storm blew up. Colonel Middleton, who liked neither Samuel nor myself, but who was a Naval Commissioner and Surveyor, accused me of conspiring to get a contract by overpurchasing supplies of the stores with kerseys and cottons for the seamen. Middleton wrote a scandalous letter to the Board which reflected on Samuel's Office, calling me a knave, and saying that I should 'lose my ears'. Samuel and I stayed up till midnight to consider our business, and felt it was 'most free' from any blame on our side, and 'horrid scandalous' on Middleton's side who was rumoured to be complaining about us to the Duke of York. But Samuel as ever marshalled all the facts clearly and concisely – showed them to Lord Brouncker, who agreed with them, and so later did the whole Navy Board. Colonel Middleton cried his excuses and all was forgiven. To celebrate, Samuel and Elizabeth and I went out in their fine new carriage to Holborn and saw the Danish lady with a beard, and then went to the Duke's playhouse and saw 'Macbeth' with the King, his mistress Lady Castlemaine, and the whole Court there. Dear Elizabeth looked beautiful – as pretty as any of the fine ladies, and Samuel heard Talbot Pepys and me saying so to each other. The King and the Duke of York, those right royal roués, thought so too – they smiled at us, but especially at the handsome woman sitting between Samuel and myself.

Early in the New Year Samuel signed an agreement with Elizabeth for a £30 a year dress allowance, which was given to me to keep as custodian! I could see the problems looming and the thunder clouds a-gathering. Samuel was gadding about, flushed with his success and popularity and money. He always had an eye for a pretty girl and the prettiest one was not enough for him – said I to myself a little bitterly. Elizabeth was still passionately in love with him. Sometimes she would send me – her silent, reliable and humble suitor – out on the Town to look for her husband and persuade him to come home! I was not a fool. I knew that she liked me and relied on me in all sorts of ways – faithful, stolid, patient Will. Hewer. It was the dashing young men like William Batelier, the silly, handsome Pembleton, the dancing master, whose brains are in his feet, and Henry Sheres (one of my Lord Sandwich's men in his Spanish Embassy) who pleased her. Once Elizabeth went to the Duke of York's house with me to see a new play 'Guzman'. After the play she and I were joined by Henry Sheres and later by Samuel, which troubled his jealous nature. I do not remember what I thought of the future. I was so happy with both of them. We lived for the day, and the morrow could look after itself.

Samuel's eyes were troubling him. He read and wrote so much, perhaps in candlelight and near-darkness, and his loss of sight worried him and his family and friends. I could take shorthand writing and Samuel often gave me verbal notes, and Elizabeth read to him in the evening. But the old Adam remained – on his doorstep shamefully with pretty young Deborah Willett. There is no doubt that Samuel behaved very badly with her. More unfortunately still they called me in to act as a kind of intermediary. Deborah had to go – this was the winter of '68 – although no fault of hers, and I was deputed by Elizabeth in Samuel's presence to be his faithful shadow (which of course I was already, in many senses) and keep him away from seeing Deborah again. I tried hard to keep the peace between the two people I loved, and by early '69 an uneasy truce existed, but I stayed by Samuel's side all the time. Early in the morning we would meet at the Harp and Ball for our morning draught, then perhaps go to the Office, or the Tangier Committee, or to the Crown Rolls Office in the Temple and back to the Patent Office. My Uncle Blackburne used to have business with Samuel at the Ship tavern and my Uncle Steventon asked him for small favours (he once sent Samuel a very fine salmon-pie).

In March '69 Samuel and I by his side survived attacks on the Navy Office, mainly instigated by Sir Thomas Clifford, urged on by the Duke of Buckingham. Sir William Coventry, an honest, capable Naval Commissioner, whom we both highly esteemed, was thrown into the Tower, where he was visited by Samuel. Eventually only Samuel survived on the Navy Board – the only man left from the Principals of 1660.

That summer of 1669, having obtained advice from Mr John Evelyn, Elizabeth, Balty her brother now a competent Muster-Master and Samuel, set off through Holland and Flanders to Paris. Elizabeth was taken ill in Brussels on the way home, took high fever, and died in London on the 10th November.

Samuel was never the same again. Nor was I.

JAMES HOUBLON'S STORY

"Others like merchants venture trade abroad" W. Shakespeare

My family have lived in London since Nicholas Houblon arrived here from Lille in the middle of the 16th century as a refugee Huguenot. Nicholas was naturalised as an English citizen in 1571 after he had been in London 20 years. His brother Jehan or John was my grandfather. My father James, from whom I take the name, was born in 1592. He married my mother, another Huguenot, Mary Du Quesne (or Du Cane in English) in 1620. My parents had no less than 12 children, all of course with traditional Huguenot biblical names, Peter, James, John, Jacob, Abraham and Jeremiah.

London has always looked after the Houblons, and modestly we say that we have helped look after London.

My father lived in Bearbinder Lane, a merchant like all of us, and I was born there in 1629. Will Hewer and I have been Samuel Pepys' oldest, and I firmly believe, his best and closest friends since 1665.

As trading merchants based in London we have a worldwide business of exporting and importing commodities, mainly with Portugal, Spain, Italy, France and the Low Countries. However it was to do with Tangier that we first met Samuel Pepys. He was then, in early '65, an up and coming young man, just 22, at work at the Admiralty. Our Mr Gifford was with me in February when we talked to him on 'Change. The following month Thomas Hill, who with Mr Bulteel usually looks after our interests in Portugal, introduced Samuel to my wife and myself at our house, where Sir William Petty was giving us a lecture. Both Samuel and Thomas Hill are keen musicians and Samuel and my mother Mary are enthusiastic singers, and these links they retained for a long time.

Talking later among ourselves we thought that Samuel had many of the natural characteristics of a Huguenot. His faith of course is ours, and he goes to both the Savoy and Threadneedle Street churches. His seriousness, his hard work, reliability and honesty all much impressed us. Although we are a pretty plain

Sir James Houblon by Sir Godfrey Kneller by permission of The Bank of England

bunch, the Houblons, the fact that he has married a very pretty young Huguenot girl, Elizabeth de St. Michel, has been carefully noted.

Later in 1665 he and I agreed on a ship venture to Tangier during the then current strict embargo on trade. We had several meetings at the Admiralty office in January and February '66 and he would sup with me and my four brothers at the Sun Inn behind the Exchange. We were all a little older than he, and well-travelled in our various businesses. We later agreed a fee of £200 and gave him an assignment on Sir Robert Viners for that sum, as payment for authorisation for our three ship's charters to get to Tangier with our cargoes – a successful venture.

We met again later that year during the disastrous fire. Isaac, perhaps the best looking of the five of us, was supervising at Dowgate, reception of merchandise from our other houses which were being threatened by the fire. Samuel recalls that Isaac was not only very well dressed at the time but extremely dirty from the smoke of the fire etc. After that we moved our trading offices to Winchester Street, where they are now.

That year we saw Samuel several times and he would sup with us and have a glass of wine, frequently at the Popes Head Inn.

I remember in February '66 my four brothers and I and Thomas Hill were invited to supper by Samuel and Elizabeth, on the occasion of Thomas' appointment to Lisbon. It was a very good supper and we all enjoyed ourselves. Young Samuel proudly showed us his new plate which sets off his cupboard very nobly. Probably presents from suppliers to the Navy! 'A fine sight it is to see these five brothers thus loving one to another and all industrious merchants' was the way Samuel described us. We went again in May and stayed until eleven at night. Later in November we saw the Pepys twice, once at the Popes Head with Dr Croune of the Gresham College.

We made a point of meeting Samuel on 'Change and discussing maritime and trading matters. From our partners in France and Holland we often knew before the Admiralty of impending action on the continent. Samuel knew too the state of the English fleets and what protection if any, they could afford to our traders. Rumours at Whitehall were frequent about the French invading the West Indies, or even invading England. We often knew the facts, and his discussions with us were of mutual benefit. Once we lost a little East Indiaman ship valued at £20,000, which was home, safe, within ten leagues of the Scilly Islands, when it was snapped up by a French caper or privateer.

When my brothers and I visited Epsom in July '67 we found Samuel and Elizabeth worshipping there in the same church. After the sermon we all walked to the inn where we were staying. I told him that he was 'the only happy man of the Navy of whom during all this freedom, the people have taken to speaking treason, but I have heard no bad word of you'.

That year Robert Offley, falsely charged Samuel with Papacy, and I offered to help in any way I could. Sir John Banks and the Earl of Shaftesbury were his main enemies at Court. The House of Commons debated the charge and deputed Sir William Coventry, Samuel's previous master at the Admiralty, and Sir Thomas Meres, a Huguenot, to decide the case, which of course was dropped.

I was so happy for him when he was promoted to be secretary to the office of Lord High Admiral in '75 and wrote to him.

During late '78 Samuel, through no fault of his own, was in desperate trouble in what afterwards came to be called the Colonel Scott conspiracy case. He was at the centre of a very high level plot. The Duke of York, a known Catholic, was in effect the Head of the English Navy, and Samuel was presumed to be his man. The Duke of Buckingham and Lord Shaftesbury sought to bring the Duke of York down by a successful attack on Samuel, the Navy's senior Administrator. His enemies at Court first charged him with harbouring a Papist musician called Caesare Morelli. I tried to persuade Morelli to turn Protestant, and found him safe lodgings at Brentwood. The government's proclamation banishing all Catholics from London was iniquitous. I think it was Thomas Hill our man in Lisbon who, as a keen musician himself, recommended the young Fleming, Morelli, to Samuel. He sang exquisitely to the theorbo and was paid £50 p.a. by Samuel for his musical services. As late as 1681 Morelli was still on Samuel's payroll at Brentwood. He and Sarah Houblon visited him there to make music.

Then Colonel Scott, Shaftesbury's henchman, attacked young Samuel Atkins, one of Samuel's Admiralty clerks, who was sent to Newgate Prison in irons, falsely charged with the murder of a Justice, Sir Edmund Berry Godfrey, in October 1678. Samuel Pepys prepared a detailed and correct alibi for Atkins which caused his immediate acquittal.

In June 1679 Samuel was committed to the Tower of London on a charge of treason brought by Colonel Scott. I visited him there several times, as did Mr John Evelyn. Samuel wrote many letters to his friends and acquaintances in Paris to help seek proof of his innocence, and accordingly of Colonel Scott's own treachery. We used our own network of Huguenot agents in Paris and Holland. M. Denise and Trenchepain were particularly helpful, as of course was young Balty, Elizabeth's brother. Naturally I put up a £5000 bond for Samuel's bail as did Peter Pallavicini, another Huguenot merchant. In fact Samuel was saved from almost certain death by his Huguenot friends, of which I am proud to be one.

Samuel's patron, Lord Mountagu, or Sandwich as he became, was Ambassador in Spain and Portugal. Frequently we sent letters of Samuel's to his patron in Lisbon through our ships. He and I talked of the proceedings in the House, which often seemed to bear little relation to the sad and distracted events outside. Occasionally we had supper at Samuel's house, and Elizabeth always made us welcome. Samuel kept a good table.

Early in '68 Samuel had shown me at the Old Exchange a serious paper he had written on the state of the Navy, and asked me to discuss it with other merchants of the Committee for Accounts. I introduced him to my father. 'A mighty pretty sight to see old Mr Houblon whom I never saw before and all his sons about him all good merchants' - was how he described the meeting.

We had met and talked at regular intervals in '68 and '69 and Samuel and I corresponded frequently. We were all desolated when Elizabeth died so suddenly on their return from a visit to Holland and Paris.

In some ways though, Samuel's links with the Houblon family became even stronger. He is very friendly with my son Wynne and his wife Sarah, with whom Samuel often sings of an evening, and they play music together. In the summer of '74 Samuel accompanied us all on a visit to Dunkirk, Mardyke and Gravelines. Samuel still flirts with my daughter-in-law - the rascal.

I wrote to Samuel in October '79 'I see the malice of your enemies increases. God forgive them for that villainous paper published yesterday. If they call the master, Beelzebub, they will not spare them of the household. You will make that religious use, no doubt you ought to make of such kind of dispensation which must be borne with Christian and manlike patience and submission'.

Colonel Scott, or his ex-clerk Don Louis, then produced a scurrilous and malicious anonymous libel entitled 'A Hue and a Cry after P(epys) and H(ewer)'. That was wicked enough but worse still it was aimed at my family too. 'For the better enabling this Hue and Cry . . . to give notice to all persons . . . if they can apprehend P. and H. or either of them or give notice of them . . . a Lady in her country house in Chelsea . . . or two merchants' daughters in London, they both being well-known to these two persons, especially P . . . before or at the next session of Parliament, they shall have a great Reward'.

Quite rightly Samuel was undeterred by these attacks. During 1680 he visited us in Winchester Street at least half a dozen times, and took Sarah Houblon to the play and occasionally took her and her children in his coach to Chelsea. When Samuel was eventually totally acquitted on 28th June of that year he wrote to me 'I could not but give you the earliest notice I could of my being at last, what I had long since been, had others been as just as you were charitable and myself blameless: I mean a free man: in every circumstance but that of obligations to you and your family, which nothing but the grave shall, or can, or ought to put an end to'.

When Samuel was recalled to the Navy onto the Tangier Committee he used to write to me frequently describing the hellish things he found and saw there in 1683.

In 1685, after dinner at his home, Samuel showed me and Mr John Evelyn, King James' 'secret' document showing that his royal brother Charles was, and had died, a Catholic. King James handed Samuel personally an attested copy of the documents which included several arguments against the doctrine of the Church of England, charging it with heresy, novelty and fanaticism. Incredible that the King should have given that document to Samuel, although it was known that he and the Duke of York had a high regard for him – but also knew of his strong Protestant views.

Two years later Samuel advised us to look to our trading ventures in the Levant and Turkey because of the naval war between Holland and Algeria, which threatened all British ships trading in that area.

Poor Samuel. There was never any respite for him. As recently as June 1690 he was actually committed to the Gatehouse at Westminster on a charge of treason – of having sent information to the French court of the state of the English Navy. Absolute nonsense of course. No evidence was submitted and he was freed in July. But he suffered the indignity of being imprisoned on a totally false trumped up charge.

I became an Alderman of London in 1691, was Knighted the next year, and my brother John and I were both made directors of the new Bank of England. Both John and Abraham Houblon had high posts with the Admiralty and with the East India Company.

The other Huguenot leaders – Louis de Duras, once Lord Blancqfort, then Earl of Feversham and senior general in the

English army, and the Marquis de Ruvigny (who believed Samuel was a Huguenot) both bear him the greatest respect. They tell me there is a Pepys family, once of the Languedoc and then of Bordeaux, and a Robert Pypas who came to London with the first Houblons in the mid 16th century. I am sure Samuel has Huguenot blood. The tender care of poor sweet Elizabeth and that rapscallion brother Balthazar – both good Huguenots – are perhaps the clues?

As I write this Samuel, Will Hewer, my brothers and I are elderly; but our thoughts often hark back to the young Samuel and Elizabeth – young marrieds – proudly showing us their new silver plate in their new London house. I remember eating a dish of ling with him on 'fish days', strolling in St James Park, or in a coach in Hyde Park – 40 years ago.

SAMUEL'S STORY

MY DEVILISH JEALOUSY AND AMOURS

"Oh love's but a dance, where time plays the fiddle:
See the couples advance: Oh love's but a Dance"
H. A. Dobson

My wife and I have now been married fourteen years. Soon we leave for the low Countries and for my poor wife's beloved Paris.

My family derive from humble stock. There is no secret to hide. To the best of my knowledge neither my simple honest father nor his brothers are people who harbour jealousy. Envy of course, we all have that, but deep savage passionate jealousy – never. It is deeply rooted in my blood and has been ever since I met and wooed my sweet, adorable, maddening little wife. Perhaps I am a throwback. There may be French relations in the Pepys family to match my passionate little Latin wife! For passionate she is indeed. She gives me every possible satisfaction in our bed-chamber, and modestly I feel that I offer her the same deep carnal satisfaction. But I am torn between my own craving for her and my stupid desire for daily petty little adventures. I need them both, and in a perfect world I would have them both. Looking back at the multitude of my silly promiscuous grapplings around London fills me with shame; time and again I resolutely promise myself to abstain. Sometimes I can keep my vows to cease from drinking excesses and too much theatre-going. Try as I can, I am unable to pass by a pretty woman.

I have the most beautiful loving wife in town, desired by all who meet her from the Duke of York and "My Lord" Sandwich downwards. And I consistently put my marriage, perhaps my own career, at risk, with my pathetic little scrambles in alleyways and carriages. And tomorrow it will be the same.

Those lines that Nicholas Burt speaks so well as Othello 'Avaunt! be gone! thou has set me on the rack' – how appropriate they are. Each day I try to destroy my happy marriage, an inch at a time. I deserve my 'rack' – my devilish Jealousy.

I think of the long line of shadowy figures hovering around my wife. Captain Robin Holmes – before, during and after our terrible period of separation, when I was huddled alone in the sad little garret at the Wardrobe, and my wife – I think – was closeted with friends in Charing Cross.

Lord John Somerset's handsome son, who knew her before I did, when she was a young girl in Paris – he offered, and she accepted, an expensive bracelet of rings. He sent shako'd footmen across London to arrange secret rendezvous which at the time did trouble my mind. Mr Coleman, the goodlooking Guardsman fills me with doubt. He is a very rogue for women; a man of whom my wife has so good an opinion. But nothing compared to the awful lustful scene she told me about, with that old goat, my Uncle Wight. That was almost unbelievable:- £500 in effect for her child – which quite disgusted me. I was at a loss to know how to deal with the situation. So of course I did nothing, and hoped it would go away.

Was she faithful to me with "My Lord" Sandwich and young Lord Hinchingbroke? I do not know, and I dare not think too much about it. She is part of the Mountagu family, but I know only too well "My Lord's" reputation with his slut in Chelsea and others. Both of them would have her if they could.

There is another subject that I shy away from. My friend Will Hewer has seen my wife in the intimate surroundings of our household. He has grown up with her, and she knows him almost as well as she knows me. I do not want to think too much about their relationship. It is clear to me that he loves her. Any man living in her company would be mad not to love her. But I trust him implicitly and in this case, I think I trust my wife, poor wench, too. Will is not handsome, not romantic, but solid, sensible and the perfect friend. Yes, I am quite sure that I trust him. I agree that he can take my wife to the theatre and to the puppets whenever they like. I agree that he should be my chaperone in my current frenzied desire for little Deb Willett, living in Holborn Hall.

'Quem Jupiter vult perdere, dementat prius' so Homer wrote and indeed some kind of madness does strike me from time to time. Last winter was such an example. I was mad to seduce little Deb. I was mad to allow my wife to catch us making love. I was mad to make her promises I could not fulfil, and my continuing madness makes me search London for the little girl.

Even Elizabeth's gentle painting-teacher, Alexander Browne made me feel a little jealous. Most of his tuition took place at Woolwich, where he had every opportunity to misbehave with my wife. Painting is a very intimate, tender creative subject, as she knows even better than I do.

Mr John Pembleton, the dashing dancing master, was altogether a different kettle of fish. I knew that logically they must be lovers. For two lessons a day they were dancing close together, whilst I was working hard at the office on affairs of state! There can be no doubt about it, although my jealous schoolboy searches of beds and closets found nothing amiss. Pembleton, after his short month of contract, turns up in such unexpected places. Obviously by arrangement he appears at our church, at various parties in London and outside London. Still he did teach me to dance, if not well, at least more than adequately. In my heart of hearts I cannot really see my wife falling in love with him but Lord with what jealousy did I walk up and down my chamber listening to hear whether they danced or no or what they did. I was so deadly full of jealousy that my heart and head did so cast about and make me fret. Once going out of the bed, Elizabeth took hold of me and would know what ailed me; and after many kind and some cross words I began to tax her discretion in the previous day's business, but she quickly told me my own, knowing well enough that it was my old disease of jealousy: which I disowned but to no purpose. After an hour's discourse, sometimes high and sometimes kind, I found very good reason to think that her freedom with Pembleton was very great and more than was convenient but with no evil intent, since I knew Pembleton was happily married.

Since then she has become mighty fond of the Frenchman William Batelier, whom I like and admire – as much as I admire and like his two beautiful sisters. They are such a lovable happy family and I am surprised, knowing myself as I do, that I have made no amorous advances to either of my beautiful Bateliers. But William does seem to be in my house rather frequently. Lord to see how soon I could conceive evil fears and thought concerning them. Pretty William and my wife were planning to go to Bow to see a dancing meeting. Quite innocent I believe. Of all my wife's admirers, excepting of course the King's brother and "My Lord", he is the only one that I care for. He and I can talk about the politics of both countries, the wine and food of France, about prints and pictures and books and music. His singing and dancing is quite incomparable. I can understand why my wife is so greatly taken with him.

Her many voyages abroad with Mary Batelier are of course a perfect guise for any other rendezvous she may wish to make with him. My better instincts tell me that I have nothing to fear with William. My wife's friends are of course my friends, and I must try to treat them with the appropriate respect. We have had some of the happiest days of our life with this handsome young family. They are so closely knit and obviously so fond of my wife, that I must endeavour not to disturb such a contented situation.

More recently, "My Lord's" man, Henry Sheres, the engineer and poet, has been seeing a great deal of Elizabeth. I saw him and Will Hewer and my wife at the Duke's House playing of Guzman and so jealous is my nature that it did trouble me though my judgement tells me there is no hurt in it on either side. My wife does delight to talk of him and to see him and she is mighty careful to have a good dinner for him. His departure for Tangier troubles Elizabeth mightily, who is mighty, though not, I think, too fond of him.

I know all the time, that these admirers press their case the more strongly on my wife for her favours, if they see that I am gadding about town with Elizabeth Knepp, or as I still do, to meet Mrs Bagwell, or Betty Martin or Becky Allen (now Mrs Jowles). I make these promises to myself, but God help me, I know next week, or the week after, I will still be gadding after beauties. My wife knows that too. She will be jealous, rightly so, of my infidelities. She will retaliate, as she is now doing with William Batelier and Henry Sheres, and my 'old disease of Jealousy' will return.

FOR TOMORROW WE SHALL DIE

"Tire le rideau, la farce est jouée" *Rabelais*

At long last, at the end of the summer of '69, Samuel, Balty and I left England to visit the Low Countries, and my country, 'la belle France'. Samuel and I have been planning this holiday for years, but problems at the Navy Office have always prevented it.

It was typical of Samuel to ask Balty to come with us. He needed additional male companionship on this long-promised venture. His own knowledge of the French language is excellent, if theoretical. To travel with two bilingual French Huguenot companions helps him immensely. Both men are dedicated to the service of the English Navy, and the Duke of York has advocated a study en route of the Dutch navy 'sur place' – our old familiar foe. Two naval men of great experience duly surveyed the Dutch maritime scene. Samuel was still fearful of the ill condition of his eyes, and Balty helped him spy out the land! Also Samuel wants to show me that 'l'affaire Willett' is over and done with. What better company for me than my dear brother – and for my dear husband to have a handsome, swashbuckling male companion. Balty was only too delighted to leave his family behind to accompany his 'patron' and sister back to his old stamping grounds.

We crossed by sea to Holland. Samuel had been there nine years before with "My Lord", at the Hague, that neat and handsome city where he bought baskets for me *and* for pretty Mrs Pierce, and saw the Queen of Bohemia. Where the 'événements' on the good ship 'Naseby' changed the history of England. Long ago it seems to me now.

We were well prepared. Samuel's friend, John Evelyn, who knows France as well as any Englishman, produced advice on where to go, what to see, and also gave us introductions. So too have the Houblon 'frères' and Sir Samuel Tuke, John Evelyn's cousin.

We spent September leisurely visiting the old beautiful cities of the Low Countries – the Hague, Breda, Antwerp and Ghent. We went to Bruges of course on our way to Paris – a voyage full of health and content. Samuel visited the University in Ghent, and we bought lace in Bruges for both of us. Here in Paris I showed him the Sacré Coeur and the palace at Versailles, where his charm as an English 'milord' quite won everybody's hearts. He asked questions all the time – his curiosity is almost greater abroad than in England. We all went on a boat on the River Seine, with a merry picnic 'sur l'herbe' – just like old days. Balty and I are so happy to be back here again. We want to stay longer than two weeks, but Samuel feels we are travelling on borrowed time – his enemies at home may be planning to attack him during the Parliamentary recess.

Our friends that we met in Paris are kind, considerate and thoughtful. Antoine Pelletier and his wife Jeanne Gaupin are particularly welcoming. My friend Madame Marie Legendre, to whom I gave a gift of an ornamental mirror, and her husband Thomas Legendre-Tunier, are both impressed with Samuel's French, and knowledge of French literature.

Samuel describes me as his 'deare and vertuous lady'. I have behaved myself very well in Paris – my first visit for fifteen years. I remember well my dear father's stratagems to rescue Balty and I from our Catholic 'prisons', and our adventurous travels to England.

In addition to my parents' old friends living in Paris – Walter Mountagu, Sir Samuel Tuke and others – Samuel and I had introductions to a variety of people. When William Hewer had my portrait and that of Samuel copied from the original, it was done by a Huguenot copier-painter called Abraham Bosse, who lived partly in Paris, partly in London. Samuel wanted to meet, through Bosse, the famous painters of the day, Le Brun and De la Fosse. But Bosse, who was a marvellous etcher, had been expelled from the Academie de Peinture seven years before our visit – because of his religion it was said.

My friends the Bateliers have given me introductions to some of their relations and acquaintances, including M. Robert Nanteuil, the famous engraver. Samuel and I visited his ateliers and dutifully admired his heads of Admirals and Sea captains!

We were also given a written introduction to an Englishman called Mr. Hughes, who lives in the Rue de la Boucherie, at the Fauxbourg St. Germain, and another to a Doctor Fitzgerald, who took us to the Jardin du Roy in the Fauxbourg Saint-Victor, where the medical students study plants and plant life.

It feels strange being back in Paris – a gap of fifteen years is far too long. Samuel and I have discussed it many times before, but there never seemed to be enough money. The last time I lived here I was a burgeoning thirteen year old, my head filled with the romance of the Court and the pretty young men. Now I am rising thirty and a married woman of fifteen years. In our wilder moments of jealousy I have several times threatened Samuel I would leave him and return to Paris. I would have made a good courtesan at the Court; La Fayette rather than Pretty Nelly!

Of course my powerful Catholic cousins and uncles are holding the stage in Paris. All of them are Carmelite priests, doubtless well known to the Queen Mother, Henrietta Maria. Jérôme and Antoine and Maurile – all intelligent dominant characters – and probably still interested in their belief and duty to convert me. I have escaped their clutches before and Samuel forbids me to get in touch with them – he is right too. On the three Sundays we have spent in Paris we have visited the Huguenot Temple of Charenton. Samuel describes it as a 'very fair and spacious room, built of freestone, with paintings of the Tables of law, the Lords Prayer and the Creed. The pulpit stands at the upper end in the middle, having an enclosure of seats about it, where the Elders sit and much harmonious singing of the Psalms'.

The day we arrived in Paris, the 10th September, the old Queen Mother died. She had left Somerset House on June 24th 1665 and then retired to her chateau at Colombes, on the outskirts of Paris. My father will be desolate when he hears the news. He has served her faithfully for nearly forty years. I thought of my father again when Samuel and I passed the wall where the traitor Ravaillac hid before killing Henri le Grand way back in 1610: the place where my father arrested and disarmed him.

We are staying in an excellent hostelry in the Rue de Tournon in the Quartier of Saint-Germain, recommended by Sir Samuel Tuke. He was described by Samuel when we met by arrangement at a bookseller's, as 'conceited but eloquent'. Come to think of it, my husband might have been describing himself!

We have an introduction to M. de Lamoignon, the first Président of Parlement, whose circle of friends and acquaintances meet together every Monday. Samuel also has an introduction to Monsieur Mignon, who was J-B Colbert's secretary when he was Minister of the French Navy. Monsieur Mignon is now Conseilleur du Roi d'Etat et de la Marine, which is very nearly equivalent to Samuel's position in London.

Our Messagerie coach from Calais rattled into Paris on the old cobble stones via Saint Denis, and ended its journey at the 'Ecu

Dauphin' in the Rue Bourg l'Abbé. There we were able to rent a coach for a month 'de Remise' with good horses, neat harness and well gilt, for 3 English crowns a day. Samuel insisted that our stay in Paris should be made in style, and who was I to contradict him? He notices everything, even if he claims his eyes are dimming: for example, the fact that Paris has more coaches trundling around than in London, that there are more monks in their habits here than in London, and many more beggars in Paris. Strolling the streets Samuel is especially critical of the fashions – the large Parisian cravats, the peculiar wigs (by English standards) and the long doublets worn by the French men of fashion. Inevitably he is greatly taken by the glamorous ladies of the stage. We wanted to see Molière playing Tartuffe but he had gone to Chambord with the Court and we missed him by a week, but we did see the actresses La Beauchasteau, La Villiers and D'Hennebault playing at the Marais Theatre at the Hôtel de Bourgogne. Samuel was in his element. He was not allowed backstage. Anyway his French is rather stilted and he has had no practice at using our elegant tongue in romantic situations. We went to Hauteroche's 'Le Souper mal apprête', and saw La Champonesle in Rosimond's 'Le Nouveau Festin de Pierre' and Visé's 'Les Intrigues de la Lotterie' at the Marais. Molière's own hall at the Palais Royal is larger than the other two theatres, and we both thought it much finer.

Samuel is very popular wherever he goes. He bustles round Paris much as he does in London. At the Bibliothèque Royale on the Rue de Vivienne he looks at Greek manuscripts of the Epistles, and visits all the bookshops. He refuses to drink French water, although I do. He holds court at the chocolate shop of David Chaliou by the Croix du Tiroir. At our hostelry he asked for his favourite 'Ho Brion' wine from Bordeaux, failed to be given it, but drank with pleasure some of the Bataillhey claret wines.

Since this is a holiday for both of us the pursestrings are untied. I have bought petticoats and a camisole from Mesdames Rémond and Prévôt at the Rue des Petits-Champs, and visited M. Bandelet, the Queen's tailor, who lives in the Rue Richelieu. I have been to M. Martial, the great glover and perfumer, bought garters at the Sign of the Cross on the Rue d'Arnetal, and fine linen at the Halle aux Toiles. I have looked at the second hand clothes market at la Fripperie, near Les Halles. Samuel has bought me Mademoiselle de Scudery's latest books 'La Promenade de Versailles' and 'Mathilde d'Aguilar'. Both of us have visited the Luxembourg Gardens near the Rue de Tournon, and the Cours de la Reine on the right bank of the Seine approached from the Gate of the Tuileries.

We are leaving Paris on Wednesday the 16th October. Bishop Bossuet of Condom will deliver the funeral oration in honour of Queen Henrietta Maria at Chaillot and I will say a little prayer for her. Although I have only seen her two or three times, I feel, after hearing my father's tales, that I knew her very well.

I will feel sad when we arrive at the Grand Cerf in the Rue Saint Denis to catch our coach for Brussels.

SAMUEL'S STORY

THOSE WHOM THE GODS LOVE DIE YOUNG – A REQUIEM

"On mourra seul" B. Pascal

A few days after our return from the Continent on the 10th November 1669, my wife died of a fever. We had been married for almost fifteen years – almost exactly half her short life.

She is now buried in our church of St Olaves. Her bust was created of white Kilkenny marble for me by John Dwight of Fulham, and overlooks the Navy Commissioners' pew in the south aisle.

In my secret diary, which may be discovered after my death and which covers our last ten years together, I have sought out some of the happy loving words that I wrote during our marriage.

Once she rode sidesaddle upon her pretty mare beside me towards Brampton and I wrote 'She rides very well – at last poor wretch begun to be tired and I to be angry with her, but I was to blame for she is a very good companion as long as she is well'.

My brother Tom had died that day 'And I lay close to my wife being full of disorder and grief for my brother that I could not sleep nor wake with satisfaction'.

On a Lord's Day morning 'Talking long in bed with my wife about our frugall life for the time to come, proposing to her what I could and would do if I were worth £2000, that is, be a Knight and keep my coach which pleased her. To church in the morning'. I was never a Knight, but we did have a coach which pleased her.

Six months later 'Talking with my wife in whom I never had greater content, blessed be God! than now – she continuing with the same care and thrift and innocence, so long as I keep her from occasions of being otherwise, as ever she was in her life, and keeps the house as well'.

In the summer of '63 'My wife and I (by my late jealousy for which *I* am truly to be blamed) have not that fondness between us which we used and ought to have and I fear will be lost hereafter if I do not take some course to oblige her and yet preserve my authority'.

That autumn at Buntingford on the way to Brampton 'My wife

by drinking some cold beer, being hot herself presently after lighting from horseback begins to be sick and become so pale and I alone with her in a great chamber that I thought she would have died and so in great horror and having a great trial of my true love and passion for her called the maids and mistress of the house . . . (she recovered) I having put her to bed with great content called in my company and supped in the chamber with her'.

At Christmas that year 'Home to dinner with my wife, very pleasant and pleased with one another's company and in our general enjoyment one of another, better we think than most other couples do'.

On a more light-hearted note I wrote down the 'Ten principles' which my rude and vulgar friends mooted to me at a christening gossip's dinner in the summer of '64. 'I began discourse of my not getting children and prayed them to give me their opinions and advice and they freely and merrily did give me these,

(1) Do not hug my wife too hard nor too much
(2) Eat no late suppers
(3) Drink juyce of sage
(4) Tent and toast
(5) Wear cool holland-drawers
(6) Keep stomach warm and back cool
(7) Upon my query whether it was best to do at night or morn, they answered me neither one nor other, but when we have most mind to it
(8) Wife not to go too straight-laced
(9) Myself to drink Mum and sugar
(10) Mrs Ward did give me to change my plat – make the bed high at feet, low at head

In the spring of '66 I was writing 'after an hour or two's talk with my poor wife, who gives me more and more content every day then another'. Of course when I use the word 'poor' it is not meant to be other than a term of affection. That summer I wrote 'my wife and I spent an hour in the garden, talking of living in the country when I shall be turned out of the office, as I fear the Parliament . . . do remove us all'. But of course it did not.

At Christmas 'after dinner to teach my wife my song "It is decreed" which pleases me mightily and my heart full of true joy'. In the New Year 'Lay long in bed, talking with pleasure with my poor wife how she used to make coal fires and wash my foul clothes with her own hand for me, poor wretch, in our little room at 'My

Lord' Sandwiches: for which I ought for ever to love and admire her, and do, and persuade myself she would do the same thing again if God should reduce us to it'.

After her flageolet lessons I wrote 'for I do foresee if God send my wife and I to live, she will become very good company for me'. That was two and a half years ago, and I have just buried my poor wife.

In February of last year we both went to the King's House to see 'Virgin Martyr' which did 'please me beyond anything in the whole world was the wind musique so sweet that it ravished me, did wrap up my soul just as I formerly been when in love with my wife . . . and makes me resolve to practise wind music and to make my wife do the like'.

Less than a year ago I wrote at the time of the Deborah affair 'I must here remember that I have laid with my Moher (wife) as a husband more times since this falling out than in I believe, twelve months before - and with more pleasure to her than I think in all the time of our marriage before'.

That perhaps best sums up our stormy, turbulent wonderful marriage together. I shall miss her mightily in the long days to come.

APPENDIX A

SAMUEL PEPYS - HUGUENOT LINKS

Over the last century there has been a great deal of research by the genealogists and antiquarians concerning Samuel Pepy's family and its derivations, in particular much work by Edwin Chappell and E.A. Greening Lamborn. Apart from disagreement about Pepys' grandfather - was he Thomas 'the Black' or Thomas 'the Red,'? (sons of John Pepys married to Edith Talbot) - the general conclusions have been consistent.

William Courtenay Pepys' 'Genealogy of the Pepys Family 1500–1800' was published in the 19th century. He wrote 'No definite link has been found with the existing pedigree which starts with certainty with William Pepys of Cottenham whose will was dated 1518/9 and proved 20 May 1519. His father is stated in the Heralds Visitations (Robert Cooke, Clarenceau Herald, Harleian MSS 4756) to have been named *Robert,* but the name does not appear in the Court Rolls. I have not been more successful with *Robert Pepys* mentioned by the Heralds, Harley and Cooke in their visitations of the County Norfolk in 1563 and 1585 (Harleian MSS BM 1101 and 1154 pp 48–50 and 17) and with whose name all former pedigree compilers have headed their work'.

Until this day the mystery has remained: who was this Robert Pepys? (The surname has been spelt in twenty different ways in the 16th and 17th century).

New research has produced evidence that the Pepys were originally a French Huguenot family.

The French Huguenot records available in London show that *Robert Pypas* appears as an Alien on the Denization Roll 36 Henry' of 11 July 1544. One could remain in the country for ten, twenty, even thirty years before taking out naturalisation papers. Moreover The Acts of the Privy Council of 1546 state that a 'pasport for *Robert Peper* to passe over to Guisnes (near Calais) to the Lord Graye of Witton for whome he had first pasport to repair thither and repaase with two horses'. Guisnes was the site of the largest Huguenot temple in France.

There was indeed a French Pepys family, for which there are five certain references. Registre 6 of 'The Armorial General de la

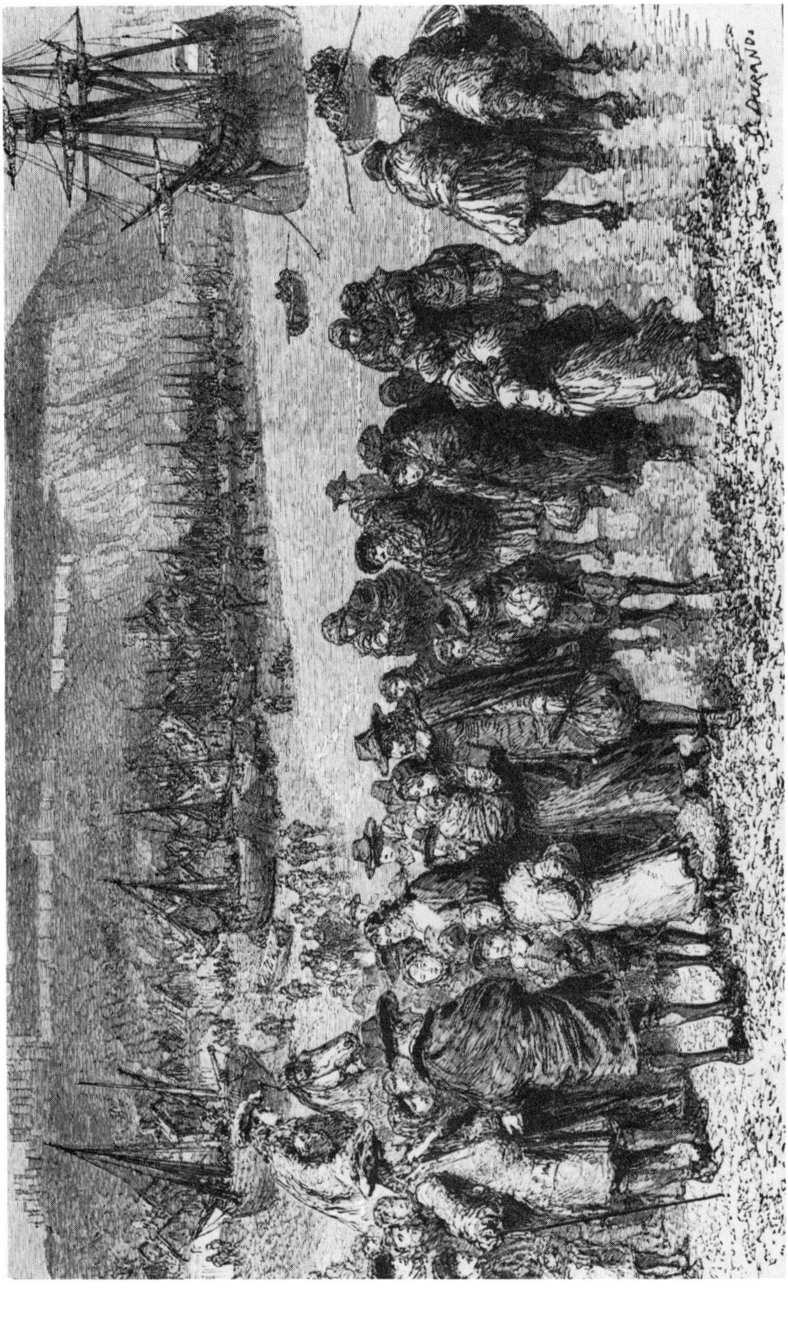

French Huguenot Refugees landing at Dover in 1685, by permission of BBC Hulton Picture Library

France' by Hozier published in Paris 1768, shows that in 1292 there was a Pepyons in an ancient contract of marriage in the Province of Languedoc. In 'Le Cabinet Historique' by Hozier III p. 12 the name 'Pepie' occurs. Sir William Betham in his 'Baronetage', London 1805 supports the view that the Pepys family came from Languedoc in France. Mr Walter Courtenay Pepys received a letter 18 Oct 1880 from M. J. Pepy-Deramez, Docteur de Sorbonne at Berne, in which he states the tradition that the Pepys family came originally from La Rochelle and Rochefort-sur-mer. A well known Doctor Pepys lived in Rochefort in the time of 'Ministre d'Etat Colbert' i.e. during Samuel's early life. A very early Italian family of that name moved to the Languedoc and then further North West to La Rochelle, the centre of the Huguenot movement. Finally a Jehan or John Pepy 'a discrete personne, maître, conseilleur et jurat' of Bergerac was living there on 21 November 1545 and on 21 January 1545 at Bordeaux. He was an acknowledged Huguenot and probably fled to the Channel Islands.

APPENDIX A-1

The Société Jervaise (of Jersey) quotes an entry from the 'Cour de Samed' in 1553 of Thomasoe Journeaux, widow of Jean Pipas'. Later on in 1629 Thomas Pepys married his second wife, a Huguenot called Marie Syvret, at St Helier Church, Jersey. Thomas was rector of that church. Their three children were baptised there in 1631. Thomas was a Roundhead in 1643 and fled Jersey to St Malo, and his wife was exiled in 1649 to Elizabeth Castle.

The research moves back to London. The Huguenot records have three references to a Jehan Peper or Pipre, naturalised on 8 November 1557 'his wif and childe, silkeweyears, born in France and goeth to the French church in 1568'. Then there are three references to a German or Jerome Pypes or Pipes in 1576, 1582, and 1583, living at St Annes in the Parish of Black Frycrs – 'a brushemaker borne under the obedience of the French Kinge and his wife came for religion and are of the French Church. He hath two children born in England'. His children were named Noey or Noel baptised 1583, Johnne baptised 1586, and Mary baptised in 1590, all at St Annes, Blackfriars. His wife Kathren Pepes was born in Paris. In 1593 she was a widow with five English born children – 3 sons of 15, 10 and 5, two daughters of 3 and 9 months: she employed three people and kept a maid.

Now the Dutch connection appears. Thomas Pepys, 'Anglus', was a student at Leyden on 20th May 1649. Oliver Cromwell's Protector's Council of State (p. 32 Entry book No. 105 London) stated on 7 August 1656 (when Samuel Pepys was aged 22) 'that passes be graunted to goe beyond ye seas to ye p'sons followeing viz. To John Pepys and his man with necessaryes for Holland bening on the desire of Mr Sam Pepys'. A year after his marriage Samuel had influence with his patron "My Lord" Mountagu to secure a pass for his father. He revisited Holland on at least one other occasion, certainly in 1666.

Much later, a Johannes Pijper, 'Brittanicus', was a student at Leyden University on 8th May 1717. Finally Pierre Pypers was born in 1749 in Amersfoort in the province of Utrecht. His family wanted him to enter the church. He refused, and moved to Amsterdam as a business man. Pierre was also a poet and a 'dramatic' author of translations of French plays – with considerable success. He entered politics and became Deputy of the States General of Utrecht and maritime Customs Collector of Amsterdam. In the period 1777–1801 he wrote many books and plays. His career showed a remarkable similarity to the famous Diarist. He died in 1805.

During Elizabeth's short lifetime 1640–69, the Huguenots in France were relatively at peace with Louis XIV's Catholic government. The notorious Dragonades and other extreme harassments and penalties, culminating in the Revocation of the Edict of Nantes in 1685, forced an influx of Huguenot refugees to England, Ireland, and the Low Countries.

On 5th March 1686 King James II published a Bill or 'lettre patente en faveur des refugies francais' i.e. the Huguenot emigrés. The main patrons were the Archbishop of Canterbury, the Grand Chancellor, the President of the Privy Council, the Dukes of Ormond and of Beaufort.

Amongst the only three 'commoners' was 'Samuel Peppys'. Any five or more of those named collectively, could dispose and distribute monies received as a result of the 'lettre patente' to deserving Huguenot familes. The two main leaders of the large Huguenot community in England were Louis de Duras, otherwise known as Lord Blanquefort, Earl of Feversham, and also Henri de Massue, Marquis de Ruvigny.

The Earl of Feversham was a Pall-Bearer at Samuel Pepys

"French Huguenot Refugees in France" by J. Luyken, by permission of Rijksmuseum Amsterdam

funeral, and was left 20 shillings and a mourning ring. He and Samuel were in patronage to the Duke of York and met frequently at Court.

In the period 1679–82 the Marquis de Ruvigny wrote at least six letters to Samuel Pepys (in the Rawlinson collection). Samuel wrote to his Huguenot brother-in-law Balty on 1 July 1679 of 'Monsieur de Ruvigny not only having a reputation of a Person of good interest in that [French] Court, but being also a Protestant and a man of great probity *he knowing mee to be of the same profession in Religion with himselfe* (we having frequently met in Our Devotions at the Savoy Church)'.

On 26th March 1680 (five years before the Revocation) Madame Bibaud Pellisary wrote to Samuel Pepys from Paris to enlist his support on behalf of her brother, who was about to resign his appointment as *Commissioner of the French Navy* and retire into England for the sake of his Huguenot religion. A major defection indeed.

Samuel employed as assistant Paul Lorrain, a Huguenot, for many years; he was patron to the De Galiniere family, a Huguenot pastor, and he employed several Huguenot servants including James Paris de Plessis. His main friends were Huguenots - the Bateliers, the Houblons, and William Hewer.

There is little doubt therefore that Samuel Pepys was so intimate with the Huguenot emigrés in England, because he himself had Huguenot blood in his veins!

APPENDIX B

THE COLONEL SCOTT CONSPIRACY

In 1673 Pepys had been charged by Sir John Banks and the Earl of Shaftesbury with being a Papist, on the absurd grounds of having a crucifix in his house, and thus 'a papist or popishly inclined'. The House of Commons debated this charge and deputed Sir William Coventry, Sir Thomas Meres (a Huguenot), and Mr Garraway to 'attend Lord Shaftesbury and receive what information his Lordship can give on this matter'. Of course there was no proof and the matter was dropped.

Pepys was then involved unwillingly and unwittingly in the so-called Popish plot of 1679. He was totally unconnected with the Roman Catholic party, but his close association with the Catholic Duke of York marked him as a target by which the Duke might be brought down, specifically by the Duke of Buckingham and Lord Shaftesbury.

A well-known London magistrate, Sir Edmund Berry Godfrey, was found murdered one night in October 1678. In December, Samuel Atkins, Pepys' clerk, was brought to trial as an accessory to Godfrey's murder, and was grilled by a Committee which included Lord Shaftesbury and the Duke of Buckingham. Pepys prepared a detailed alibi for Atkins, which caused the jury to acquit him without leaving the box. But Shaftesbury and his friends kept up the attack.

A Colonel John Scott had fraudulently sold large tracts of land in Long Island, New York, to a Major Gotherson. His wife, Dorothea, helped by the Governor of New York, ascertained and proved the fraud, and a petition for redress was presented to the King. He asked his brother, the Duke of York, to command Pepys to collect evidence against Scott as to his dishonest proceedings in New England, Long Island, Barbados, France, Holland and England. In 1678 Scott visited Lord Shaftesbury. As a result Scott then sought revenge by accusing Pepys of betraying the Navy and of sending secret particulars and documents to the French government – furthermore a plan or design to dethrone the King and 'extirpate the Protestant religion'. Pepys and his close colleague, Sir Anthony Deane, were committed to the Tower under the Speaker's warrant on 22 May 1679. Pepys' place at the Navy was taken by Thomas Hayter, Pepys' clerk. Initially bail was refused by the Attorney-General, but eventually Pepys was allowed out on bail of £30,000 (the enormous sum depicted the seriousness of the charge of treason). It was not until 9th July that bail was eventually granted – £10,000 on his own surety and £5000 each from James Houblon, Richard Dutton, Sir Thomas Beckford and Peter Pallavicini. Houblon and Pallavicini were known Huguenots.

Pepys knew that he and his friends had to work quickly to refute the grim charges that he and Anthony Deane faced. The key people involved were his Huguenot friends, James Houblon, his brother-in-law Balty and various Huguenot merchants. Pepys provided the energy and the ideas, which in the main consisted of building up a huge dossier on the truly iniquitous activities of Colonel Scott, over a period of years and in several countries. He also secured refutations of the charges alleged to have been made about him in France. James Houblon provided a ready-made merchant network in various countries, and almost certainly considerable funds to help clear his friend. Balty (perhaps to everybody's surprise) surpassed himself in tracking down considerable evidence in France about Scott's activities.

Pepys sent out scores of letters through Houblon to contacts who could help, in France, Brussels and Holland, including John Brisband/Brisbane then in the Paris Embassy: Pepys kept copies of all of these letters, now available as Rawlinson MSS A. 194 folio 1–2. Colonel Scott had named two Frenchmen – the Marquis de Seignelay and Monsieur Pellissary, a Naval officer, whom he alleged had been asked £40,000 each for receiving England's naval secrets from the two accused.

John James, an ex-butler of Pepys, was produced by William Harbord (Shaftesbury's spokesman) and he accused Pepys wildly of Papacy (crucifixes, beads, daggers, and of employing his Catholic musician Morelli). The King and many of Pepys' friends, including John Evelyn, rallied to his support. As a result mainly of the immense dossier which Pepys, Houblon, Balty, Denise and Trenchepain had accumulated, Colonel Scott was now most reluctant to appear in Court. Shaftesbury and his man Harbord realised they had gone too far when Pepys demanded a trial. Eventually after quite incredible charges, and countercharges involving fresh witnesses; Donluis, the Harris brothers, John Joyne and many others; on 28 June 1680 the Attorney-General declared in Court to the Lord Chief Justice that he had 'Nothing' to say against Pepys' and Deane's Motion for a discharge – and they were both set free.

Although Scott refused to acknowledge that his original deposition was not true, John James confessed on his deathbed in 1680 that he had trumped up the whole story relating to Pepys' alleged change of religion, at the instigation of Mr William Harbord, MP for Thetford. Harbord became Surveyor General of the Crown Land Revenues, and was Pepys' most vicious enemy.

Scott had cheated the States of Holland out of £7000. In 1682 he murdered George Butler, a hackney coachman, fled to Norway where he stayed till 1696, but later secured a pardon to return to England.

Pepys' correspondence in 1679/80 was mainly to Balty, to James Houblon, and frequently concerned three more Huguenots who were of considerable help to him – M. Claude Denise, merchant, M. Francois Trenchepain, merchant, and Henri de Massue Marquis de Ruvigny, who was naturalised British in 1680, and although living in Greenwich, had considerable influence still in Paris.

On 25 June 1690 Pepys was again committed to the Gatehouse at Westminster on a charge of having sent information to the French court of the state of the English Navy. There was no evidence and he was freed in July.

There is no doubt that the concerted effort of his Huguenot friends and relations saved him from the scaffold. The opposition was controlled by the Duke of Buckingham, probably the most influential man in England – dominating the King. The penalty for treason was, of course, death.

APPENDIX C

PAINTINGS OF ELIZABETH - A MYSTERY

Most art experts agree that the original paintings of Elizabeth Pepys no longer exist. The paintings by Saville (1661), John Hayls (1666), and the miniature by Samuel Cooper (1668) appear to have been lost or destroyed. Curiously enough their paintings of her husband exist, and one by Sir Godfrey Kneller of Samuel, painted in 1689 when he was 56 years old, also still exists.

Nevertheless research recently carried out does indicate that there *are* paintings of Elizabeth in being.

The two paintings by Saville of Samuel and Elizabeth were for many years in the possession of the Pepys - Cockerell family, a legacy from John Jackson, Samuel's nephew. At the John Pepys - Cockerell sale at Sothebys in London on Wednesday 1st April 1931, the Saville portrait of Elizabeth Pepys was not included in the sale, possibly because of doubts of its provenance. In the following month, May 1931, the Connoisseur Magazine vol. LXXXVII p. 357 showed an advertisement by the Grafton Galleries of London. It was a photograph of a head and shoulders oil painting of Mrs. Pepys *attributed* to Sir Godfrey Kneller (1646–1728). He came to England in 1674/5 and may well have been commissioned by Samuel to 'copy' Elizabeth's portrait by Saville. The familiar sloping shoulders, the heart shaped sensuous mouth, the hair ringlets, the long, straight, strong nose (seen from a different side) do have similarities to the known likeness seen in John Hayls' work. So do the décolletage and full bosom. She wears a necklace of rings - no doubt those given to her by her handsome admirer of early Parisian days, the young Lord Somerset with the shako'd French footman.

The conclusions must therefore be: either that this portrait is indeed the original Saville, or that Samuel Pepys, when he was painted by the then famous Sir Godfrey Kneller in 1689, also commissioned from him a copy of the Saville.

John Hayls was a pupil of Miereveldt in Amsterdam, but accepted commissions in London and in Italy. During 1666 he painted Samuel, and Elizabeth as Saint Catherine. Legend has it

Samuel Coopers 'lost' miniature, by permission of BBC Hulton Picture Library

Elizabeth Pepys attributed to Sir Godfrey Kneller, by permission of Witt Library, Courtauld Institute of Art

Mrs Pepys, by Sir Joshua Reynolds, by permission of Witt Library, Courtauld Institute of Art

that this painting was destroyed in 1830 by a prudish Scottish nurse in the 19th century Pepys family, on account of the rather attractive décolletage. Luckily the excellent engraving by James Thomson of the Hayls painting can be seen today at the National Portrait Gallery in London.

The 'Catalogue of Engraved British Portraits' p. 333 shows that Sir Joshua Reynolds painted Mrs Pepys in the winter of 1780/81 'Half left nearly full face. He also painted Mr. Pepys in January 1781. Presumably this commission came from the Pepys - Cockerell family because 'Country Life' of 6th April 1961, 'Problems of Pepys Portraits' refers to a copy 'by some skilful *18C* hand of the *Greenwich* portrait'. This portrait of Elizabeth may be in Earl Cowley's collection. It shows her wearing a large white stock and cravat. Again the long sloping shoulders, mouth and lower lip, her strong nose and high arched brows are reminiscent of the John Hayls' portrait of Elizabeth. It seems logical to suppose that Reynolds based his copy of Elizabeth on the John Hayls original.

We know that Samuel Cooper (1609–1672) painted both Samuel and Elizabeth in miniature in 1668. The Diary states that Samuel was not satisfied with Cooper's painting 'in the greatness of the resemblance nor in the blue garment' she wore. The invaluable BBC Hulton Picture Library have unearthed photographs of two miniature paintings of Samuel and Elizabeth Pepys, which may be engravings or even the originals of Samuel Cooper's 'oeuvres' of 1668. When Mr Owen Morshead was Pepys librarian at Magdalene College, Cambridge he discovered a photograph of a miniature portrait of Mrs Samuel Pepys which was shown at the annual dinner in Feb 1921 of the Samuel Pepys Club. Derek Pepys Whiteley who was later assistant Pepys librarian thought that the photograph might have been of the 1668 Cooper miniature.

So this book ends with a mystery. It shows four portraits of Elizabeth Pepys. Both the author and the publisher, and doubtless the Pepys family, would be delighted to hear from any readers who can shed more light on paintings of Elizabeth.

CHRONOLOGICAL SUMMARY

1616	Death of Shakespeare
1620	James Houblon, Huguenot merchant married. His son James is Samucl's lifelong friend
1624	Richelieu becomes Chief Minister in France
1625	Charles I comes to the throne
1633	Samuel Pepys born in Salisbury Court, Fleet Street
1640	Elizabeth St Michel born in Bideford, Devon
1641	Massacre of Protestants in Ireland
1642	Outbreak of Civil War in England, Battle of Edgehill
1642	Balthazar de St. Michel born in Bideford, Devon
1643	Mazarin becomes Chief Minister of France
1646–50	Pepys at St. Paul's School, London
1646–7	Charles I surrenders to Scots, then handed over to Parliament
1648	Second Civil War in England. Alexandre St Michel imprisoned in Dunkirk
1649	Charles I executed
1651	Cromwell rules Britain
1651–4	Pepys at Magdalene College, Cambridge
1653	Cromwell becomes Protector
1654	Pepys appointed secretary to his cousin, Edward Mountagu
1655	Pepys marries Elizabeth St Michel at Margaret's Church, Westminster
1658	Pepys has operation for stone removal. Death of Cromwell
1659	Pepys visits Baltic for Lord Mountagu
1660	Pepys begins the Diary – by ship to Holland with Mountagu to bring Charles II to England. Appointed Clerk of the Acts to the Navy Board. Meets de Cretz (painter) Blondeau (coin minter) Eschar, Delabarr
1661	Coronation of Charles II. Louis XIV reigns in France
1662	Pepys appointed to Tangier Committee: also made Younger Brother of Trinity House. Balty marries Hester Watts

1663 Alexander St Michel (Samuel's father-in-law) obtains patent for curing smoky chimneys
1664 Pepys brother Tom dies. Samuel and Elizabeth visit Huguenot church in London. Pepys family meet the Bateliers. Balty is a soldier in Holland
1665 Pepys elected Fellow of the Royal Society (Gresham College). Appointed Treasurer of Tangier Committee. Meets M. John Brisband and Lanier (the musician). Great Plague starts in London. First mention of James Houblon in Diary. Meets Mrs Lethieuller. Moves family to Woolwich, but takes lodgings at Greenwich at Navy Office. Second War with Holland until 1667
1666 When the Plague is over Pepys' family and the Navy Office return to London
1666 The Great Fire of London in September - sees Isaac Houblon - Balty and wife help Samuel move his household goods. Samuel meets the King. Merchant venture to Tangier with Houblons.
1667 Dutch ships sail up the Thames and Medway. Parliamentary Committee on Navy Board Miscarriages. Samuel negotiates Balty's promotion with Duke of York. William Batelier visits Marseilles
1668 Pepys' sister Pall (Paulina) marries - Mary Batelier is bridesmaid. Defends Navy Board before House of Commons. Turberville prescribes for Pepys' eyes. William Batelier visits France, brings back many gifts for Pepys family
1669 Commissions of Accounts accuse the Navy Office of corruption and inefficiency, which Pepys rebuts. He ceases writing his Diary. Meets Lord Blanquefort, future Earl of Feversham, the leading Huguenot at Court. Travels to Low Countries and France - meets John Loton (painter) - Cabal formed. 10 Nov Elizabeth, his wife, dies. Secret Treaty of Dover between Charles II and Louis XIV
1670 Council again attacks the Navy Board and Samuel defends them, against false sale of seamen's tickets. Pepys has affair with Mary Skinner. Balty is Muster-Master at Deal
1671 Pepys makes tour of West Country
1672 Pepys admitted Elder Brother of Trinity House. Declaration of Indulgence by the King. Third Dutch War begins. His patron Lord Sandwich dies at battle of Sole Bay

1673	Pepys appointed Secretary to Admiralty commission. Elected MP for Castle Rising, Norfolk. Navy Office burns down
1674	End of Third Dutch War. Pepys attacked in Parliament over naval materials and press gang. Pepys accused of Papacy. Begins reform of Navy
1675	Pepys makes major speech in Parliament
1676	Pepys elected Master of Trinity House. Demands 30 new ships for Navy
1677	Pepys has 30 new ships laid down for building. New victualling contracts for tender
1677–8	Colonel Scott prepares the Great Plot, backed by Duke of Buckingham, to bring down the King and the Duke of York by attacking the Admiralty, and Pepys specifically.
1678	Samuel Atkins, Samuel Pepys' clerk arrested on false charge of Papacy
1679	James Houblon, Mr Pallavicini, Mr R. Dutton and Sir T. Beckford put up £5000 bail each for Pepys to be released from the Tower (22 May–9 July). Balty visits Paris to obtain defence evidence
1680	King recounts escape from Battle of Worcester to Samuel. Book of Mornamont written by Pepys about Scott conspiracy. Balty made Agent to Navy Commission in Tangier
1681	King abruptly dissolves Parliament. Pepys ill with ague. Balty returns from Tangier
1682	Pepys sees Duke of York's ship sunk on journey to Scotland
1683	Rye House Plot. Pepys visits Tangier and Cadiz. James Houblon gives him letter of Credit
1684	Pepys appointed King's Secretary for Naval Affairs. Elected President Royal Society for 2 years
1685	Revocation of the Edict of Nantes by Louis XIV: 100,000 refugees leave France for Holland, Germany, England and Switzerland. Death of Charles II: Duke of York becomes James II. Pepys becomes MP for Harwich. James II shows him confidential documents about King Charles being a Catholic
1686	William of Orange invited to England, lands, and James II flees to France. Lord Feversham, a Huguenot, commands James II's army. Marshal Schomberg, a Huguenot, commands William's army. Pepys secures berth on Navy ship for his nephew and godson Samuel St Michel.

1689	Balty marries Margaret Darling. Pepys defeated in Parliamentary election, resigns his Secretaryship, Mastership, of Trinity House. William and Mary become King and Queen of England. Young Samuel St Michel writes to his godfather from Londonderry.
1690	Pepys imprisoned for one week on suspicion of Jacobitism. Battle of the Boyne on 1st July: Huguenot troops fight for William's army against James II
1697	William and Louis XIV sign peace treaty of Ryswyck
1699	Pepys made Freeman of City of London for services to Christ's Hospital
1701	Pepys lives with Sam Hewer in Clapham
1703	Samuel Pepys dies. Leaves Mourning Rings to Lord Feversham, the St Michels, Paul Lorrain, the Houblons, other Huguenots amongst other friends and family, including John Evelyn. William Hewer is Executor.

BIBLIOGRAPHY

Pepys commenced his Diary in January of 1660 and ended it in May 1669 due to his declining sight. The Diary was first discovered at Cambridge in 1728 but was not transcribed until 1819 when Lord Braybrooke, the Visitor of Magdalene College, entrusted the task of deciphering the six volumes, covering 3,000 quarto pages and containing 1,300,000 words, to a young Bachelor of Arts named John Smith. The Diary was first published in 1825 under the title 'Memoirs of Samuel Pepys'. Subsequent editions with additional matter were published in 1828, 1848–51, 1854 and 1858. Further editions have been edited by the Rev. Mynors Bright, Mr H. B. Wheatley and more recently, by Mr Robert Latham.

Pepys mentioned his wife in practically every daily entry, always as 'my wife' and never as 'Elizabeth'. Lord Braybrooke's edition of the Diary is therefore the prime source for this book.

Sir Arthur Bryant's invaluable trilogy – 'The Man in the the Making', 'The Years of Peril' and 'The Saviour of the Navy' have provided background material.

Balthazar le Marchant de St Michel, Pepys' brother-in-law, wrote Pepys a significant letter on the occasion that the latter was under attack in Parliament as a suspected Papist. It contains so many intriguing clues to the St Michel family that it has been included in full.

Extract from 'Brother Balty's letter to me giveing an account of the ffortune of his ffamily, perticulerly done for the cleareing the imputacion layd on mee in Parliament of my turning his Sister from a Protestant to a Catholique'.

'ffirst my ffather, Sonn to the High-Shreeve of Boge (in Anjou in ffrance) a Papist, and all his ffamely, in which religion, allsoe my ffather was bread, and continued in, till hee was 21 yeares, at which time, (hee being then in the German service) turned Protestant, and without trubling you with the rest of his life there, till hee returned to ffrance, I shall only say that hee did soe: where hee ffound his ffather Dead, haven given all hee had (hearing of my ffathers being turned Hugenot as hee termed it) in mariage with his Daughter (my ffathers only sister) soe that my ffather, being disinherited of all for his religion-sake, had nothing lefte but his sword and ffreinds to preferr him in the world (though an Uncle of my ffathers a Chanoine of Paris who loved [him] soe well, that hee promised to make him his Aire and give him 200,000 livres Tournois, which is about 20,000*l.* sterling, if hee would but goe to mass againe, but all (to this deare man whoe lived and died a saintely life) nor any thing could shake his resolutions of Continuance in the true Protestant Cause; at last ffortune in this world seemed to smile one him againe, hee being (as you know sir) a Gentleman, extreamely well-bread, got him the ffrends (together with his Name and Quality being of a very Good house in ffrance) to preferr him when the Match was concluded between his Majesty Charles the ffirst of Blessed memory, and the Daugher of ffrance* to be of her retenue, in the Place of one of her Gentleman Carvers, soe he came over with her Majesty, but longe had hee not continued heere in her service, but the cloudes of his Misfortunes (as to the Losse of his place) ffrowned on him againe, being tooke notice of by some of the ffriers that hee came not to Mass, was by it imediattly knowne to be what he was viz: a very strong and ffirme Protestant, soe that the Queen dismissed him his imployment, hee having in discourse and Controversy of religion struck a ffrier: Well (as I said before and as your Honour knew) hee being a man not only Extreame Hansome, but allsoe of mightey winning Courtely Partes, went ffor Irelande where hee soone by it wone the Affection of my mother, Daugher, to sir ffrancis Kingsmill and then late widow to an Irish esquire, so my ffather, after hee had maried her, though much to the dislike of her ffreinds (my Lord Moore dl) with what moneys they could then raise being 1500*l.*, intended for ffrance againe (with his wife my mother) to indeavour by Law with his sister (to recover if Posible some parte of his ffathers Estate): but in his prosedure, haveing turned the moneys hee had into Goods marchandable ffor ffrance, at sea hee and goods were all tooke by the Dundirckers, and hee also prisoner some months, so that hee and my mother were againe to begeen the World, but hee, being bread to Nothing but the sworde: (that was his recourse, and by it had in his time many very Honourable Comissions both in ffrance, Holland and Germany as well as England:) hee for some time settled himselfe upon that litell hee hadd in Devonshire at a Place called Bidiford, where, and

*Henrietta Maria

thereabouts my sister and wee all ware borne. Sir my Small age at those times hinders my giving you soe exact accompt as I would wish: how-that, at last my ffather, Mother and ffamily went for ffrance againe, neither cann I tell on what accompt only at ffirst I remember that he caried a Compagny of ffoot under his Comande by order of Englande, to Assiste the ffrenche against the Spaniard in the taking of Dunkirk, and Arrass which was about the year 1648 or 9 neather any further acompt cann I say wee went to parris about but that my ffather (at last) grew full of wheemsies, and Propositions, (of Perpetuall Motions &c.) to Kings, Princes and others, which soaked his pockett, and brought all our ffamely sow low (by his not minding any thing elce spending all hee had or had gott and getting no other imployment to bring in more) of nothing more, and my mother (for ffeare of her childrens want) brought into extreame trubles, at last shee was persuaded by some deluding Papists, namely Madam Trouson, a Rich Counselers wife, Mr. Duplesis a Rich Advocat of the Parlement, with many others pretended Devouts, that if my Mother with her children would gett ffrom her husbande my ffather, that Damned trublesome Hugenot (as they cauled him) they woold provide for all of uss namely my mother, sister and selfe by allowing her a considerable allowance ffitting a Gentle-wooman of her Quality, Give a Rounde some of moneys and make my sister a Nunn and my selfe Page to the Popes Nuncio (by which i might since I have thought on it [be] either a Cardinall or a Bardache*) then at Parris resident; in order to theese persuasions my Mother agrees, apointes the day and Hower, when exactely, came 2 Coaches on of Madam Trouson aforesaid, and the other of Mr. Duplecy and Madam Trouson in hers caries mother and sister a way as sweete as litening ffor ffeare on my ffathers interest and furies, and putts them both into the Nouvelle Catholique of Weemen, and I in M. Duplecys convaid to that of Garsons, at last my deare sister being extreame Hansome was deluded into the Nuneries of the Urselines (all this about *her 12 or 13 yeare of age* where shee was received with gladness, thinking to have her there sure enough it being the stricktest Nunerys in all Parris, but shee was not there longe I meane not 12 days eare my ffather by some strategeme or other I know not well How, gott her out, and uss all, hee having bine allmost distracted about it (Poor Deare man) but in ffine hee gott us al ffor England againe, where after some time wee had the Honour to be related to you my my Dear sisters match, which was of extreame Content to my ffather, that his deare child had an other fferme Protestant Protector, and giude.

*catamite

The Huguenot Society of London and their equivalent in Paris provided in their many publications valuable clues to the Pepys, St Michel, Hewer and Bataillhey families.

Mr Walter Courtenay Pepys and Mr Edwin Chappell's books on the 'Genealogy of the Pepys family' provided information about the French family connections. Mr J. R. Tanner, Mr Walter H. Whitear and Mr H. B. Wheatley have also written significant books about the Pepys family.

The Calender of State Papers for England and for Ireland provided additional material for the Pepys, St Michel and Bataillhey families.

The Index Society volume XIII provided information about the Pepys family at Leyden University.

Burke's 'Landed Gentry of Ireland' and O'Hart's 'Irish Pedigrees' produced information about the St Michel family and Elizabeth's mother, Dorothea Kingsmill, in Ireland.

The 'Memoires du Duc de Sully', the 'Journal de Jean Herouard, Medecin du Roi' (Henri IV et Louis XIII), 'The Weekly Intelligencer' of Sept 30 1645 and the Duke of Portland MSS vol 3 p. 150 – all produced significant items about Alexandre de St Michel's life and exploits.

The Dictionary of National Biography carries a profile of Edward Mountagu, 'My Lord' Sandwich and of the Houblon family.

The Latter Day Saints (the Mormon Church) International Genealogical Index produced information about the Pepys and Hewer families in the 17th Century.

INDEX